SECRET
THOUGHTS

For Jim,
Enjoy the ride!

H.S. CLARK

Published by Grand Media
www.grandmediacompany.com
grandmediacompany@gmail.com

ISBN-10: 0988427400
EAN-13: 9780988427402
Library of Congress Control Number: 2012918449
Grand Media, Puyallup, Washington

For Luba, my wife,

because love is the greatest mystery

"Nothing is at last sacred but the integrity of your own mind."

-RALPH WALDO EMERSON

PROLOGUE

The thermometer beeped, and Joline snatched it from her daughter's mouth, angling the LEDs toward the lamp and squinting at the readout. The red crystalline numbers faded in and out of focus as Joline struggled for more light, tilting the pink dollhouse roof that was the lampshade. But no matter how she adjusted the light or twisted the plastic gauge, the LEDs still read the same.

"One hundred and two. Come out from under the covers, cutie. Otherwise, I'll have to put you in the bath, and you wouldn't like that," she said, tapping Kayla's runny nose.

"OK, Mommy," said the five year old, pouting as Joline removed the blanket, leaving only a sheet. Kayla coughed and shivered, grabbing one of her teddy bears in a fierce embrace.

Joline knew that every child in her daughter's preschool class had already been sick. Kayla's illness was not a surprise. But Joline couldn't shake her feeling of impending doom. What a terrible weekend for her husband to be out of town. The child's blue eyes, watery and dull, frightened Joline beyond reason. She kept trying to reassure herself that Kayla had nothing more than a cold.

Kayla looked so small and helpless in her big bed, surrounded by colorful dinosaur sheets and stuffed teddy bears. At the first sniffle, she'd lost her stubborn toddler independence, regressing to the dependent infant she'd once been. She's beautiful even when she's sick, Joline thought. Fine blond hair fell in tangled honeycombs over Kayla's face, cheeks as fever-red as the painted faces of her plastic dolls.

Joline headed for the master bathroom. The fever had to be brought down, no matter what. Kayla needed medication, and fortunately, Joline had just bought a bottle of acetaminophen. It was a great fever reducer, and Kayla had done well with this medication in the past. Reaching into the medicine cabinet, Joline trembled. Something wasn't right, and again she wished her husband hadn't gone. She needed him now. But Kayla hadn't been this sick when he left. "Why am I getting so upset?" Joline asked her image in the bathroom mirror. "Calm down. It's only a cold, she'll get over it."

After pulling the shrink wrap off the white plastic bottle, Joline struggled with the childproof cap. Cap off, she peeled back the foil barrier, teased the cotton out with her pinky, and shook out one of the amber colored gel-caps. The soft gelatin capsules cost a bit more, but they were worth it. Kayla could swallow these soft capsules. One would be enough.

With the capsule in one hand and a glass of cranberry juice in the other, Joline returned to her daughter's room. The stuffed bear played "Twinkle Twinkle Little Star" and then "Frère Jacques" in electronic tones. Kayla sneezed and snot ran down her upper lip.

"Bless you, baby." Joline wiped the child's nose with a tissue.

"Will I get better, Mommy?"

"Yes. Yes, I promise. Now, I have a jelly-pill for you. Will you take it for me?"

"OK, Mommy."

"Sit up, please."

Kayla tried, but seemed too weak. After Joline set the juice on the night table, she lifted her daughter to a sitting position. Supporting her with one arm, Joline fed Kayla the soft capsule, placing it on her hot, furrowed tongue. The rubbery ball stuck there as Joline put the juice up to her daughter's pale lips. Kayla sipped and gagged a bit, spilling some of the juice, but the pill went down.

"There now, you're such a good girl. That'll make you feel better."

Kayla giggled, swinging the bear around her head, pretending as if it were flying. She jumped up, bouncing on the bed.

"Kayla! What are you doing? Stop it. Please."

A hideous howl filled the room, like the distressed call of a wounded animal as a predator closes in. The howling stopped abruptly, and the room was silent except for the shrill chimes of nursery rhymes. Then Kayla grabbed her head. It vibrated. Sweat poured from her forehead. "Mommy, it hurts," she said, and then collapsed on the bed, her fragile arms twitching as if electrified.

Joline wanted to grab Kayla and run to safety. But there was nowhere to go. The flush in Kayla's cheeks turned gray and her heart could be seen pounding through her chest. "Kayla! Honey! Wake up! Wake up!" Joline shook her, but the child didn't respond. Her eyes rolled up into her head and she gasped, shallow, rapid. Then her pupils dilated widely and her breathing stopped.

Kayla arched her back and vomited. Viscous yellow fluid tinged with cranberry juice filled her mouth and leaked out the sides. Joline turned the stiff child onto her side and emptied her mouth. Scooping up Kayla, hugging her tightly, Joline put her mouth on the dark face, covering the nose and mouth, and breathed for her daughter, sucking in a strange taste. The stiff child went limp, and the throbbing of her racing heart against Joline's breast began to slow, more and more, until the only pulse Joline felt was her own, palpitating in her throat, choking, suffocating. The miracle that had started within her womb, with the first kick, ended abruptly in her arms.

For several minutes, Joline continued to blow into the lifeless child. Finally, wrenching her mouth from the blackened face, she groped at the matted hair. "No, no, no," she cried, rocking the flaccid child in her arms. "You're going to get better, baby, I promise, I promise, I promise." Kissing Kayla's mottled cheek, Joline tasted her own bitter tears.

CHAPTER 1

As Dr. Paul Powers entered Lakeside Hospital, he noticed a difference right away. It was subtle to any casual visitor, but loud as a trumpet to him. It wasn't going to be an ordinary day. Perhaps it was the buzz of conversations in the hallway, or the cluster of whispering physicians and nurses around the espresso bar. The hum was a washing undercurrent that spelled trouble. And before he made it through the lobby, he got the story. One of Lakeside's own had been admitted to the ICU that morning.

Running late as usual, Paul hurried to the operating room. Today's surgery schedule was packed. If he didn't get the anesthetic for his first patient started within thirty minutes, there would be hell to pay with the surgeons and the nurses.

Unlike in his anesthesia residency, the surgeons at Lakeside worshiped speed, hard work, and most of all, themselves. Paul reluctantly catered to their workaholism and bloated egos, even as he admired their technical skills.

The clientele of Lakeside, in Bellevue, a yuppified eastern suburb of Seattle, demanded the finest of medical care no matter what the cost. Residents of Bellevue displayed their wealth with pride, but Paul suspected that much of the city's opulence was a fragile illusion, with reality lurking one missed payment away.

He'd been lucky a few months back to land his first private practice job with the anesthesia group at Lakeside, a feat he owed primarily to Dr. Valdimire Zhazinsky, a staff radiologist. Zhazinsky had taught Paul at the University of Washington in both undergraduate classes and in the medical school. Efficiently known as Dr. Z, the Professor had left his prestigious post at the University of Washington, but not before achieving recognition as a brilliant research scientist. It was no wonder Lakeside Radiology used an outrageous first-year package to lure Dr. Z into private practice.

Pounding up the stairs, Paul banged the large silver button on the wall and ran through the double doors of the operating suite, panting, almost colliding with Ben Hinkley. An internist first, Ben specialized in intensive care medicine. Seeing him leaving the operating suite so early in the morning was a bad sign. Paul figured Ben had come to mooch off the donuts and coffee the hospital provided to the OR staff every morning.

Paul grabbed Ben by the tweed sleeve of his Armani suit. "I know you hate to eat and run, but what the hell's going on today, Hinkley?"

Ben's fat bulldog face wrinkled. "Look, I've had a long night, Powers. No games, now, please."

"Long night?"

"There's a VIP in ICU, and I'm losing the battle. It's crazy. And there's media coming." Ben tried to pass, but Paul blocked his path.

"Media? So what's happening and who is it?"

"Cyanide poisoning, from an over-the-counter pill. A radical cure for the common cold. I think you know him. A new doc here named Zhazinsky. Radiologist."

Paul froze.

"You OK? Were you close?"

Paul stared. "Is he dead?"

"Probably, just a formality now. Wait for the cyanide levels to drop, then run the EEG again. You know the routine."

"I'm going with you," said Paul.

"But, they're already looking for you in the lounge."

"Sorry, Ben, the OR will just have to wait."

On the walk to intensive care, Paul remembered the many fatherly encounters he'd had with Dr. Z. During medical school, they'd talked all night in the cozy confines of Dr. Z's private library, the musty smell of old volumes of wall-to-wall books mingling with the vapors of mint tea. Tchaikovsky played softly in the background as Tolstoy, Solzhenitsyn, and Chekov came alive. Dr. Z fancied himself a great student of Russian art and history. So often Paul had almost broken beneath the stress of becoming a physician, trying to understand his profession's awesome responsibilities. But Dr. Z was always there for Paul. Z had a way of making sense out of all the insanity of the world.

In intensive care, Paul looked on as Dr. Z lay motionless, eyes taped shut and his face dark blue. A breathing tube originated from his mouth and connected to a ventilator. Blood percolated intermittently from a smaller tube emerging from the right side of his nose. The high-pitched, rapid beeping of his pulse punctuated the slow, cyclical rush of air from the ventilator to his lungs. Paul held his hand to his face at the sight of the usually rosy-cheeked Dr. Z. Whatever Paul expected to see, it wasn't this. He'd never seen cyanide poisoning before, and he hoped never to see it again.

Dr. Z's wife, Natasha, sat at the bedside. When she saw Paul, she jumped up from the chair and embraced him.

"Paul, oh, Paul, I'm glad you're here." Tears streamed down her cheeks. "Val had a cold, a co..." She choked on the last word.

"I'm sorry, Natasha, I just heard. Ben's doing all he can."

She released her grip, nodding her head as her hair fell over her wet face. Bright, green eyes peered through the curly brown tangles of her hair. "I know, but who would do such a thing?" Reaching up, she parted her hair gracefully, sweeping it past her dark, red lips, over her cheeks and behind her shoulders. Above her nose, Paul noticed more wrinkles than ever before. Natasha seemed to have aged years overnight.

Paul stroked his mustache. "I wish I had something to tell you, to make sense of all this, but these kind of things never make any sense." Natasha sat back down, sobbing.

Ben approached the bedside. Speaking softly out of the corner of his mouth, without making eye contact, he said, "I'm working with a preliminary diagnosis of cyanide poisoning from a tainted acetaminophen pill, but I'm still waiting for toxicology and levels. We had to send the samples out."

"How do you know it's cyanide?"

"Oh. Well. Clinical history, presenting signs, and a mean smell of bitter almonds."

Paul moved closer, placing his hand on Dr. Z's cheek. To Paul's surprise, Dr. Z's cheek felt hot. His face had swollen like a balloon and his arms felt ridged. Lifting his eyelids revealed moderately dilated pupils.

"When did he come in?"

"About four a.m.," Hinkley said.

"I can't believe it."

"And there's more. At least six other cases reported so far. One's a little girl, DOA in our ER about an hour before Dr. Z."

"How come Z wasn't DOA?"

"Who knows? He's a big man, well over three hundred pounds. That could explain it."

"How'd you treat it?"

"You've got to realize, fourteen years in practice, I'd never seen a case before tonight. Of course, the ER passed a stomach tube and washed him out. Then I used a standard cyanide poisoning protocol, from a kit. Amyl nitrate inhalation, then sodium nitrite and sodium thiosulfate intravenously. And, of course, mechanical ventilation and one hundred percent oxygen."

"That treatment's the same as it was twenty years ago," said Paul. "You're using the blood itself to scavenge for cyanide. Isn't there something else you can do?" He felt Dr. Z's wrist. The pulse bounded rapidly.

"They've got a drug in Europe, a cobalt compound that mops up the cyanide and turns it into Vitamin B12," said Ben, "Not FDA-approved in the USA."

"Damn," said Paul. "Has he any brain activity?"

"First EEG was flatline, no brain waves at all. I'll do the next one tomorrow. I'm sorry."

A respiratory therapist, dressed in protective gown, mask, and gloves, disconnected Dr. Z's breathing tube from the ventilator. The therapist passed a plastic suction catheter into the breathing tube. Dr. Z didn't respond to the stimulation of the catheter entering the passages of his lungs. This was a bad sign; even a severely comatose patient usually has some response to poking in the lungs. Brain-dead patients, like patients under deep anesthesia, lack brain wave activity and don't respond to pain or other stimulation.

Paul detected a fruity smell coming from the breathing tube just before the therapist reconnected Z to the mechanical ventilator. Paul leaned in and sniffed.

"I wouldn't snort too much of that, if I were you," said Ben. "That's hydrogen cyanide gas. Smells like almonds."

"More of a fruity smell to me," said Paul. "A slight citrus tang, kinda like anesthetic gas, but not as sweet."

"Strange stuff," said Ben. "A lot of people can't even smell it, and those that do perceive it differently. All I know is, it's definitely not good for you." He left the bedside.

Natasha stood at the bedside, her slender torso bent over the bed rail, running her fingers through her husband's thin, sandy hair.

"Paul, why's he so hot? What's happening to him? Can he survive?"

"He needs a miracle, Natasha. But he's a strong man. It's a wonder that he's made it this far. The cyanide prevents his cells from using oxygen."

Her eyes widened. "You mean he's suffocating?"

"On a cellular level, internally, yes," Paul answered. "Some of his cells are using oxygen in a useless fashion, producing heat instead of energy. That's why he's hot."

"Paul," she said, grabbing his hands. "I love him."

"I know, he was like a second father to me. I wish there was something I could do."

"There is," she said. "I want you to find out who did this."

"What? That's for the police."

"I've no confidence in police, I want you. Most of my childhood, in the old country, I hid from the police. I can't rest until I know the truth. But if you won't do it for me, that's all right, Paul. Do it for him. Val helped you through school, residency, and got you this job. Although he'd never say it, I know he loved you like a son. I want his killer brought to justice."

Releasing her hands, Paul recoiled. "It's a random, serial murder. There are others..."

"That doesn't matter," she said, hanging her head, leaning over her husband. Clutching the bedrail, her pale hands turned red, matching her fingernail polish. Turning her head toward Paul, with eyes blazing green, she glared at him. He felt her desperation compelling him to obey. Now he realized Natasha had spoken the truth, that she'd never be whole again until the killer had been found. "Paul, I need this one favor."

The ventilator cycled, sending air rushing noisily into Z's congested chest. "All right, I promise I'll look into it. And if the police can't find the killer, I will."

Natasha smiled. Her hands relaxed their death grip on the bedrail, and her fine, white fingers flowed off the metal bar. "Thank you, Paul. You're a very special kind of friend." She wiped the tears from her eyes. They were cool, green, and bottomless.

Paul wondered just how deep he'd fallen into the abyss.

CHAPTER 2

Late the next day, Dr. Valdimire Zhazinsky's repeat EEG showed no brainwave activity. Paul paid his respects at the bedside in ICU as Ben Hinkley shut off the ventilator. It died with a sickening whoosh as the last breath left Z's body. His chest sank, and Ben shut down the monitors. It made no sense to monitor a dead man.

Natasha stood over the lifeless form of her husband for several minutes after all the life support systems had been terminated. Her black chiffon dress hung motionless and her eyes looked ready for tears, but none came. Paul wondered if she'd already started to come to terms with her husband's demise, or was she holding back, in denial? She leaned over the bedside and planted a single kiss on Z's dark cheek. Then she stepped away from the bed, stumbled, and would have fallen if Paul hadn't caught her in time.

"Let me take you home," said Paul.

"Thank you. I guess you'd better."

He started to lead her out of the ICU. Ben approached, shaking his bowed head. In his slate-gray, double-breasted suit, he looked like an undertaker. "I'm sorry, Natasha," he said, without making eye contact. "I did what I had to do." It struck Paul as an odd thing to say. He'd never known Ben to be apologetic or to openly examine his decisions. Paul couldn't think of anything more Ben could have done to save Dr. Z. His care had been timely and complete.

Natasha took Ben's hand. "It's all right, Ben, I know you did your best." Ben's fat lips turned pencil-thin, and tugged upwards at one end, like a smile was trying to escape. It never did. He jerked his hand away, back to the safety of his pocket, the tapered lapels of his suit flapping as he stretched the fabric. Natasha opened her mouth, her tongue flirting with her upper teeth, daring them to form a word. She sighed, shut her mouth, and said nothing.

Paul escorted Natasha through the hospital. Her dark dress flowed on her tall, thin frame, following like a shadow. Every time they entered a new corridor, heads turned. Natasha's maturity and natural beauty combined into a blend both rare and majestic. She'd been aged to perfection.

The cold, tan leather of her Mercedes C55 warmed up quickly as Paul slipped behind the wheel. Natasha snapped her seatbelt together and ran her hands downward, smoothing out her dress. She handed Paul the car keys.

"Still driving the old truck?" she said.

He took the keys. "What just went on back there?"

She pulled her head back, the kind of impossible movement you'd expect from a rooster. "What do you mean?"

"Between you and Ben. Natasha, if you really want me to help you find out who killed Val, you can't hold back." He started the engine. Three hundred and sixty horses rumbled. Natasha reached over and turned it off.

"For several years," she said, "I've suspected Val was having an affair."

"And now?"

"I don't have any proof."

Paul stroked his mustache. "And Ben knows?"

"Val and Ben were old friends. One way or another, Ben knows. And the way he looked at me tonight..."

"I'm sorry, Natasha."

"Don't feel sorry for me, Paul. Val loved me very much. I've got to believe it, because I still love him. That's why I've got to find out who killed him. I want justice."

Paul grabbed the car keys, looking at the drab, cement walls of the garage. "Take me home," said Natasha. "And please stay the night. I couldn't stand to be alone."

Paul nodded, realizing that Natasha wanted revenge more than anything, and he'd unwittingly become her avenging angel.

CHAPTER 3

The Mercedes hugged the road, twisting through overhanging boughs of evergreen trees, a fine drizzle falling off the branches. About every fifty feet a private driveway flashed by, some paved, others turned to mud. Overcast skies combined with thickening limbs to accelerate dusk, and night seemed to fall instantly. Paul turned off the road, stopping at the gateway of the Zhazinsky estate. Twin stallions of black iron reared on top of tall, brick sentries. Natasha touched a button on the car ceiling, and the wrought-iron gate slid open. As Paul drove up the cobblestone driveway, short, electric torches came to life and a cascade of light flowed along the edges of the path ahead. The gate closed behind them as Paul pulled up to the house. Spotlights lit the entryway as the driveway torches extinguished. The car stopped in an oasis of light, surrounded by blackness.

A massive weeping willow formed a canopy over the entryway. The house was a two-story English Tudor with irregular brown stones topped with square hardwood beams. A large dormer protruded high above, and Paul knew this loft room well. It had been Dr. Z's study, where they'd spent many hours together.

Paul ran around the car and opened the passenger door. Natasha slid out of the seat, unfolding her long legs and rising gracefully, like a newborn faun. She smiled as he took her arm and shut the car door.

They walked up three giant, stone steps to the elaborately carved oak door. Paul fumbled with the keys.

"It's the large, bronze one," said Natasha. Paul found the key and opened the door.

The parquet floor clicked as they entered, echoing. A winding, wooden staircase in front of them disappeared to the second level. Antique statuettes and vases on pedestals decorated the foyer and living room. In the entryway hung an oil painting of Natasha and Val, both young, their youth enhanced surrealistically by impossibly reddened cheeks.

In the painting, Paul could appreciate how broad-shouldered Val had been, even in his youth. A look of determined possessiveness filled his dark eyes. It clearly said, "This is my woman, stay away," and Val's big, hairy hand engulfing Natasha's waist reinforced the sentiment. But Natasha's face had the look of innocence, as if she'd just been born in Val's nurturing arms.

Paul found it difficult to imagine Val cheating on Natasha, unless Val subscribed to a double standard of faithfulness. If this double standard did exist, Paul could always explain it as a trapping from the old country. Maybe a married man in the old country needed to have an affair to reaffirm his manhood. Perhaps it was a rite of passage.

But where did that leave Natasha? Paul wondered if she'd ever strayed. She certainly attracted enough attention from men. All she'd ever have to do is reel one in. Paul's instincts told him that Natasha's love of male attention had a limit, and Val was it.

"Would you like some tea?" Natasha asked.

"Can we take it in the study?" said Paul. "Or is that..."

"Everything will remind me of Val, Paul. But I never want to forget. Yes, the study." She left to fix the tea.

Paul ascended the wide wooden stairway. His footfalls echoed with a reverberation more hollow than he'd ever remembered. He flipped the switch at the door of the study. The warm glow of a hanging electric lantern filled the room. The study contained a plush burgundy carpet, matching leather chair and couch, office furnishings, and wall-to-wall books. He sunk into the red leather chair next to the couch and ran his fingers along the ornate, brass tacks that held the upholstery together. It hit him that Val, his friend and mentor, would never again return to this room.

Natasha entered with a china tea set, put it on the coffee table, and settled onto the couch. The room filled with mint vapors and a trace of fresh perfume. Paul poured both of them a cup of tea.

"Whatever you need to know, Paul, just ask. I already told the police everything."

"Everything?"

"No. Not about that. Just everything they asked. Probably routine things."

"Natasha, I need more than that. I need it all."

"It started with his hunting trips."

"Duck hunting?"

"Yes, you know he had a passion for it."

"I know," said Paul. "We hunted together more than once."

"Yes, well, Val's passion became an obsession. He started going out of state. Finally, he found a good trip guide in South America, in Colombia, that's where he ended up going mostly. Dove hunting. Weeks at a time."

"You don't think he was hunting?"

"Oh, he was hunting, all right, but not doves."

"Other two-legged animals?"

"Uh-huh. That's what I suspect."

"Why?"

"You know his special edition Remington?

"He loved that gun," said Paul. "Wouldn't shoot without it."

Natasha frowned. "He left it home several times."

"Maybe he bought another one to keep in Colombia," said Paul. "Transporting a firearm to some countries is a difficult process."

Natasha shook her head. "But he had no bruises. How could he hunt for a week and come home without bruises? Even after a few rounds of skeet, Val always bruised his shoulder."

Paul sunk deeper into the leather. It was warming, molding to his shape. "How did it affect your relationship?"

"I pleaded with Val to stay home more. But his eyes would glaze over. He said he had to perfect his hunting skills. At first, I believed him. You know how much of a perfectionist he is." Paul nodded.

"He asked me to be patient," said Natasha. "Be patient and it would all soon be over. I guess, in a strange way, he was right." Tears filled her eyes.

The tea had gotten cold before Paul could drink it, and a chill filled the room as well. Natasha may have been right. Val could have been cheating, running away to Colombia for a secret rendezvous. Right now, it wasn't relevant to finding the one who'd poisoned the pills. He needed to change the subject for a moment.

"Where did Val purchase the pills?"

"In the local Thrifty Mart. I gave the bottle to the police."

"Can I see where it happened?"

"Of course. Follow me."

They went to the master bathroom on the first floor, a huge room tiled in black and gold. Paul opened the wooden medicine cabinet. It was empty.

"The police took everything," said Natasha. "Even the garbage."

"Where did you find him?"

"On the floor. On his back."

"Did he have a head injury?"

"No, he didn't. I remember asking Ben about that. Ben said it didn't matter. Val was as good as dead before he hit the floor anyway." She tore a tissue from a box and wiped her eyes.

Paul tried to picture a man of Val's size having a cyanide induced seizure and falling onto the tile floor without injuring his head. "We can do this tomorrow, if you want."

"No, that's all right. Can I show you anything else?"

As Paul walked around the immaculate bathroom, on the tiled deck of the nearby

Jacuzzi, a sparkle of light caught his eye. He leaned closer. A tiny shard of glass was stuck in the grout groove between the tiles. The shard appeared to have survived the police vacuum. He pulled his mini mechanics tool out of his pants pocket and coaxed out the tweezers. Carefully, he grabbed the tiny piece of glass with the tweezers, wrenched it from the grout groove, and placed it on a tissue. Held up to the light, the glass looked thin and fragile.

"What is it, Paul?"

"Have you broken a light bulb in here lately?"

"Not that I recall."

"It could be a piece of an ampoule, a glass drug ampoule. When glass drug ampoules are cracked open, they often shatter, leaving pieces that look a lot like those from a broken light bulb. Glass ampoules are used to package drugs for physicians and nurses, only."

"Why would Val have that?"

"I was going to ask you," said Paul. "Sometimes, I bring home samples or leftovers that would otherwise be thrown away. Maybe Val did, too."

"I don't know," said Natasha. She eyed the sliver and shook her head. "What will you do now?"

"There's nothing more here. Tomorrow, I'll call the police, quietly make some inquires. I have some friends there. Maybe I'll go down to the station, too. Then I'll decide what to do." He thought about visiting some of the other victims, and the Thrifty Mart, too.

"Won't they miss you at work?"

"I have some vacation coming, gave them notice already. I'd like to sleep on the couch in the study, if that's OK."

She nodded. "Good night," she said, and gave his hand a warm squeeze.

Paul reentered the study. The ampoule bothered him. Maybe it was nothing, but it didn't fit. Neither could he fathom Val miraculously escaping serious injury in the sudden fall. He scanned the books that lined the walls. Val's library was very impressive, especially the volumes on Russian literature of all kinds. Val and Paul had discussed many of the authors.

In any discussion on Russian literature, Paul had the disadvantage, for he knew little beyond what Val had taught him. Several old volumes caught Paul's eye. The worn covers only held together because they'd been made at a time when covers were sewn with devotion by hand. Dozens of fine golden ribbons marked places Val had frequently visited in the books. Pulling one book out, Paul angled the embossed, leather cover to the light in order to make out the title. It read, simply: *Rasputin*.

CHAPTER 4

Sunlight barely penetrated the thick curtains of the south-facing dormer windows of Dr. Z's study. Paul's first deep breath sucked in the earthy taste of mildewing paper. As his eyes opened a crack, he realized there was something heavy on his chest. An open book. Now he remembered, he'd been reading the thick volume of Rasputin's complex life.

Evidently, Dr. Z had studied Rasputin, in addition to all of Russia's most respected artists and scientists. But Grigori Yefimovich Rasputin had a scandalous reputation as an evil faith healer, a wizard of the black arts. In his youth, he'd earned the name Rasputin. It meant "debaucherer."

Rasputin won the support of the Empress Alexandra by successfully treating hemophilia of her son, Alexei. The Empress, in turn, influenced her husband, Czar Nicholas II. Rasputin, as a trusted advisor, wielded great power over Russia's imperial family from 1907 until the sorcerer's death.

But Rasputin abused his power, engaging in outrageous, immoral sexual exploits that irrevocably damaged the credibility of the government. A group of conservative noblemen conspired to kill him. They poisoned him with little effect, even though Rasputin received ten times the dose of poison required to kill a normal man. Shooting Rasputin didn't work, either. Finally, he was thrown into the Neva River and drowned in 1916.

Paul thought it ironic that Dr. Z, a student of Rasputin's life, would succumb to poison. Whoever poisoned the capsules must have had a motive, more than just wrecking havoc with strangers' lives. Seven people had now died as a result of one person's anger. Paul wondered what could have prompted someone to strike out in such a random fashion.

Grabbing the phone, Paul called his direct number for King County Sheriff Jackey McCann. She'd saved his life once and he'd returned the favor. That kind of experience was good for some no-questions-asked insider information. He got through.

"Jack, how've you been?"

"Powers, I can't believe it. You getting involved in this crap, again?"

"What tipped you off?"

"Your timing. And surveillance on the widow. Did you have a good night?"

"Very discreet."

"I'm warning you up front, Paul. This is a high profile case. All information is on a need-to-know basis."

"So? Tell me what I need to know," said Paul.

"Not a damn thing."

"OK, OK. Some generic info then. Theoretically, what motivates someone to strike out randomly?"

"Don't think random," said Jackey. "Think a specific goal."

"For instance?"

"Like destroying the drug company, becoming a celebrity, or making a difference in life."

"What about murder?" said Paul.

"Possible. That's partly why Natasha's under surveillance. The random killing could be a smokescreen. But there's seven dead, and no indication yet that any were targets."

"And the method, Jack?"

"Need to know."

"I do," said Paul.

"That's a stretch, but you are an anesthesiologist. I could be asking you for expert advice. Especially since Muhammadan dropped out, literally."

"The chief medical examiner?"

"Uh, huh. Hit the floor. Might be a brain tumor. He got an MRI scan yesterday. They any good?"

"Very good," said Paul. "Dr. Z taught me a lot about them. He helped develop the technology."

"Muhammadan's at Lakeside, so I'm sure he's in good hands. Do me a favor and check up on him."

"Sure."

"OK. So let's say I need your expert advice. The killer removed medication from the soft gel-caps with a syringe, replaced the drug with cyanide, and reassembled the packaging. A real professional job. We found one unopened bottle. Nearly undetectable. And all from the Thrifty Mart. We're trying to trace the cyanide."

"How?"

"Each batch has a unique chemical signature, so sometimes we can trace it to the source. It's easy stuff to get, but the feds require a mound of paperwork. There may be a trail."

"Thanks, Jack, from your expert."

"Powers, I bent the rules for you, so I expect you to call me with anything, no matter how small."

He thought about Dr. Z's alleged infidelity. "Need to know, only," said Paul.

"Christ. Stay out of trouble." She hung up.

Paul walked to the window and parted the velvet curtains. Beyond the iron gate, on the shoulder of the paved road, sat a black sedan with a shadowy figure inside. Paul had to admit Natasha's lack of faith in the official investigation was well founded. The police were wasting their time. Paul didn't know anyone who would benefit from Z's death.

Z seemed to be loved and respected by everyone. But Paul realized if Z had been unfaithful he might have made an enemy, and jilted lovers sometimes turned into killers.

Natasha appeared at the door barefoot, dressed in a white silk bathrobe. The frictionless fabric defied gravity and looked like it might slip off at any moment. She held a carved wooden tray with a breakfast of fruit, cereal, juice, espresso, and a single yellow daffodil. Rose perfume filled the room as she seemingly floated to the desk, leaving the tray on the felt blotter, in front of the desk chair. Dr. Z. had never let anyone share the tall, upright chair. Natasha smiled, as if she had no idea Paul would find it strange to usurp Dr. Z's sacred chair.

Paul swallowed, hurried back to the couch, and sunk in. He felt like he'd suddenly grown roots as tough as the leather. "I'll take it on the coffee table, please," he said, trembling. This woman had raw power that Paul couldn't fathom. She bobbed her head once, like tipping a hat, and moved the tray to the coffee table.

"Thanks, you didn't have to bother."

"No bother. You fell asleep in one of Val's books. They are quite boring, aren't they?" She'd obviously been to the room earlier.

"Nah, just tired, really. Did Z ever talk about Rasputin?"

"A favorite topic of his. The magic, the wonder, the mystery. You know."

"I'm beginning to," said Paul, running his hand through his bushy brown hair. He hadn't even combed it, yet. What a mess he must look.

"Did you find out anything?" she asked.

Paul choked on a bit of watermelon, finally forcing it down. Did she know he'd been on the phone?

"Not much more than I've read in the papers, except..."

"Except?"

Paul held the espresso at his lips, savoring the scent, sipping gently, eyes closed. He remembered duck hunting, on a clear fall day, Val and him, hiding in the blind, with only the warmth of coffee and friendship to combat the cold.

"Paul, whatever it is, I can take it."

He opened his eyes. "Did Val leave you well off?"

Natasha leaned back on the desk and crossed her feet, causing the bathrobe to creep upward. Her creamy calves and sculptured ankles looked like Michelangelo carved them from marble. Her face, too, seemed carved in stone.

"So, I'm a suspect, too?"

"No, please don't take it like that."

"You shouldn't listen to the police," she said. "They asked me already. Val left me very well off. I spoke to the insurance adjuster this morning. They're transferring two million dollars tax-free to my account tomorrow. Except for a small mortgage on the estate, we have no liabilities."

"How long has Val had the insurance?"

"Many years, but he did recently increase the policy limits from half a million to two million dollars. It was just after taking the job at Lakeside. He said we could afford more." Natasha folded her arms, leaned back, and sighed.

Paul's empty espresso cup chimed against the saucer as he set it down. "You're holding back again, Natasha."

"It's nothing, really. But all our finances, down to the last piece of paperwork, are in perfect order."

"So?"

"No, Paul, you don't understand. I mean absolutely perfect order. Every file complete. Every document labeled. Val provided every form and phone number I needed. And detailed instructions. He left me a step by step guide in the event of his death."

"You never knew about it?"

"No. Val handled all our finances and legal affairs. I never realized he was so organized. Maybe he had a premonition."

Paul shrugged. He didn't know what to make of Natasha's obvious surprise. Wives probably discovered many new things about their husbands after losing them. "He loved you, Natasha. That's all it means."

She pointed to the book on the coffee table. "And what did you ask Rasputin?"

Paul scratched his head. "I've been trying to figure out why Val lived for a while after taking the poison, when all the other victims died instantly. The noblemen poisoned Rasputin, fed him poisoned cakes, enough to kill ten men." Paul jumped off the couch, circled the coffee table, and paced on the carpet in front of Natasha. "That's it! Don't you see? Rasputin didn't die."

"I know the story. So?"

"That's what I fell asleep thinking about." Paul held up his open hands. "Why didn't Rasputin die?" He made a fist with one hand and struck the other. "That's the key."

"And?"

"Maybe Rasputin knew he was going to be poisoned, figured out what kind of poison, and took an antidote..."

"Unlikely," she said.

"That's what I thought, too. So, another explanation is dose. Maybe they messed up the dose."

"You think Val got a lower dose."

"Yes. The killer's methods may be inexact, essentially, he estimated. To inject enough cyanide into a gel-cap, he'd first have to remove all of the original drug. If he leaves some of the original drug in by mistake, then less cyanide ends up in the pill."

Natasha nodded. "I understand. He figured two pills full of cyanide would kill a big adult, but he didn't fill every pill the same. I feel so good having you here, Paul." She moved toward him and held his hands. Her warmth spread through him like an electric shock.

Paul let go gently and returned to the couch, putting the coffee table between them. "That's why Val lived for a while," said Paul. "Val got a lower dose. In 1916, it wasn't easy to measure drug dosages accurately. Rasputin probably got a gnat's dose of poison due to a fouled-up measurement."

Natasha walked to the window and parted the curtain, gazing out, her sharp profile etched against the glass. Paul wondered if she knew about the police car. "But unlike Rasputin," she said, "Val didn't survive the first attempt." She turned around, tears in her eyes, and her stone face melted.

CHAPTER 5

Paul took the Mercedes to Lakeside Hospital, leaving the Zhazinsky estate as a continuous line of visitors began arriving to offer Natasha condolences. Valdimire Zhazinsky had been a well-known and popular physician. Paul planned to question Ben Hinkley further, and to stop in to visit Dr. Muhammadan. Paul had promised Jackey McCann he'd visit the ailing medical examiner.

Dr. Z's funeral was to be held outside in the late afternoon, if the weather held. By some miracle, today looked like one of those rare dry spring days in the Pacific Northwest. Natasha expected Paul to be one of the pallbearers, so he needed to wrap up his business at Lakeside without delay. He'd have to go home, clean up, and change into something appropriate.

Paul found Dr. Muhammadan on the neurology ward in a private room. Heavy blankets swallowed Muhammadan's small body, and he looked like a mere lump in the bed. Only his large, bald forehead gave away his presence. As Paul walked closer, he noted Muhammadan looked pale, remarkable for a man with dark brown skin.

Paul observed Muhammadan as he slept. He breathed irregularly, with occasional coughs and sputters. A green tube by his nose provided supplemental oxygen from a jack on the wall. Paul remembered Joff Muhammadan as a vigorously healthy man, an energetic forensic scientist, tireless and exacting, who'd helped solve many difficult crimes. But the normally robust medical examiner now looked like a terminal man.

"Joff, it's Paul Powers. Joff." He shook him gently.

Joff gasped, choked, and then opened his eyes slowly. His pupils were cross-eyed and he seemed blind. "Paul, is that you?"

"Yes, Joff. How are you?"

"No damn good. Can barely focus, hard to talk, too."

"Just close your eyes and concentrate on talking. One thing at a time."

"Right." He closed his eyes. "Better now. Hit me like a bomb."

"What hit you?"

"Sudden headache. Got so weak I couldn't stand up. If Ben hadn't been there..."

"Hinkley?"

"Yes, we were going over the Z case."

"Anything new?"

"I don't know. I tried plotting the decay of the cyanide levels, some of it didn't fit the normal nomograms." Joff sighed and seemed to dose off.

Paul leaned over the bedside and shook the frail man. "Joff, Joff, don't fall asleep on me." Joff stirred, but didn't open his eyes.

"He's had enough for now, Powers," said Ben Hinkley from the doorway. His burgundy suit looked like it had been slept in, the purple tie sported a greasy stain, and his hair needed combing. "You'll wear him out."

"Ben, what did Joff mean by that bit about the cyanide decay? You were there."

"Oh, that. He tried to run the cyanide levels through normal decay nomograms, but he said the numbers didn't fit. The decay fell off too fast.

But he didn't account for the cyanide scavenging treatments I gave Val."

"That should have been obvious," said Paul.

Ben shook his head, his fat cheeks wobbled. "Should have been, yes, but Joff has a bleeding AVM. He's lost some of his cognitive abilities. Take a look at the MRI."

Ben pulled up the MRI scan of Joff's brain on the bedside computer. The report read, "Subcortical mass suspicious for small Arterial-Venous Malformation with peripheral extravasation and mild edema."

"What's the prognosis?"

"Good, he'll probably recover after a few months of rehab. The AVM has already bled. I don't expect any more trouble from it as long as we keep Joff's blood pressure down. Neurosurgeon said it should scar over, no reason to operate."

"That's the best news I've had today," said Paul.

"So leave the poor man to rest, and I'll see you later. I assume you're also one of the pallbearers?"

"Yeah."

"Well, you better get home and change. And me, too. We both look like hell." Ben put his arm around Paul and coaxed him toward the door.

"Wait a second, Ben." Paul slipped free of Ben's grasp. Ben turned around, his fat lips hanging open inches from Paul's face. "One more thing," said Paul. "Do you have any new ideas on why Dr. Z didn't die right away?"

Ben's face filled with color. "What is it with you, Powers? Morbid curiosity? The man is dead. Let's leave it at that. I haven't been looking into the nuances. He took cyanide and it killed him. That's all I know, and all I care to know. If you're smart, you'll drop this detective shit. You're a doctor, not a cop." He stomped out of the room and slammed the door.

Hinkley might have a point, Paul realized. He needed to start thinking more like a doctor than a policeman. He picked up the bedside phone to call the Medical Examiner's office. The receptionist left to find Dr. Poulos, the assistant medical examiner who'd taken over for Muhammadan. Paul knew Poulos, a neophyte more concerned with procedure and his own job security than with substance.

"Hello, Dr. Powers?"

"Hi. I'm with Muhammadan at Lakeside. He told me he was working on the Zhazinsky cyanide decay nomogram before the illness hit."

"How is Joff?"

"Very tired, but they believe he'll eventually recover."

"Thank God," said Poulos. "Yes, I reran the cyanide decay pharmacodynamics this morning, myself."

"Tell me about the discrepancies."

"What discrepancies? Everything checks out."

"Muhammadan said the cyanide levels fell off too fast."

"Nothing doing. Joff forgot to include the last few cyanide levels in his calculations. And some levels he used were wrong. Understandable mistakes, considering the shape he's in."

"Was Joff's math correct?" asked Paul.

"Oh, sure. But he entered the wrong data."

Paul paced in the tiny space by the bed, whipping the phone cord back and forth. It puzzled Paul how Muhammadan could do complex math, but neglect to include the correct data. If his mind had started failing, higher math ability should have been the first thing to go. "Could anyone have altered the data?"

"Never. Our data is treated as legal evidence. It's in a doubly encrypted computer database. You need a password to enter the system and an encryption code-key to access the numbers."

"Who knows the password and the code-key?"

"Only Muhammadan and me."

"Thanks," said Paul. "I won't take up any more of your time."

"Keep an eye on Joff, and wish him well for me."

"Yeah, OK."

Paul hung up the phone, wondering how Muhammadan could have made such a big mistake in his calculations. It might be worthwhile to check into the deaths of the other victims. Perhaps others had noticed odd circumstances surrounding the cyanide poisonings. Maybe it was intuition, but Paul suspected more was going on then a random poisoning by a madman.

There was the matter of Dr. Z's remarkably uneventful fall to the bathroom floor, his delay in succumbing to the cyanide, the strange piece of drug ampoule Paul found near Z's hot tub, and now a question raised by the medical examiner about mathematical inconsistencies in the cyanide levels. Taken alone, none of these minor events meant anything. Paul searched for a common thread to link these oddities together, but he couldn't come up with anything. It didn't surprise him. Maybe he was scrutinizing the whole affair too closely. The straightforward explanation of a random product tampering still seemed to provide the best fit to all the available evidence.

Tomorrow, he decided, he'd pay a visit to the parents of the little girl who'd been admitted DOA to Lakeside on the same night as Dr. Z. For starters, Paul planned to contrast the young child's poisoning and rapid death to the slow demise of Dr. Z. Paul hoped to find significant differences between these deaths if he examined the two tragedies carefully.

The irregular breathing of the chief medical examiner continued. He looked tiny, helpless, and vulnerable. Perhaps Poulos was correct, that Muhammadan's judgement may have been affected adversely by the malformation in his brain, even before the major bleeding began.

Muhammadan couldn't help Paul anymore. The man needed time to recover. Paul couldn't extract a straight answer from Ben Hinkley. He got annoyed when questioned, too annoyed. He seemed either remorseful or guilty over Dr. Z's death. Paul didn't know which. Maybe if he kept a close eye on Hinkley, his behavior at the funeral would offer a clue.

CHAPTER 6

The windswept grass of Forest Glen Cemetery surrounded the central amphitheater. Actually, the amphitheater was little more than a stone block surrounded by a lush lawn dotted with folding chairs. Beyond the lawn, gravesites divided by paved pathways spread out over many acres, like spokes on a wheel. Tall evergreen trees circled the long perimeter of the cemetery.

In the center of the amphitheater, on top of the block, sat a dark oak coffin. It was adorned with elaborate gold and draped in purple velvet. Nearly a hundred well-dressed people crowded around the monument, their hushed conversations drowned out by a stiff, gusting wind. Sun tried to poke through dark, stuffed clouds that hung ominously ready to drop their load on the mourners below.

A few warm days in a row had fooled the bulbs into sprouting, and daffodils and tulips sparsely decorated the dirt walkways of the cemetery. Starlings, just returned from their long journey south, skittered about in the branches of budding red leaf maples surrounding the amphitheater. Insects, the earliest hatchlings of the season, buzzed around the visitors.

Paul stood in the front row, with Ben Hinkley at his side. Hinkley's face was stern and unreadable under a sheen of sweat. Natasha, dressed in a heavy black gown with matching shawl, greeted all those who approached the coffin to pay their final respects. She never cried. Dr. Z insisted on a closed coffin, one of the many intricate details covered in the papers he'd left Natasha in the event of his early demise. Dr. Z had never set foot in an American church, apparently haunted by memories of corruption in the churches of his childhood. So, by Dr. Z's wishes the entire funeral would occur at the gravesite.

This had been an unusual forensic case for the medical examiner, because he had done most of the legally required toxicologies before Z's death. The cause of death had been investigated and proven by numerous physicians. And flat EEG's don't lie.

There hadn't been much for the medical examiner to complete after Z was declared dead and taken off of life support. Z's instructions had been overly specific, like all the instructions he'd left for Natasha. Z wanted a speedy funeral, outdoors in the great Northwest, rain or shine. So far it still looked like the weather would hold, although Paul knew Northwest climate could not be trusted, especially in the spring.

Paul recognized a few of the mourners as physicians he'd met at the university.

"Greetings, Master Paul, good to see you again," said a voice from behind.

Paul turned. The voice belonged to Horace Yardley, a British researcher Paul had worked for in residency, and a close friend of Dr. Z's. Horace stood about five-ten, pale, skinny, with a thinning crop of red hair. Yardley had left the University of Washington for some sort of private sector job, the exact nature of which Paul had never been certain. "Dr. Yardley, long time no see. I wish we could meet for a happier occasion. Where did you get off to, anyway?"

Yardley smiled. "Remember that bloody mess, picafentanyl?

Paul nodded. How could he forget? They'd worked together on the superpotent synthetic narcotic picafentanyl, under a grant from Edward Rose pharmaceuticals. The drug got all the way to clinical trials, and looked like a breakthrough anesthetic. It was developed on the basis of the paradoxical theory that stronger narcotics depress breathing less than weak narcotics. The powerful painkiller picafentanyl produced unconsciousness, but didn't impair breathing.

Unfortunately, the drug is partially excreted on the breath, like alcohol. During the clinical trial, in the operating room, Paul unhooked an unconscious patient's breathing tube for a few seconds for routine suctioning. The next thing he knew, he found himself in ICU with a nasty bump on his head and a drip of naloxone, a narcotic antidote, running into his veins. Apparently, the entire surgical staff had passed out in the midst of surgery. Rescue proved interesting, since no one could safely enter the operating room.

"Of course I remember picafentanyl," said Paul, "I still have the bruises."

"Quite. Edward Rose picked me up after they yanked picafentanyl from clinical trials," said Horace, handing Paul a business card.

Paul looked it over. "What are you working on these days?"

Horace looked over his shoulder and then leaned closer to Paul. "I can't say, exactly. Let's just say that a certain branch of your government took an interest in picafentanyl after the news got out."

"You're still working on it?" Paul asked.

Horace nodded. "Your tax dollars at work," he said. "Let me thank you again for backing me through the board of inquiry. I'd never have escaped intact if it weren't for you. I never told you, but they threatened to deport me. I'm forever indebted, old chap."

Paul couldn't believe it. The feds must have hired Edward Rose pharmaceuticals to develop picafentanyl for military purposes, or as an antiterrorist agent. No doubt defense contracts paid better than university research grants.

"OK, I get it. Don't ask, don't tell. No wonder you've been in hiding for a few years. At least they let you out for funerals. Good to see you." Paul slapped Horace gently on the back.

Conspicuously absent was Z's immediate family, for he had none. No sons or daughters. Natasha had never been able to have children, though not for lack of trying. The childless couple had endured years of in vitro therapy and experimental fertility treatments. But all the high-tech reproductive science known to mankind had not been enough to allow Natasha and Z to bring a child into the world.

Although he had not been an avid churchgoer, Z's instructions asked for a Russian Orthodox priest to officiate at the funeral. Natasha had retained Father Superior Alexis Novikov from the Northwest Russian Orthodox church in Kent, Washington, where Natasha frequently went to worship. Father Novikov was an octogenarian who wore his age well. He was stooped from either age or perhaps years of bowing in supplication to God, but Paul could tell the Father had stood over six feet in his youth. His black, flowing robes hung wide on his linebacker shoulders, hiding fifty or more excess pounds inside. The Church had been good to Father Novikov.

The Father raised a crimson bible until it almost touched his full, bushy beard. Small eyes, wrinkled from wisdom or stress scanned the pages. Dark, centipede eyebrows ran from the bridge of his fleshy nose, darting upward and disappearing under the edge of his black, pullover cap. The upper part of his beard parted slightly, and a melodious voice emerged from the dark opening.

"It's springtime. A time of renewal and rebirth. Valdimire loved the springtime, and the outdoors. And he was well traveled. Of all the destinations on the planet, Z chose the beautiful Northwest to live. As I read through Z's final instructions, I was puzzled as to why he insisted on an outdoor funeral, rain or shine. And it stuck me that Z would have been pleased to be buried here in the dead of winter, or the heat of summer, or the storms of the fall. He understood the holy alliance of God and nature, a wonderful trait for a man of science. And he channeled his profound awe of God into some of the greatest medical advances in history, for the betterment of mankind. I see the Holy Spirit in this man, his belief in God propelling him to an outstanding level of community service. His love for his community was only exceeded by his love for his dear wife, Natasha. Such is our belief in Christ. In Christ we all shall live and give our service to the Holy Spirit. In Christ shall we find truth. Only in our good works done in the name of Christ shall we ascend to the kingdom of heaven, to eternal life. For Christ told us that whosoever lives and believes in me shall never really die."

Natasha slowly scanned each of the mourners through her black veil while the priest droned on. When she locked eyes with Ben Hinkley, he looked away abruptly. Hinkley pulled a neat handkerchief from his suit pocket and wiped sweat from his forehead. He shuffled his feet a bit while awkwardly attempting to refold the handkerchief. Finally, he stuffed the sweaty rag back into his pocket.

"Today," said the priest, "we'll read verses that testify to the resurrection of Christ. Our faith is tested by belief in the resurrection of Jesus Christ. We're reminded that Luke did not at first believe that the Lord had returned, but later found his faith. Our faith in the resurrection should be as unshakable as belief in the wonders of spring, as clearly evidenced by this glorious day. Christ gave us the gift of eternal life in heaven. Let us pray in silence for the soul of our dear friend, leader, and devoted husband, Valdimire Zhazinsky." The crowd bowed their heads in silent meditation.

The priest continued the ceremony and brought many in the congregation to tears, dwelling on the sadness of the occasion. Bible verses mixed with hymns arose and dissipated into the gusty wind. The Father burned holy incense in a golden censer on a chain, swinging it by the coffin to symbolize the return of Dr. Z's spirit to God.

One of Dr. Z's university research associates delivered an upbeat eulogy, focusing on Valdimire's life and accomplishments. Paul learned more about Z's brilliant radiologic advances in MRI scanning and medical computing. Previously unknown to Paul, most of the advanced scanners and medical computers in use today contain complex software developed by Dr. Z, and hardware, too. The speaker referred to Valdimire Zhazinsky as the "Einstein of radiology."

The weather held for the amphitheater ceremony, and then the priest slipped two poles into brackets on top of the coffin. Paul took the right side, in front of Hinkley. Four other men, friends of Natasha that Paul didn't know, stepped up to the coffin, one man behind Hinkley, and three on the other side. Together, three abreast, they lifted the coffin from the stone.

They followed Natasha, who followed the priest, and the other mourners formed a double line behind the casket. The grim procession reminded Paul of Dr. Z's long trek from persecution in the old country, to notoriety in a new land. What a waste for such a brilliant life to end so soon. Paul's eyes welled up with tears, and he stumbled slightly, but somehow managed to hold up his end of the coffin. It seemed light, but Paul didn't know what to make of it. He figured the overwhelming sadness he felt must be playing tricks with his mind and muscles. He wasn't good at funerals.

Down the pathway through the expanding circle of gravesites they walked to the Zhazinsky plot. The pallbearers lowered the casket onto a canvas platform at the gravesite. Thick leather straps held the canvas platform aloft between two brass poles, suspending the casket above the grave. The dank scent of earth arose from the freshly dug grave, overpowering the sweetness of the evergreen trees and budding flowers. Something stung Paul on the leg, and he rubbed the painful spot. The vicious bite, part of the usual rites of spring, reminded Paul that life continued in spite of the untimely passing of his friend and mentor.

The priest finished. "This good earth is to be Dr. Valdimire Zhazinsky's resting place. Any turmoil he knew in life has ended. Here he shall know everlasting peace. As a final tribute, I'd like his friend and colleague, Dr. Ben Hinkley, to say a few parting words."

Ben stiffened and his jaw dropped. Natasha's lips drew to a thin line. Paul knew the priest's instructions hadn't originated as one of Dr. Z's numerous requests. Natasha had planned this. Ben couldn't back out. He was surrounded by devoted mourners. But from the expression on his face, they could have been a pack of wolves.

Trembling, Ben looked directly at Natasha before turning to face the crowd. He took a deep breath and swallowed. "I, I love Valdimire," he said. "Yes, I love him dearly, for his counsel, his generosity, his humor, and his professionalism. His presence will be missed by all who knew him. But a man of his stature can never truly die." Ben pounded on his left chest with his fist, "In here," he said, "Valdimire still lives."

A cold wind rustled through the evergreen trees and Paul shivered. Natasha approached Ben and put her arm around him. The priest signaled the gravediggers, and the straps holding the casket were released.

Paul watched the ornate casket settle deep into the earth. He bowed his head and swallowed hard. For the first time since Dr. Z's death, Paul felt empty. He'd lost a great friend and mentor. Looking for the killer was Natasha's idea. But the effort served Paul well, feeding his denial, keeping him preoccupied so he didn't have to admit his loss. Natasha had used Paul's inability to complete the grieving process to enlist his aid in securing revenge.

As the coffin finished the journey to its final resting place, Paul could no longer deny Z's death. No more would Paul need Natasha's skillful manipulations to push him to continue his investigation into the murder of her husband. Now Paul also yearned to see the murderer brought to justice.

Paul felt dizzy, hot, and shaky. A fire burned in the pit of his stomach and the air smelt burnt. He imagined grief must be making him ill. He never remembered getting so overwrought about anything in his life. Suddenly, a lancing pain seared his head. There were two Natashas, both out of focus. Grabbing his head, he doubled over and the lawn rushed toward him, a blunt impact on cool wet grass. Several strong hands grabbed him and turned him over. Looking up, a swirling circle of blurry faces stared down at him.

"Are you all right?" said a voice from the fog.

"911," he gasped. The words came out like spitting taffy.

CHAPTER 7

Paul looked up to see a comforting sight. Dr. Christine Mason, neurosurgeon and ex-lover, hovered overhead. Her bright, green eyes examined him beneath perfectly sculpted bangs of short auburn hair. For a brief moment Paul thought about what they'd had together, and why it didn't last. In the end, Chris' overwhelming love of medicine left little passion for him or anyone else. She remained his closest friend.

"Chris, why can't I move my head?" He tried to sit up

"Don't move. You're strapped down. You've been semi-conscious for over an hour. I'm running you through an emergency MRI scan."

"What's going on?"

"I don't know, yet, silly. That's why I'm getting the MRI. Now sit still."

Paul felt too weak to offer any resistance, especially against a set of restraints. Chris disappeared, and the cold table supporting him began to move slowly toward the oversized circle of metal that was the MRI scanner. Refrigerant coursing through the huge magnet hummed in Paul's ears as his head slid into the round, metal chamber. The faint scent of ozone crept up his nostrils, and the skin on his face seemed to be tickled by the magnetic flow.

The monstrosity clicked and whirred, reaching into the deepest recesses of Paul's head to find the answer to his sudden collapse. Paul knew Chris was hovering around the computer terminal in the control room, trying to glimpse each magnetic slice of his brain as it formed on the screen. Each individual imaginary magnetic image slice would peel off the screen as the next slice replaced it. Chris might have to review a semitransparent printout of all the slices in order to make sense of it.

In less than twenty minutes, the MRI scan ended. Paul awaited the verdict. No matter what, he'd be glad to be rid of the restraints. Chris reentered the inner chamber of the MRI scanner. He didn't need a high-tech scanner to read her face. The news was not good. "That bad?" he said.

"I'm afraid so, Paul." She removed the restraints from his head, and then his arms and legs. Tears formed and she tried to hold them back. Her dispassionate doctor persona withered in his presence. She still cared.

"Give it to me straight, in doctorese."

"You've got a small tumor in the posterior midbrain. Probably not an operable location."

"Prognosis?"

"Control and possible temporary remission with directed radiotherapy. But long-term outlook depends on the type. I'm afraid there's no easy way to get a biopsy."

"So we wing it, huh? Hope for the best?"

"Exactly."

The reality of Chris' statements struck like an axe. Primary brain cancer killed its victims quickly, and it was a young person's disease. Paul knew it would never go away, he'd have to learn to live with it. This would be his greatest challenge yet, living with the specter of early death.

"When do I start radiation?"

"Since your symptoms are serious already, I've arranged for you to start tomorrow. We'll do repeated MRI scans at intervals to follow your progress."

"OK, you're the boss," said Paul.

She smiled. "Paul, I..."

"You don't have to say anything, Chris, except that you'll stop by later."

"You know I will." She left the room.

An attendant wheeled Paul to a private room on the neurology floor, right next door to Dr. Muhammadan. It seemed ironic, both Muhammadan and he experiencing similar symptoms. They both had the sudden onset of headache, blurry vision, and extreme weakness. Many different neurological disorders manifested the same final, common problems. This is what makes neurological diagnosis such a challenge, and high-tech diagnostic tools like the head MRI scanner so indispensable. The MRI scanner can quickly differentiate between diagnoses such as bleeding malformations and tumors. An MRI diagnosis is regarded as accurate and infallible.

***

The next morning, after Paul returned from his first radiation treatment, Ben Hinkley came to visit. Seeing Ben depressed Paul almost as much as the diagnosis of cancer. Ben always seemed preoccupied with his medical duties, or perhaps he had other personal problems. Today, he looked like he'd gained twenty pounds.

"What's happening to all you doctors?" said Ben with a smile. "You're dropping like flies."

"They don't make them to last anymore," said Paul, struggling to pronounce each word. His lips, dry and stiff, wouldn't obey his commands without a fight.

Ben puffed out his big red cheeks. "Whoa, you need some rest, I won't stay long." Paul felt relieved. "I heard your treatment went well. Chris says if the repeat MRI is good, you can go home."

"I'm bored here. I don't do TV well."

"I heard your group is granting you a leave of absence. I suggest you use it." His jelly-like face solidified as he smoothed the front of his pale blue suit, running his hands over his enormous stomach. Wrinkles fled from the fine fabric like ripples on the surface of a pond. "Stay home for awhile and recuperate."

Coming from Hinkley, the fatherly advice seemed out of character. Why, Paul wondered, this sudden interest in his welfare? The last thing Paul wanted to do was stay at home and do nothing, especially if his days were numbered. He intended to continue his investigation into the murder of Dr. Z. As soon as Chris released him from Lakeside, he planned to question the parents of the young child victim.

A nurse entered with a wheelchair. "Free ride to the MRI scanner, any takers?" Paul smiled and threw his legs over the side of the bed. His control of his muscles had improved greatly overnight. After sliding his feet into thin plastic slippers, he tried to support his weight. The nurse quickly grabbed his arm to assist, even though he felt he could go it alone. He didn't blame her for helping; he still felt shaky.

Hinkley said goodbye and left, and Paul took the long ride to the MRI scanner. It amazed him that Chris expected to see any difference after one radiation treatment, but evidently Paul's specific tumor demanded frequent MRI scans for successful treatment.

CHAPTER 8

Chris gave Paul a temporary reprieve. He'd be free for two days, until his next radiation treatment and MRI scan, or until new symptoms developed. If all went well, he'd be able to get outpatient treatments from now on. This made him happy. He'd be able to handle outpatient therapy much better than weeks of hospitalization. In all the hours he'd spent working in hospitals, he'd never felt as helpless and cooped up as he did now. Being a caregiver didn't prepare you for being a patient.

A volunteer pushed Paul in a wheelchair to the entrance of the hospital. He walked to his Toyota pickup in the parking lot. Natasha had arranged for the truck to be driven back from the cemetery. A wet memo under the wiper blade said: *Go home and take it easy, we need you back at Lakeside-Ben.* The piece of paper came from a drug company "freebie" pad for Spasmol, a new muscle relaxant for severe spasticity. Paul thought the detail men must be desperate to try marketing Spasmol to an internist. As far as Paul knew, only rehabilitation specialists prescribed the drug. And only in extreme cases, because it had a lot of bad side effects.

Getting back behind the wheel of his truck felt unbelievably great, at least compared to yesterday, when Paul couldn't walk. He called the medical records department at Lakeside from his cell phone, on the pretense of needing billing information, and got the address and phone number of the cyanide DOA, a little girl named Kayla. Since he might be dying from a brain tumor, he wasn't going to worry about violating federal privacy laws.

Paul called the phone number on the girl's account, but it went directly to voicemail. He'd have to show up unannounced and hope for the best. Friends of his had once lived in Kayla's neighborhood and he knew the area well. After a short drive, he found the house, a brown, two-story affair with a thick shake roof. With the exception of a huge three-car garage, the house seemed conservative for this neighborhood.

He rang the bell. A woman opened the door, the side edges of her dirty blond hair swayed against a yellow pullover that hung casually over the waist of her white jeans. She could have been one of a thousand suburban moms, fortyish and a little too thick in the hips.

"I'm Dr. Paul Powers, a close friend of Dr. Valdimire Zhazinsky."

She held a hand to her mouth. "Oh, my. You mean the doctor killed in the poisoning?"

"Yes, I'm looking for Kayla's parents."

"I'm Joline, Kayla's mother."

"I'm so sorry for your loss. Could we talk for a bit?"

"Would you like to come in?" she said. He nodded.

She led Paul inside, through a brightly lit hallway to the living room.

"Thank you for meeting with me," said Paul.

"Can I get you some coffee?" she said, with a wide smile finished in peach lipstick.

"If it's no trouble," said Paul, softly. In reality, he could kill for a cup.

"Just a minute," she answered, and hurried out of the room in what Paul imagined to be the direction of the kitchen.

The living room sported a baby grand piano, an overstuffed couch, and two tall chairs. He quickly took full advantage of the comfortable couch, relaxing while viewing an array of family pictures on the wall. One photo showed a little girl, an angel with blond hair and blue eyes. He arose to examine the picture more closely.

"That's Kayla," said Joline. "She was our only daughter."

"She's beautiful," said Paul. "I'm so sorry. Why are you alone today?"

"My husband left for a few hours to close up things at work, but he'll be back soon. So many friends want to stay with me, but I need to be alone for a while. They'll all be by later." She set two full cups on the coffee table with napkins. The bitter aroma woke his nose.

"I can come back at another time." He stood up to leave.

"You were friends with the Russian doctor?"

"Yes. Close friends. Almost like father and son, at times."

"Sit down." He did. She sat opposite Paul on a stiff chair. "What can I tell you?"

"You bought the pills at the Thrifty Mart?"

"Yes, Kayla looked bad that morning, fever and such. So I. Yes, I bought them."

"Did you notice anything different about the bottle or the packaging?" He drank the coffee black, it was strong and hot.

She shook her head. "No, yes, I don't know." Tears pooled on her prominent cheeks.

"It wasn't your fault. You couldn't have known." Paul handed Joline one of the napkins. She wiped her eyes.

"I had a premonition."

"Anything you can tell me will help."

"I was so worried about Kayla, and so upset at my husband for being out of town."

"Where?"

"L.A. I had a lot of trouble getting the cap off. It stuck."

Paul wondered if extra glue added to the inner safety seal by the killer might have adhered to the threads of the plastic cap. It confirmed his suspicions that the killer's methods were not as perfect as Jackey suggested. Then it struck him.

"When did you give Kayla the pill?"

Her coffee steamed as she sipped it for a moment. "It must have been after 2 a.m. She was pronounced dead at 2:29 in the Lakeside emergency room."

"But you bought the pills early? When?"

"I don't know exactly, why? Does it matter?"

"It does."

She put down the coffee and ran her fingers through her hair several times. "Maybe 11 a.m., or a little after."

"Did the police ask you, too?"

"I don't recall. They asked so many questions. I wasn't in the best of shape to answer at the time."

Paul jumped up, fishing his cell phone from his pocket. "Excuse me, but I need to make a call."

"Sure, I have a mess in the kitchen, I'll leave you to your call." She left the room.

He called Jackey McCann.

"I hope you have something for me this time, Powers."

"I may, Jack. When did Z buy the pills?"

"According to forensics, the store video shows him there at 10:45 a.m. A cashier remembers seeing him sometime between 10 and 11 a.m."

"When did Natasha call 911?"

"At about four a.m. that night."

"Any other pills missing from the bottle?"

"No."

"Any other empty pill bottles found in the house?

"None. Powers, what's your point?"

Paul paced the living room. "Why does a doctor with a cold wait seventeen hours to take his medication?"

The line went silent.

Finally, Jackey spoke, "I want answers, Powers, not more questions."

"Yeah, well you can work on that one for a while."

"In my spare time," said Jackey, and she hung up. Paul settled back down on the couch.

"What was that all about?" asked Joline, as she reentered the living room.

"Another piece of a puzzle that's making less sense all the time," said Paul. "You bought medication in the morning, but waited until Kayla was sick enough to need it. I understand your reluctance to medicate a small child. But Dr. Z also waited all day to take his medication. I think an adult would normally take medication early, at the first sign of illness. Especially a physician, and especially Dr. Z. I remember him taking medication for every ache and bruise."

"I feel better talking to you, Paul. All these deaths. So senseless. We deserve to know the truth."

"I have one more question. It's just..."

"Please, ask me." She sat down stiffly on the hard chair, bracing her palms on the side for support.

"How did Kayla die?"

Her eyes widened. "You know, everyone knows."

Paul leaned forward. "I don't want to be told what I already know. What did you see, exactly?"

Joline's eyes glazed over, their focal point somewhere past Paul, beyond the wall of the lonely house. As if in a trance, she began.

"She was so weak, so frail. Her skin reddened with fever, the scary kind children get, the kind of fever that kills an adult. Had to get the fever down. She swallows gelatin capsules, can't take a pill. Only soft capsules, with juice. I remember..." She grabbed her head in both hands, holding it as if it might explode. Paul felt like a demon, but did not dare to stop Joline. He needed to know the truth, to see Kayla's death through her mother's eyes.

Joline continued. "I put the pill on her tongue, washed it down. And she started jumping, suddenly, she had energy. Until the seizure, a moment later, shaking, turning blue, falling limp. I couldn't save her. I couldn't. Oh, God, Kayla." Joline stood up suddenly, unsteady, shaking, as if she wanted to run away.

Paul got up from the couch and hugged Joline, her tears flowed as she trembled in his arms. The embrace seemed wholesome, natural. A horrible murder had linked the two bereaved strangers together. He held her until she stopped shivering.

"I'll be all right," she said, gently pushing him away. "There was one more thing."

"What was that?" Paul asked.

"It all happened so fast. Not even time to call 911. So I tried to breathe for Kayla. She had a strange aroma, a weird cross between burnt almonds and macaroons. I'll never be able to forget that awful scent."

Kayla's death had been swift and brutal. She would have fallen if Joline hadn't been there. If Dr. Z died the same way, his death would have been quick, and the seizure activity should have caused some noticeable damage.

Joline's description of the hydrogen cyanide smell didn't match what Paul had experienced at the bedside of Dr. Z. Paul remembered Hinkley said that people often perceive the deadly cyanide gas differently. But the different perceptions bothered Paul, in spite of Hinkley's explanation.

"I have to go now," Paul said.

She wiped the tears from her eyes with the back of her hand. "I hope I've helped."

"Yeah, you've helped a lot."

"What will you do, now?" She led him to the front door.

"Keep asking questions, keep looking." He decided his next stop would be the Thrifty Mart.

"What are you looking for?"

Paul smiled. "I don't know," he said, stroking his mustache. "Something unexpected. Maybe the missing piece of the puzzle." He left the house. Halfway down the cement walkway he looked back. Joline stood in the doorway, watching him. From this distance, she looked exactly like Kayla. He waved, and she reciprocated before closing the door.

Back on the highway, it was raining enough for Paul to use the mist setting on his wipers and turn his lights on for safety. He noticed a red Mustang, with its lights off, tailgating him in the right lane. Cars that followed too close made him a bit nervous. He slowed down to encourage the Mustang to pass in the left lane. The red car swerved into the left lane and pulled alongside him briefly, matching his speed.

The Mustang's passenger window lowered halfway, revealing a bearded head in a baseball cap. Paul heard sudden acceleration and was thankful the annoying car had decided to leave. As the car pulled ahead of him, a hand reached out the window, and Paul expected to get the finger. Instead, the passenger released what looked like a handful of snow. It crashed against the truck's windshield, shattering it. A million pieces of wet safety glass mixed with metal buckshot flew into Paul's face, and he lost control of the truck, braking, skidding, almost flipping the vehicle, running off the road, coming to rest on the grassy shoulder. Highway traffic zoomed by as he tried to catch his breath.

The inside of the truck looked a mess. He examined his face in the rearview mirror. The few bleeding scratches could pass for shaving cuts.

Other than the fright taking a few years off his life, and the truck needing a new windshield, he'd survive. He'd heard of road rage leading to violent acts on the highway, but he always thought it happened to other people. At least they hadn't shot him. Paul didn't see any reason to remain on the shoulder and wait for a cop. Chances of finding the offending car were slim. Red Mustangs had safety in numbers.

He thought about calling 911, and saving some of the buckshot for evidence. But spending the rest of the day answering questions and filling out forms would probably prove to be a waste of time. He'd have to pay for the repair out of pocket, anyway. There wasn't enough damage to merit filing an insurance claim.

Paul decided to go on his way. After finding his sunglasses in the glovebox, he slowly merged back onto the highway, glasses shielding him from the wind. He gritted his teeth, wind whipping through his hair, hoping his luck would soon change for the better. He doubted it could get any worse.

CHAPTER 9

Paul drove his Toyota pickup to a glass shop, and told them he'd been sprayed with rocks from a gravel truck. If the shop found any ball bearings in the truck, his story would be suspect, but he didn't care. For the moment, his cover story spared him a long stream of annoying questions.

He found a car rental company that agreed to pick him up, and then went into the bathroom at the glass shop to clean up. The scratches on his face had bled and clotted, leaving streaks of dried, crusted blood. His cheeks seemed hollow, probably a reflection of several days of minimal food, IV fluids, and stress. He looked sick, and certainly didn't feel well.

Washing out the scratches made them bleed again. So he stood there for a long time, dabbing the wounds with paper towels until they stopped oozing. Now, they looked like shaving cuts, and he hoped they would draw little attention. Paul finished fixing his face just as the rental agency ride appeared.

The rental agent never questioned Paul's altered account of the accident. After the usual paperwork, Paul drove out of the rental agency in a late model Hyundai sedan, headed for the Thrifty Mart.

While driving, Paul rubbed the scratches on his cheek, and they responded with a slight sting, but his fingers came back clean. For a moment, he angled the rear view mirror so he could catch a glimpse of his tattered face to reassure himself that the bleeding had really stopped. Then he eyed the drivers around him. From now on, he'd do his best to drive defensively and to watch out for crazy people on the highway.

The Thrifty Mart shared a small strip mall with the usual assortment of hairdressers, travel agents, card shops, and others. The parking lot was half empty and he easily found a spot. As soon as the twin sliding glass doors magically opened, Paul read the newspaper headlines: *Still No Leads in Cold Pill Murders, Northwest Stores Pull Liquid*

Cold Pills. Business at the store didn't seem to be affected. Random killing from product tampering, Paul thought, like violence on the highway, is an easy crime for the public to ignore, as long as you are not the victim.

Just as the headlines stated, all the cold remedies that came in a gelatin capsule were gone. But in addition, Paul noted that the Thrifty Mart had taken all liquid cold formulas off the shelf. He supposed the police were testing other medications from this store, looking for possible tampering.

Paul pulled a bottle of aspirin from the shelf and looked both ways down the aisle. From the cold pill display shelves, he could see thirty feet to his left and twenty feet to the right. The long aisle sported everything from over-the-counter drugs to books, candles, and greeting cards. To his left, a cashier stood behind a counter and register at the front of the store scanning items and handing out lottery tickets. Two video cameras hung over each end of the aisle.

Sneaking into this store and putting tampered vials on the shelf would be a difficult task. It occurred to Paul the best way to sneak bad drugs onto the shelf would be to purchase the same drug. Telling the difference between browsing and a product exchange on a security video might be difficult. The killer would probably have purchased some cold medicine on that day, and left a paper trail. Paul wished he could get access to the daily receipts. He placed the aspirin bottle back on the shelf.

Jackey must know how many people the video caught in this aisle on the day of the murders. Paul believed one of these people must be the killer. He'd have to get the film, somehow. Perhaps Jackey could access a copy for a little trade of information. He'd consider revealing Dr. Z's alleged affair. It probably had no bearing on the case, anyway.

As if Jackey could read his mind, she appeared at the end of the aisle. In full uniform, six feet tall, her sudden presence startled Paul. Slowly, she approached, until he could count every crevasse in her richly tanned, weather-beaten face. Unlike her face, her biceps and shoulders pressed all the wrinkles out of her green jacket, as if the sleeves had fallen behind her resistance training. Each brown stub of her close cropped hair stood at attention. He'd never seen her look so fierce.

"Unbelievable timing, Jack," said Paul. "We need to talk."

"Sure thing, but first, let me see your hands."

Confused, Paul complied, holding his hands outstretched and open. Jackey fixed her eyes on his, and reached out and grabbed his hands. He felt cold steel, heard a ratchet clatter, and looked down at his cuffed wrists, dumfounded.

"I'm sorry," said Jackey.

A blur of King County SWAT team soldiers rushed in from both ends of the isle, and grabbed him. For an instant, Jackey locked her uncomprehending eyes to his, as one of the SWAT team members roughly patted him down. "He's clean," said the man. "Get him out of here." Two helmeted men on each arm, clad in heavy Kevlar, shoved at the small of his back and it cracked, knocking the wind out of him, propelling him forward, uncontrollably. Tripping over his own feet, battered, the SWAT team carried him away. A dry, constricting ring gripped his tongue. He tried to move the hot, thick mass, to speak, but he could barely breath around it. Coughing, he gasped for breath as the team shoved him through the doors of the Thrifty Mart.

Outside, icy rain poured, chilling him, like falling naked into a snowdrift. The parking lot was jammed with police cars and SWAT trucks, red and blue lights flashing. A fire engine and a red ambulance sat ready just beyond the police vehicles. A crowd gawked from behind police barricades, and a TV camera turned to follow the action, red light glowing. Behind the TV camera, the satellite dish from a news truck hung twenty feet up from its hydraulic lift. It seemed everyone in the world knew about the SWAT team assault, except him. Another team in full body armor toted heavy equipment into the store. On their backs, he saw the logo: *Bomb Disposal Unit*.

Bundled roughly into the back of a police car, Paul fell across the seat as the door locked shut. The seat's dusty fabric smelled like a locker room. With considerable difficulty, he raised himself to a sitting position, face pressed against the wire barrier separating him from the driver's compartment. Jackey jumped into the front, passenger seat, shut the door, and turned around. The driver started the engine.

Paul found his voice. "Jack, what the hell are you doing to me?"

"Paul Powers, you are under arrest for the poisoning and murder of seven people by product tampering, and conspiracy to commit murder by discharging an explosive device in a public place. You have the right to..."

He knew the rest of the speech. Sitting back on the hard bench seat, Jackey's Miranda dialogue faded into road noise and rain, as his thoughts raced. Unreal! His quest for truth had made him the prime suspect. No one knew where and when he would be today. He hadn't told anyone. He felt like he'd been stalked by a psychic, but he refused to believe in psychics or mind readers. The informant was precise enough and timely enough to plant a bomb in the drug store and frame him for it. There had to be a logical explanation. I must be getting closer to the truth, Paul thought, and the killer is nervous. Paul shivered. It occurred to him everyone now believed he was the killer.

"Powers, do you understand these rights? Powers?" He looked up. Jackey had finished her required reading.

"Yeah."

She shook her head. "Jesus, Powers, an anonymous caller said you were about to bomb the Thrifty Mart. They wanted to let the SWAT team take you down. I convinced them you'd listen to me."

"What bomb? You don't believe any of this, do you?"

"I believe we caught you in the Thrifty Mart with a bunch of C4. What do you want me to believe?"

Paul rolled his eyes. He knew this wasn't happening. Surely he was dreaming, having a nightmare. Soon he'd wake up panting, covered in sweat.

"Where were you on the day of the murders?" Jackey asked.

"I had a bad evening on call the night before, I was in bed, alone."

"Do you have an alibi?"

"Look, the cyanide killer had to be on one of the store's security videos. That ought to clear me."

"I don't think so, Paul."

"What?"

"I reviewed the videos for the first time this morning, trying to match faces with names."

"And?"

"At 10:08 a.m., a man pulled several packages from his pocket and put them on the shelf among the liquid cold pills."

"Did you get a look at his face?"

"Yes."

He leaned forward, halted by a sharp back spasm, the legacy of one SWAT team member's fist. "Can you ID him?"

She nodded.

"Well?"

"It's you," she said, frowning.

Paul sunk back, deep into the seat. He wondered if he could trust his own thoughts. Maybe the brain tumor had turned him into a mad man.

CHAPTER 10

In the Bellevue Police station, a swarm of blue uniforms in brass buttons and badges clashed with the ragged delinquents filtering through the station. Simultaneous conversations and a steady charge of phones, beepers, and faxes blended into a loud rumble. Above the noise, a distraught woman yelled at a young officer behind a desk as he attempted to fill out a report. Jackey led Paul through the chaos, into a room where he was fingerprinted and swabbed for DNA. In the next room, he signed a form and watched his few possessions packed into a plastic box.

At last, Jackey allowed Paul access to a phone. He decided to call Milton Freeman, his attorney. Perhaps it was a bad sign that Paul knew Milton's personal number by heart. Milton had gotten Paul out of tough spots before, and he trusted him. Paul dialed.

Someone answered. "Hello?" they said. Paul had expected a secretary, but Milton had picked up himself.

"Thank God you're in."

"I'm not in. I'm in Arizona. Who is this?"

"Paul Powers."

"You're not going to let me finish my vacation, are you?"

"I'm in jail, in Bellevue."

"Whoa! Who did you kill, this time?"

"Seven of them. They think I'm the cold pill murderer, and a terrorist."

"What? How did you get tangled up in this? Playing detective again, are you?"

"Yeah."

"I'm on the next plane out, at your expense. You've got to stall' em. Waive your right to an attorney, temporarily. Plead not guilty. Don't give a statement or answer any questions until I get there. And stay out of the shower. OK, Powers?"

"I can handle it."

"Good luck."

"Yeah, thanks." He hung up. There went his freedom, his reputation, and his savings, all in one day. Now the only thing he had left to worry about was his life.

As the door of his holding cell shut with an eerie clang, Paul wondered if he'd ever again see daylight. Would they agree to bail? And if they did grant him bail, could he even afford it? The cold cell smelled of vomit and urine, scents with which Paul, as an anesthesiologist, had more than a passing familiarity. He thought Jackey must doubt his guilt, because he suspected she'd used her influence to get him a private cell. Judging by the assortment of tattooed misfits in the adjoining cell, Jackey's kindness probably saved his life. Paul knew he wouldn't last five minutes with the characters next door.

He lay upon the hard cot, closed his eyes, and tried to convince himself of his innocence. Perhaps the brain tumor had confused him to the point of committing the crime and then searching for the killer. He'd surely need elaborate psychological and physical testing to determine his fitness to stand trial. And what about his radiation treatments and MRI scans? Would he be allowed out of prison for high-tech medical care? He wondered if medical care still mattered. A quick death from a brain tumor might be better than sitting on death row.

Despite the cold, uncomfortable surface, Paul dosed off, losing track of time. He dreamed of duck hunting with Dr. Z, only Z looked like a shotgun-toting skeleton, with a huge, toothless smile. As Z unerringly picked off ducks one by one, they screamed in terror and fell to earth, whistling progressively louder, like buzz bombs, exploding on impact, closer to Paul each time, zeroing in on the blind. He looked up at a wounded, shrieking, duck-bomb, heading straight for him. At the moment of impact, he awoke, shaking violently. The duck's shrieking turned into a loud whistle, a human catcall from the next cell.

"Paul, wake up, please." He opened his eyes, and shifted his shivering, stiff body off the cot. Covered with sweat, he stood up, struggling to focus.

"You look terrible," said Dr. Christine Mason through the bars.

"I feel worse," said Paul.

"Tumor or not, I don't believe you did this."

"That makes one of us," said Paul, grabbing the bars for support. He loved her taut face, creamy skin, and perfect bangs. Even in jail, Chris never dropped her guard.

She took his pulse. "Your heart's racing, you're so pale. I've got to get you out of here."

"Good luck. I may not even get bail."

"No, but I told them you're sick, in my care, and I need you at Lakeside for testing and treatment as soon as possible." She put her hands over his and looked deeply into his eyes. She's so beautiful, he thought, I hate for her to see me like this. "It'll be OK," she said, but her wrinkled brow said the opposite. In her face, he saw his own physical and mental deterioration.

"Never thought I'd be so glad to have cancer. Strange world."

"Don't say that, Paul, please. Where's your lawyer?"

"In Arizona. But I called him. Milton will come through, he always does."

"I'm going back to get your medical records, the public defender is helping me for the time being. They may need to have another physician examine you."

"The jail doc?"

"Yes. Don't give up, Paul, I'm sure it's all a mistake."

"An elaborately crafted, well orchestrated, ironclad mistake, better known as a setup. They thought of everything, Chris, except the lynch mob. And funny thing, it might be true, for all I know."

Chris shook her head and started to walk away. He knew as the words left his tongue he shouldn't have spoken with such despair. He'd like to blame it on the brain tumor, but in reality, he often didn't know when to shut up. "I'm sorry, Chris. It's great to see you. Thanks for trying to help."

She turned around and smiled, tears in her eyes, her auburn bangs tossing. "That's better. I'll be back soon. Bye."

Paul walked back to the cot. If he wasn't already crazy, this drab enclosure would drive him nuts. He'd have to hold on to what little sanity he still had until Milton arrived. There was no way to make sense of the day's events. Paul closed his eyes and tried to sleep. He figured any nightmares he might have tonight couldn't be any worse than his reality.

CHAPTER 11

The next day Paul was whisked away in a van to the King County Courthouse and Jail in Seattle for his arraignment. The van was loaded and unloaded in police garages to avoid the media. Paul never got even a glimpse of the outside world. Attorney Milton Freeman arrived just in time to give Paul a short briefing. Handcuffed, Paul was paraded by two deputies into the judge's chambers, along with an assistant prosecuting attorney and the arresting officer, Sheriff Jackey McCann.

The room was lined with metal shelves, stuffed with books. Judge Ryan was a sixtyish man with two horizontal tufts of gray hair protruding from either side of his bald head. He leaned forward from his perch behind an old desk, wood heavily stained from years of abuse, and gazed at Paul over the top of a pair of moon-shaped reading glasses.

In front of the judge stood Milton. He sported a deep Arizona tan topped by a receding cap of curly white hair. He asked the deputies to uncuff Paul, and the judge did not object.

Judge Ryan ruffled through a stack of papers in front of him. Triple chins could not hide his puzzled look.

"Doctor, these are serious charges. Do you have anything to say before I read them?"

Paul saw Milton shake his head. "Nothing, Your Honor," said Paul.

"Very well. You're charged with one count of product tampering, seven counts of second degree murder by means of product tampering, and one count for the unlawful attempt to discharge an explosive device. Prosecutor, how do you justify these charges?"

"Your Honor," said the assistant prosecutor, a stiff young woman in a dark blue pants suit. "A security video shows the defendant illegally exchanging the retail products in question in a timeline consistent with the product tampering and murders. And on a different day an anonymous caller claimed someone planned to bomb the same store. Then the defendant was found at that store in close proximity to a potent C4 explosive device."

"All circumstantial, Your Honor," said Milton. "There are no direct links from my client to the crimes in question."

"But more than enough evidence to support the charges," the judge finished. "Sheriff McCann, is the defendant here the same person you apprehended as per your report and are the prosecutor's charges consistent with your knowledge of the crime?"

"Yes, Your Honor."

"Dr. Powers, do you understand these charges?"

"Yes, sir."

"How do you plea?"

"Not guilty."

"So noted."

The prosecutor spoke up again. "We ask that bail be denied due to the horrific nature of the crime and the imminent threat to society posed by Mr. Powers. We wish to point out that Mr. Powers is also suspected of domestic terrorism."

"That's Doctor Powers, madam," said Milton. "I note that the doctor is in good standing in the medical community, has no prior record, and has pleaded not guilty to the charges. And no terrorism charges have been filed at this time."

Judge Ryan leaned forward, removing his reading glasses, and looked at the assistant prosecutor. "Does the prosecutor's office still believe in the presumption of innocence?" the judge asked.

The color ran from the assistant prosecutor's face. "We do, Your Honor," she said.

"Very wise. Bail to be set at two million dollars. Dismissed."

Paul's heart sank into the pit of his stomach. He knew two million dollars bail was almost the same as no bail at all.

"Don't worry," said Milton. "We can fight this. The good news is they don't have enough concrete evidence to make the charges stick."

"So what's the bad news?"

"No one will issue a bail bond for two million dollars unless you put up one-hundred percent collateral. The usual ten percent payment won't work. You'll have to put up the whole two million in securities, real property, or cash."

"I don't have that kind of money."

"I know. But I'll get you out, somehow."

Paul felt a bit reassured. Milton did his best when working against all odds, and he never made a promise unless he planned to keep it.

As the deputies ushered Paul out of the judge's chambers, Jackey McCann shook her head and flashed Paul a stone-faced and detached look. The deputies took Paul back to a holding cell in the King County jail. As his head cleared a bit, he started to make a list of all the little things that didn't make sense in the investigation. One item, the discrepancy in the time it took for Dr. Z to medicate himself, bothered Paul greatly. How had Z escaped a head injury? Why hadn't he died immediately? What of the shard of strange glass in Z's bathroom? Paul added his arrest to the list of unexplained phenomenon. Clearly, Jackey would no longer provide him with any inside information from the ongoing police investigation.

Suddenly it occurred to him, what if the road rage incident wasn't random? What if someone had tried to kill him or discourage his private investigation? After failing to knock him off the track of the killer, the next logical step might be to frame Paul for the murders. He hadn't told anyone about his plans to go to Joline's or to the Thrifty

Mart. Yet, someone had waited for him at both places.

Somehow, his plans had been discovered before he'd revealed them. As far as Paul knew, he hadn't been followed. Even if he had been followed, how could anyone have set him up in advance? How could they have anticipated his trip to the Thrifty Mart and placed a C4 bomb in the store before he'd arrived? So what had the killer done, read Paul's mind? Not likely. The more he thought about it, only one conclusion remained. The brain tumor must have turned him into a mass murderer, without his knowledge or consent.

After all, Jackey identified him on the security video from the Thrifty Mart. Unless he was the killer, how could the video show Paul stocking the shelves? Maybe the killer looked like Paul. He had an average face, nose a little too full, with a common brown mustache and hair style. He was of average build and stood five-nine height, an average height. A million guys fit his basic description. But Jackey knew Paul very well. Without question, she could pick him out from a million other guys. All Paul's convoluted reasoning led right back to the same logical conclusion. He must be guilty as charged.

A guard approached the cell. Paul thought it might be dinner time, but they had taken his watch. The guard pulled a key from his belt, unlocked the door, and swung it inward. "You're free to go," he said.

Paul stared out the open door. "What?"

"You can go, now, I said."

Paul looked up. The guard twirled his key ring on his finger. "Unless you'd like to stay." Paul stood up, painfully unbending his lower back.

"Did they drop the charges?"

"Oh, no. You made bail."

Paul tried to think of anyone he knew with two million dollars to spare. He doubted the anesthesia group would post bail. He'd only been on the job a few months, and from the looks of things, he'd probably never work again. Collecting his thoughts, he slowly followed the guard out the door and into the precinct offices. Uniformed police swarmed around like bees. One officer was dragging a hooker, kicking and screaming. Rings and jewels sparkled on her pierced face. A line of handcuffed men, almost identical, waited for processing. Paul had seen these generic faces before, the homeless druggies of greater Seattle, begging or stealing for their next fix. The police station rounded them up, digested them, and excreted them back on to the streets in a never-ending cycle of tragedy.

In the merchandise room, the desk clerk returned Paul's wallet, watch, comb, pocket tool, change, cell phone, and half a roll of antacids. As he followed the guard to the front of the station, Paul chewed two of the tablets. The chalky powder coated his throat with dry grit. At the door, dressed in a black leather coat, carrying an umbrella stood Natasha. The guard left, and Natasha handed Paul an extra-large, black, hooded overcoat.

"It's Val's old coat. Put it on, it's pouring outside."

"The insurance money? That's not wise," said Paul. "I'm a bad investment."

"I know you're innocent. And you're the only chance I have of getting to the truth."

"I have a brain tumor. Who knows? Maybe I killed Val." His face stung and his ears rang. Sudden dizziness nearly knocked him down. After staggering briefly, he regained his balance. She'd slapped him, hard. He rubbed his cheek. It bristled with pain. Even the hair on his moustache hurt. His fingers came back spotted with blood, because the glass cuts had reopened. Once again, he confirmed that he didn't know when to shut up. He deserved more than a slap. For the price she'd paid, Natasha should have clobbered him with the umbrella. "I'm sorry," he said.

She squinted her eyes and gritted her teeth. "Come along, Paul. We have a lot of work to do." He had two million reasons to obey, so he took her by the arm, letting her lead the way. As he left the captivity of the police station for the free world, he felt like the handcuffs still remained. But now Natasha held the key.

Paul looked around as they walked away from the station. He'd half-expected an ambush from a crowd of reporters. Pedestrian and street traffic was light and no one seemed to notice that an alleged mass murderer had just been released from jail. Paul inhaled deeply the damp fresh air and realized how good it felt to be out of the musty cell.

Natasha had somehow managed to post bail without attracting immediate attention. They made it to the car without being accosted by a single reporter. She drove the Mercedes this time, while Paul slouched in the passenger seat, exhausted. He'd gotten himself too deeply involved in investigating the poisoning murders to be able to stop. Besides preparing a defense, he'd have to do Natasha's bidding or go back to jail. He didn't know which alternative frightened him more. As he examined her intense face in profile, with her eyes fixed on the road, he understood for the first time the indomitable woman who'd survived and thrived against all adversity in the old country, where she'd had no one to rely upon but herself.

Natasha's indefinable, raw power had drawn Paul into her struggle to find her husband's killer. Besides her willpower, of course, there was the small matter of two million dollars in bail. He couldn't get rid of a nagging thought, or perhaps intuition, that Natasha knew much more than she was willing to reveal. But he'd never discover her secrets by asking. Whatever she knew, he'd learn only by investigation and deduction.

More than anything, Paul needed a shower, and a good night's sleep in a real bed. Rain washed against the windshield, scattering the glare of the oncoming headlights. Black night engulfed him as multicolored lights, traffic, and advertising, blended into a haze. The city smelled stale. He closed his eyes, leaning against the window, trying to doze, butting his forehead on the frosty glass during stop and go traffic.

"Don't pass out yet," said Natasha. "We're going to a party tonight."

Paul forced his eyelids open. He couldn't have heard her correctly. "You're joking."

"I'm not. There's a suit in the trunk from Nordstrom, I think it's the correct size."

"I don't believe this. You're for real." He sat up. "You paid two million dollars to take me to a party?"

She smiled, licking her cherry red lips. She had the type of lip gloss that never smeared. "Mmm, yes, it does seem a bit pricy for a date."

A sudden rush of adrenaline hit Paul, perking him up. "You want to explain?"

"The security video. Twi Chang owns the company."

"How do you know about the video?"

"Anyone who reads the papers knows."

Paul realized he hadn't had access to any news since his arrest. He wondered if he was now a tabloid sensation, or the most hated man in the Northwest, or both. "You're going to question Twi Chang?"

She nodded. "I know it wasn't you on that video. I want to know what happened."

"Isn't it a little too soon for you to be partying?"

"Perhaps, but the invitation came long before Val's death, and everyone will be there."

Paul sighed. Now he understood. "You need me with you. A bereaved widow at a high society ball, with her husband's murderer on her arm. You want to start a shock wave. Why?"

She caressed the leather covered steering wheel, wrapping her arms around it. "To shake out some information. Someone in this town knows more than they're telling."

Natasha might be describing herself, Paul thought. But her crazy idea had merit. People tended to talk more under duress, and alcohol helped, too. The party would give him an opportunity to find out more about the security system that might cost him his life, and to question all the richest and most influential players in Bellevue. Since the whole town probably thought him guilty, what did he have to lose? The powerful grapevine of executives and community leaders had access to privileged information, and more informants than the FBI.

"It's at the country club," she said. "We'll shower and change there."

City lights gave way to patches of country blackness as they left the highway for the backwoods of Bellevue. Even in darkness, the unmistakable rolling arrogance of an eighteen-hole golf course came into view. The road twisted and turned, and the dank scent of freshly cut, wet grass engulfed them. Natasha took her anxieties out on the car, taking each turn a little too fast, rocking Paul back and forth in his seat, his stomach churning. He felt like he'd been swallowed by a huge snake, with powerful peristaltic waves pushing him down a slimy meandering gullet toward eventual doom. Hunger disappeared in a wave of dizziness and nausea. Another shove of acceleration confirmed Natasha didn't want to be late for the party.

She circled the main building of the Eastside Country Club, a round, poured concrete structure, large enough to be a small stadium. A three-story glass-and-aluminum prow framed the front entrance. Beyond the packed parking lot, shadowy figures in dark suits and light, flowing dresses funneled into the glass entrance, like bits of glittery sand flowing through an hourglass.

Natasha parked in the rear of the round building, in a deserted lot. "The health club," she explained, popping the trunk. "Grab your suit, I have a key to the locker room entrance." She started to slide out of the car, but Paul grabbed her arm.

"Natasha, what are you keeping from me? What do you expect me to do tonight?" Once again, he hadn't been able to keep his mouth shut.

She smiled, lips wide, eyes fixed on his, probing him with some kind of sixth sense she handled so well. Maybe Natasha really could read his mind. She patted him softly on the knee. "Keep asking questions, Paul, that's all I want." Paul let her arm go. As he suspected, the direct approach couldn't pry any more information from Natasha, but at least he'd tried. If he stayed sharp at the party, perhaps her behavior would reveal her true intentions.

A strong cup of coffee would go far in restoring him to an alert frame of mind. Right now, he wanted to go home, wash off the jailhouse stench, and get some sleep. The last thing he wanted to do was go party, and this party promised a long night of hard work. His future and his life hung in the balance.

Whatever Natasha's motives, she had bailed him out. For the time being, he thought it logical to assume she was on his side. But with the tumor growing in his brain, he wasn't sure if he could even trust himself.

CHAPTER 12

Natasha's keen sense of style hadn't failed her. Paul's transformation in the locker room was nothing short of miraculous. As he stared in the mirror at the new Paul Powers, he found it hard to believe he'd just come directly from jail. He felt like some Mafia family hotshot, back on the street, looking good, and ready for hors d'oeuvres. The gray pinstriped suit gave him a bold, vibrant look. A delicate rose-colored shirt and coordinated power tie sparked a virtual explosion that demanded attention. It was perfect for tonight, for he needed all the attention he could get.

No detail of his outfit had been left to chance. A richly carved leather belt, jet black Ralph Lauren Oxfords, socks, and Calvin Klein underwear had been provided. All of the necessary toiletries for a quick cleanup came in a traveler's kit, neatly organized. Straightening his tie, he reached into the inner coat pockets to find a leather-bound memo pad and Montblanc pen on the right, and *Paul Powers, M.D.* business cards on the left. The phone number on the cards belonged to Natasha. This had always been her investigation, he thought, but now it was official.

Natasha had even provided two energy bars, Starbucks instant coffee, and a cup to mix it in. He hungrily devoured the energy bars and washed them down with two cups of hot coffee. Sugar and caffeine had always been his two most important food groups. They had the intended effect, coursing through his body quickly and restoring his vitality.

By the time the new Paul Powers emerged from the locker room, he realized Natasha had bought him, down to the underwear. Although he didn't like being owned, he could think of no alternative. At least he hadn't come cheap. Natasha had given him the freedom and resources to prove his innocence, an opportunity he couldn't afford to pass up. So he waited for her in the dark entrance to the gymnasium, outside the women's lockers.

And out she came. "You look wonderful," said Natasha. He thought the same of her. She wore a black gown with a French cut slit. A fine lace held up the almost bare right shoulder, an effective fashion tease. The open shoulder fell into a thin slit, revealing a sliver of smooth, olive skin. It curved toward her right breast, reversing halfway there, tracing downward, providing a peek at her strong hip. Skirting the front of her thigh, the window of flesh darted daringly toward her inner loins, diving down her leg to finish in a split evening dress look. As the seductive slit released Paul's eyes, air hunger choked him. He took a breath.

"A Gianna Versace original," she said, walking toward him like a model down a runway. "Do you like it?"

"I was right. You are out to start a shock wave." More like a tsunami, he thought.

"I have an eye for style," she said, smiling, "and you're not bad yourself. Almost worth two million bucks." She straightened his tie, the soft warmth of her fingers brushing his chin. His moustache twitched electrically.

"I've never been to this kind of party before."

"Follow my lead, you'll do fine."

This time, Paul drove. He took the Benz out the back parking lot, reentered the main approach road, and drove to the front entrance of the club as if they'd just arrived. Now Paul had joined Natasha for an evening of deception and detection. A doorman let her out, while Paul surrendered the keys to a valet in uniform.

A silver metal prow framed the building entrance. Beneath the prow, a row of glass doors trimmed in gold foil stood open, indifferent to the environmental and financial cost of admitting the chilly, Northwest night air. Tall evergreens bordered the building, a bit of nature inserted between cement walkways and poured concrete walls. Mature rhododendrons, ten feet high, swayed on either side of the doors.

Milling about in the foyer, Paul recognized Michael Buchanan, CEO of Aquatech, the largest marine technology firm in the country. His picture had often appeared in local papers. In his late fifties, Buchanan had to be one of the richest men in the world. Streaks of gray highlighted his dark hair. His wife looked perhaps twenty years old, a blue-eyed, short-haired blond in a black, silky, spaghetti-strap dress. The dress was covered with cloth butterflies that matched a tattoo above her ample left breast.

"Natasha, you look lovely," said Buchanan. "How are you getting along without Val?"

"Paul's taking good care of me," she said. Buchanan's lips twitched, collapsing into a thin line, his gaze drifting somewhere over Paul's head. Buchanan's right hand circled his wife's thin waist, his fingers pressed gently into her buttock. He didn't introduce her.

Paul was disgusted. He wondered why Buchanan didn't just mount his wife's head on a wooden plaque over his fireplace and be done with it. But Paul didn't blame Buchanan for ignoring an accused killer out on bail. Buchanan provided a good sample of the kind of reception Paul might expect tonight. Cool was certainly better than overt hostility.

"How's your health, Michael?" said Natasha.

"Steady as she goes, all watching and waiting now." He stroked his wife's behind. "I'm very upbeat about the future."

"Wonderful," said Natasha, giving Buchanan's free hand a quick squeeze. Buchanan gave his wife's rear a subtle push toward the ballroom door, like a rider guiding a horse. She responded like a well-trained thoroughbred, trotting off through the ballroom doors, her husband in tow, both laughing about God knows what.

"Why the health question?" Paul asked, "Buchanan sick?"

"Yes, multiple sclerosis, in its early stages."

Paul thought this odd. Multiple sclerosis rarely affected men. It was primarily a woman's disease. "What are they doing for it?"

"Some new kind of drug treatment. Supposed to slow it down. And lots of brain scans, just like you."

"MRI scans?"

"Yes. Poor man. He's had a lot of setbacks this year."

"The Aquatech embezzlement scandal? I read about it in the Wall Street Journal. As I recall, he had to pay the money back to the stockholders."

"Yes," said Natasha, "fifty million or so, give or take, out of his pocket."

Paul's jaw dropped. "Fifty million! Did they ever find the person responsible?"

"No, but Buchanan is still a prime suspect. He was one of a select few with access needed to transfer funds offshore. Now, they've taken his access away. Fifty million is pocket change to him, and worth it to stay out of jail."

"Two million to keep me on the street is a bargain by comparison."

"I thought so, too." She smiled, taking his arm and drawing him close as they entered the huge ballroom. Inside, chatter filled the room like feeding time at a duck pond, intertwining with soft jazz from a band at the far end of the room. Tuxedoed waiters darted about with trays of hors d'oeuvres and wine. Pungent scents clashed from an unknown number of musky perfumes, with an overwhelming dominance of alcohol.

The line for hard liquor formed at a bar, left of the entrance. Some of the guests obviously had a head start. Nearly passed out, they sunk deeply into overstuffed chairs or sofas. Less pickled, more animated groups sat at small, round tables, while the newly arrived, mostly sober, milled about the room in search of food, drink, and gossip.

Paul knew half the people, although he'd never met them. They came right out of Forbes' Fortune 500. Their names, pictures, and private lives were common knowledge. He felt crushed by ego and charisma.

Crystal chandeliers reflected soft, shimmering shadows on the plush, burgundy carpet. Pleated velvet tapestries in forest green with gold inlay covered much of the walls. Woven wallpaper covered the exposed sections of wall in beige, twine-like fibers.

"What's the occasion?" Paul asked.

"Donald Unger's sixtieth birthday."

"The real estate tycoon?"

"The same."

Natasha took Paul by the arm and led him through a crowd of immaculately dressed couples, decked out in gold and diamonds. She led him toward a short Asian man, bald, except for a few wisps of white hair combed over his scalp. Age spots covered his face, his skin wrinkled and thin, like a crumpled piece of paper after a futile attempt to flatten it out again. He held a drink in his left hand while he conversed with a portly man. At the sight of Natasha, the Asian flipped up his right hand stiffly, abruptly ending his conversation. Taking a few steps in Paul's direction, the old man reached out for Natasha and they shook hands.

"Tasha, Tasha, good to see you at happy occasion." He kissed the back of her hand. She gently pulled it away, eyes smiling.

"Twi Chang, I'd like you to meet Dr. Paul Powers." He grasped Paul's hand firmly, pulling Paul to within inches of his face. Paul felt a slight tremor in Chang's hand.

"She believes in you, doctor, and I believe in her," he said softly. The noise and music of the ballroom made the conversation private. "Do not disappoint her, for I am old and can not tolerate disappointment." Chang smiled, but the left side of this face remained in a frown. Paul realized Chang had a facial droop.

"I'll do my best," said Paul, wondering whether he had just been threatened or encouraged. Twi Chang released Paul's hand and Paul took one step backward.

"So good, so good." Chang's smiled widely, his lopsided grin revealing a perfect set of unnaturally white teeth. They sparkled like the chandeliers. "You both need drinks," he said.

"It can wait," said Natasha. "I need help with a more urgent matter."

Twi Chang looked around the room. "The video?"

"Uh-huh."

"Tasha, you know it's out of my hands, all gone, legal evidence."

"I know."

"What do you ask of me?"

"How could it be mistaken?"

Chang pouted and looked Paul in the eye. "It cannot."

"Mr. Chang," said Paul, "is there anyone in the company I can talk to, someone with technical expertise."

"You speak of my daughter, Lin. She's my expert, now. Soon, the company is for her. If she will. There..." He waved his hand for a few seconds, beckoning to someone in the crowd. Again, Paul noticed a mild tremor in Chang's hand. A tiny Asian woman in a plain, gold dress walked toward Paul. Thick, black glasses framed her oval eyes, and they looked like brown marbles as she got closer. A silver necklace on a fine chain hung from her frail looking neck. Her shoes, more like sandals with heels, showed off her little toes, with the nails painted in glitter. Jet-black hair, parted in the center, had been balled together at the back of her head with a scarab clip. Paul wondered about the length of her hair. A miniature purse with a traditional Chinese pattern hung from her narrow shoulder by a thin, white cord.

"Dr. Powers," said Chang, "this is my lovely daughter, Lin." She smiled, small, thick lipped. Paul offered his hand and she shook it, her fingers so fine he was afraid to squeeze them.

"You are the doctor from the drugstore," she said. "I thought you were in jail."

"Yeah, I was. I'm out on bail."

"I see," But the scrunching up of her bridgeless nose told Paul that Lin really didn't understand.

"Lin is a graduate of computer science from MIT," her father said. "Lin, Dr. Powers has questions for an expert."

Lin looked at her father, bowing her head very slightly. "Yes, father."

"Tasha," said Chang, taking her by the arm, "about your drink."

"Excuse us," said Natasha, walking off, leaving Paul with Lin.

"They have a videotape," said Paul, "and they say it's me. But it can't be."

"I need a drink," said Lin, grabbing two glasses of blush from a passing waiter. She held one up to

Paul. "I imagine you need this, too." He nodded and took the glass. "It's not a tape," she said.

"What?"

"It's a DVD."

"A digital video?"

"Correct. Sentry Security is totally computerized. The video data from each account is digitized and sent by modem to our office, where we store it on compact discs."

"None of the data is stored on-site?"

"Only briefly, in a buffer, until it is sent to Sentry by digital cable or phone line. That way we don't need much more than simple cameras and a modem at each location."

"You're saving money."

"Correct. And no one at the site can tamper with the video."

"What about at your office?"

"Never. Only father and I have the codes needed to edit the accounts. And he doesn't work much any more since he got sick."

"Has your father had a stroke?"

"Why do you say that?"

"His face droops and his hand trembles."

"Can I ask you a question, doctor?"

"Yeah, shoot."

"They say he has too much fluid in his brain, and they put a tube in to drain the fluid into the abdomen."

"A shunt. I'm familiar with them."

"But now all they do is monitor him with MRI scans, and wait."

"They are doing the right thing, MRI scans are very precise. I'm being followed with MRI scans, too, for a tumor."

"Oh, I'm sorry." Her crescent shaped eyes widened, dark eyebrows rising, pressing wrinkles into her forehead. "Will you be all right?"

"Only time and the MRI can tell. I feel OK now."

Lin's worry lines receded. "The DVD security system is as infallible as the MRI," she said, eyes distorted by her thick glasses.

"What would be involved in altering the security output?"

"Oh, my. We'll have to sit down for this." They found two rounded, padded lounge chairs facing one another. Paul massaged his forehead. His life depended on Lin's response. One computer nerd held his future in her hands. And his real accuser wasn't even human. How, Paul wondered, do you cross-examine a computer?

Lin held her hands in the praying position, but open, as if the answer to all the mysteries of the universe fit between her delicate palms. He hoped it were true. "It would have to be done at the main studio," she began. "We have storage and editing equipment that could be misused to alter video effects."

"How?"

"Digital magic. You don't think we really brought the dinosaurs back, do you?"

Paul stroked his moustache. "I get it, just like Hollywood special effects. Digitally recreate me in another role." She nodded. "Who has the knowledge and the access?" he asked.

"Only me."

"Anyone else in the company?"

"No."

"What about your father?"

"He has access, but he couldn't make the digital changes, not possible. He wouldn't."

"Could you tell if the DVD had been altered?"

"Depends how good the job is, and it takes time."

"And the prosecuting attorneys have the DVD."

"I know, I gave it to them. But I kept a backup copy."

"You did? I've never seen the video."

"Would you like to? I could run a few tests, look for tampering."

"How about tomorrow at 10 a.m.? I have an MRI scan in the morning."

She opened her tiny purse and found a business card. "I'll be there, but come alone. I'm going to find an excuse to empty the office. I don't want anyone to know we're doing this. I'm not even sure if what we're planning is legal."

"I won't tell a soul, I swear," said Paul, holding up his right hand.

"Good. Because if the DVD has been altered," she said, "I'll be the one in trouble, instead of you." She smiled, her high cheeks rising and flushing.

Paul gave Lin one of his cards. "If anything else comes up, call me."

They strolled around the ballroom, the conversation turning to lighter subjects, college and professional school, likes and dislikes, and the inevitable romance history. In precise, almost clinical fashion, they probed each other's strengths and weaknesses. For two triple-A personalities, they related well. Paul forgot about his troubles for a while, as he realized how much he enjoyed Lin's company.

He trusted this woman. She seemed too sweet to lie, or perhaps too intellectual. In Lin's world, Paul imagined lying didn't make rational sense. Computers, after all, never lied. Paul felt no physical chemistry between Lin and himself. She wasn't a sexy or stylish person. Perhaps the computer analogy fit her sexuality, too. Paul couldn't envision falling in love with a computer. Lin finally excused herself to return to her father. Paul watched her five-foot silhouette disappear behind tall heads in the crowd. He looked forward to meeting her tomorrow.

Shrill chimes sounded, a spoon-on-glass signal. The room quieted. Donald Unger prepared to blow out two candles in the shape of a giant number sixty on top of a table sized birthday cake. The cake stood on its own wheeled cart. A drunken version of the happy birthday song filled the room, and Unger blew out the candles to a chorus of cheers and applause. Music started up again, as did the gossip. Paul walked over to

Unger. Paul thought he might as well meet the birthday boy.

"Damnedest thing in the world," said Unger, his belly pushing out his cumberbund, white, except for food stains. Pouches of skin hung loosely beneath his eyes, and a string bowtie, untied, dangled from his neck. His shinny lapels, and the tuxedo jacket, too, were wrinkled. "How the hell World Development outbid me, I'll never know. I thought I had the deal in hand. I spoke to Turner, I knew what he wanted. Hell, we played golf the day before, for Christ's sake."

"There's got to be a mole in the board room," said a thin man at the table, as he nervously rubbed his bald head.

"Look, Jarrard," said Unger, "I swear, I didn't tell anyone. Not even the board. And I certainly didn't tell those damn South American raiders."

Six others sat at the table. A waiter wheeled off the cake to a serving area as Paul approached. "Happy birthday, Mr. Unger," said Paul. "Great party."

Unger shifted his sizable bulk, tilting his baggy face. "Do I know you?"

"Dr. Paul Powers,"

"The Paul Powers?"

"Yeah, out on bail."

"A pleasure." He frowned. "What misguided shit put up the two million?"

"Natasha Zhazinsky, I'll tell her you said hello." Paul grabbed some white zinfandel from a passing tray and then sat down at the table.

"The widow herself? Cute. But you came to the right place. I need a doctor's advice."

"Free advice, worth the price," said Paul.

"Know much about spongiform enceph-alopathy?"

"Yeah, a little. CJD, Creutzfeldt-Jakob Disease, Mad Cow, Kuru, to name a few."

Unger tapped on his forehead with his index finger. "That's what's in my brain, little holes."

"The biopsy showed it?"

"No, serial MRI scans. Can't treat it, they say, so no reason for a biopsy."

Unger had a good point. "Do you have symptoms?"

"A little dizziness or disorientation at times, very mild. Does this all make sense to you? Sometimes I think doctors are all a bunch of quacks." Unger covered his rubbery mouth with both hands. "Oops, sorry, no offense intended."

"None taken," said Paul. "Spongiform encephalopathy is a rare disorder, poorly understood. Caused by a prion, a weird protein particle. No one knows what a prion really is or how it's supposed to behave. Even if you are exposed, it can take twenty or thirty years to develop the full-blown syndrome. Serial MRIs can help you predict how fast it's spreading. But there's no cure yet, as I'm sure you know."

Unger polished off a tall shot of scotch and breathed a sigh of relief. "So you think I might die of old age, huh?"

"Yeah, most likely."

"Thanks, you're reassuring." He leaned back in his chair. "So, who do you think killed Val? I suspect you have an opinion."

"The same one who framed me," said Paul, "and killed all the others. I was apparently getting too close to the truth. The killer seems to be able to stay one step ahead of me, almost like he's reading my mind."

"But they've got it on video, for Christ's sake." Unger laughed.

"They caught King Kong in Manhattan, too," said Paul. Unger stopped laughing. Paul gave

Unger a business card. "You know a lot of people in this town, sir. If you hear anything unusual, I'd appreciate you letting me know." Unger glanced briefly at the card and buried it in the inside pocket of his tux jacket. It will probably go to the cleaners, Paul thought. He was guilty until proven innocent. It would take a miracle to get anyone in this town to help him.

Paul found Natasha nursing a screwdriver and conversing with Anthony Wallick, president of Pacific Rim Bank, the largest banking conglomerate in the Northwest. His territorial dominance included Washington, Oregon, Alaska, Idaho, and recently, Hawaii. Rumors placed his scouts last month in California. Anthony stood too erect, an imposing six-foot-plus, with sharp features chiseled into an unchanging dour expression. Poker with Wallick would be a nightmare.

Single and in his forties, Wallick had risen to become one of the most feared and respected CEOs in the country. Speculation on Wallick's future ambitions ran rampant in the press. No wonder he had a reputation for being a ruthless negotiator, for he looked like a warrior ready for battle.

"Tony, dear," said Natasha, in a deep voice, as she ran her hand against his white shirt. "Mmm, so soft and lovely."

"Satin darling, a Richard Taylor, you should treat yourself to one. As I was saying, I only started the Hawaii expansion to work on my tan."

Wallick's blue suit, of panne velvet, seemed to light him from within. Intense blue eyes stood out from his deeply tan face, topped by a flaming torch of blond hair. "All I'm asking," said Natasha, "is for you to keep your ears open, and call me if you hear anything about the poisonings."

Wallick tried to speak, but Natasha put a single index finger against his lips. "Shh, just say you'll do it." Her fingertip parted Wallick's lips and entered his mouth. He gently grabbed her hand, pulled the fingertip out, sucking it on the way.

"I'll call you with the slightest news," he said.

"You're a dear." She stroked his cheek. "Hi, Paul," she said, apparently noticing him for the first time. "Anthony, have you met Paul?" Natasha staggered as she pivoted to introduce him. Paul caught her.

"Maybe you've had enough," said Paul. She grinned.

"Dr. Powers," said Wallick. "I feel I already know you through the media and the gossip tonight."

"So they're talking about me?"

"Quite a bit, I'm afraid the trial has already begun. Not to worry, impatience is a disease. Use it to your advantage. That's why I win all my negotiations. The other side thinks it's already won."

"But I don't have your composure," said Paul.

"Life takes its toll on my insides, I'm afraid I'm on borrowed time, and one day I'll have to make the balloon payment."

Paul noticed Natasha staring blankly, not able to follow the conversation. "I'd better take her home while she can still stand." Wallick nodded.

"Keep fighting, never give up," said Wallick.

"Thanks," said Paul, putting his arm around Natasha and coaxing her toward the door.

Natasha perked up for a moment. "Leaving? We're leaving?"

"Yeah."

"But we haven't found the killer yet."

"It's a good start," said Paul. Natasha had ceased to make sense. "We can do no more good here. Let me take you home."

Natasha pulled herself roughly from Paul's grasp. She staggered forward and dropped her screwdriver, glass and all, shouting, "No, I'm not leaving!" The room quieted and all eyes turned toward her. Paul moved in, but Natasha tried to swat him away, as if he was an annoying insect.

"Val left me. Val would never go away and leave me. He loved me too much." She started to cry, her arms flailing at the empty air, as if she was daring anyone to stop her.

So, thought Paul, she's not made of stone, after all. "He would never leave you, someone took him from you, someone killed him, remember?"

"What if he's not dead?" she said loudly between sobs. "What if he left me? What if he didn't love me?" She was hysterical. Paul bent over and charged Natasha sideways, hoisting her on his back, her legs dangling. A path formed in the crowd, a gauntlet of gawkers enjoying the spectacle. She pounded her fists on his back, and he could smell her heavy, alcohol breath.

"Let me go, I'm not finished here!"

Paul carried Natasha through the crowd and out the ballroom door. The astute wait staff had already fetched the Mercedes from the valet lot.

He poured her into the back seat, activated the childproof door locks, and took off like a madman, leaving the grinning, well-entertained crowd behind. He wondered if the party had been an investigative success, or a boondoggle. In either case, tonight had made him realize that finding the killer not only meant freedom for him, but also peace for Natasha.

CHAPTER 13

After the morning MRI scan, Paul headed for Sentry Security. He'd left Natasha sleeping soundly, softly snoring. Likely she'd remain asleep until the late afternoon. He wondered what she might have learned at the party, but he'd have to wait until she sobered up enough to question her. If her drunken outburst was any indication, her doubts about Z's fidelity were deeply rooted and haunting her.

Natasha obviously wasn't afraid to use all her assets, including some seductive prowess, to get her way. Maybe the fidelity problem in her marriage worked both ways. Paul had undressed her last night and put her to bed, trying hard to remain clinically detached in the process. But although he'd denied it all morning, tucking Natasha's nearly naked body under the sheets had aroused him. Thinking about it now was worse.

Sentry Security had its main offices in the Centennial building in downtown Bellevue. The downtown bustled with auto and pedestrian traffic. After struggling for parking, he found Sentry on the eighth floor. A metal, windowless door with a gold foil name and a padlock logo identified the office. It had a digital combination lock, and a sign on the door said: *Closed*. He knocked, but got no answer. A doorbell to the side of the door caught his eye, and above it a square of black metal mesh. He pushed the button, but it made no sound.

"Who's there?" said a tinny voice from a speaker behind the metal mesh.

"Paul Powers." The electronic door lock buzzed. "Come in."

Inside, it looked like any other office, with a utilitarian receptionist desk against an off-white wall, computers, and a small waiting area. Corridors spread out on both sides of the reception desk, and Paul noted the dark glass windows of several offices off each hallway.

Someone approached from the darkness of the right corridor. It was Lin, but he hardly recognized her. She wore a gray, pleated schoolgirl skirt suit. The short skirt made her legs seem impossibly long, while the jacket broadened her shoulders. A low-cut, white cotton T-shirt showed off her slender neck and unblemished upper chest. She'd parted her hair on one side, pulled it toward the other, and pinned it behind her neck in a sculptured tuft, once again leaving its length a mystery. Her fingernails were glossy black.

"Lin, you look so, so..."

"Different?"

"Yeah, but I was going to say great."

A smile started at the corners of her eyes and poured over her cheeks. "I wear what father likes for social functions," she said, "but in the office, I'm in charge." Paul felt underdressed in his simple blue jeans. She took his hand and squeezed it warmly. "Glad you're here, I started working on the DVD as soon as everyone left. Follow me."

She led him through several hallways, turning a few times. The office was deceptively big. At the dead end of the last hallway, the sign on the door read: *Data Management.*

Inside, the windowless room smelled of ozone, and the air hummed. Computers stretched wall to wall, about thirty feet on each side. In the center, unfamiliar electronic equipment crowded the surface of two long workbenches. A tower of modems along one wall flickered with hundreds of red lights.

"I'm astounded. What a setup."

She took him around the room. "These are the modem links for our various accounts, downloading raw data twenty-four hours a day. Next to the modems are computer terminals for data processing. We keep a strict inventory of everything that comes in."

"So you don't lose anything?"

"Yes. And these are banks of writable DVD drives, where the information is converted for permanent storage. With the compression algorithms I've added, our storage capacity is virtually unlimited."

"Where's the backup system?"

"You'll notice every DVD drive is double-stacked. Two discs are burned for every piece of data, a very cheap method of storage. And the hard-drive buffers here hold the last several months of data."

"Where do the finished discs go?"

"We keep both copies here, in a vault, unless one is turned over to the prosecuting attorney."

Paul swallowed. "I think it's time."

"Over here." She gestured for him to follow. In one corner, a bank of six monitors hung above a complex computer terminal. "You'd better take a seat."

He sat in one of two padded office chairs on wheels. "What is this area?"

"These CPUs are specialized for manipulation and analysis of digital graphics."

"Disneyland?"

"You could say that." She laughed, holding up a shiny DVD. "This is an exact copy of what we gave the prosecuting attorney."

"A death sentence?"

"Watch the movie."

Lin loaded the DVD into the drive. It whirred as the drive reached operating speed. "Here's the painkiller aisle camera view, time index 10:07 a.m."

Paul watched the monitor. Time progressed as an overlay on the bottom corner of the screen. He watched a man in a dark overcoat walking down the aisle. At 10:08 a.m., the man took several bottles off the shelf, put them in his coat pocket, and then replaced them. It looked like a switch had been made. The man faced away from the camera. As he turned to walk back down the aisle, for a brief instant his face became visible. Lin froze the video and blew up the image.

Paul stared at himself on the screen. "They're going to execute me by lethal injection. An ironic death for an anesthesiologist," said Paul. "Unless you can prove it's a fake."

"So far," said Lin, "I found no evidence of tampering." She looked Paul in the eyes. "It's a real dilemma, because I believe you're innocent. You're too kind and dedicated to be a murderer. And too sane."

"You have proof of that?" said Paul.

"In my heart, yes," she said. She stood up, leaned over and kissed him. Warm and wet, probing, confident. He received the kiss passively, too shocked to respond. But he enjoyed it. She tasted sweet, silky, and fresh. A glow colored her prominent cheeks. He felt warm, and realized he must be blushing, too. She sat back down.

"If you'll kiss me in court, I'll be acquitted for sure," said Paul. How wrong he'd been to rush to judgment of Lin's fashion sense and sexuality. Clearly, it was another case of guilty until proven innocent. He'd make an awful juror.

"I've run some preliminary tests on the video. There's no dithering or layering to indicate a cut-paste process. But the face shot is brief, and a computer expert could have substituted your face for another. I estimate the subject's height and weight are the same as yours."

Paul stroked his mustache. "So, you're telling me I'm still dead."

She frowned and shook her head. "Don't hang yourself, yet. I've just started." Once again, he'd spoken too soon, frustrating Lin before she'd had a chance to finish her analysis.

"Sorry, I appreciate what you're trying to do. Everything's been happening so fast, I can hardly think straight."

"Forgiven, this time."

Paul sat in silent admiration as Lin's fingers danced on the keyboard and the trackball. She pulled a square plastic board from a slot under the computer."

"What's that?"

"A drawing tablet. I have an idea." With unbelievable precision, Lin circled parts of the frozen video picture. "What time did Dr. Z buy his pills?"

"10:45."

She ran the time index to 10:45 a.m. and let the video run. Z entered the isle, snatched a box of cold pills off the shelf, and walked out of view. Lin froze the picture and circled a part of it. After a few commands, the two circles appeared side by side on the screen. "And now," said Lin, "we shall see."

Numbers appeared, in lumens, under each circle, 7.9 lumens under Paul's circle and 7.2 lumens under Z's circle. "Yes!" Lin said. "Do you see?" Paul shook his head. Lin explained, "These numbers represent the estimated lumens per square foot in the store at that exact location when each of these videos were taken. There is a subtle difference in ambient light in these videos, but it should be the same."

"How do you account for it?"

"Fluorescent light deteriorates slowly over time. New bulbs are brighter."

Paul jumped up, rolled the chair away and ran his hand through his hair. "So, you think these videos were shot on different days?"

"Probably months apart, unless..."

"Unless?"

"Unless one bulb failed altogether, on the same day."

Paul shook his head. "Not good enough to prove tampering, but I have an idea." Lin pushed back from the keyboard, folding her hands on her lap. "Getting a shot of my face would be easy enough," Paul continued, "but the body had to come from somewhere, probably from another day of Thrifty Mart video."

Lin's eyes brightened, filling her thick glasses like a computer screen. "I'd have to use a graphical search algorithm, with the fake body as a reference. I can do it." She began typing furiously.

"How long have you had the Thrifty Mart Account?"

"Six years. Behind us is a multiple DVD player, like a jukebox. Before you came, I loaded all the Thrifty Mart DVDs." She outlined the fake body on the video and cropped it out. He watched in silent awe as she stuck indicators into each part of the digital body, like cyber-voodoo, writing incomprehensible incantations in machine language. She bit her lip, fingers flying furiously, mercilessly punching the keys. Squinting her eyes into narrow slits, she wrenched her neck around and blew air through pursed lips.

Paul touched her neck from behind and massaged it gently. She responded with a soft, "Mmm," like purring. After about ten minutes, she leaned back in her chair and stroked Paul's massaging hands. "It's a matter of time, now," she said, softly, "Hours, maybe days. Then I have to check all the close matches one by one."

Paul leaned forward and kissed the nape of her neck. She rubbed her cheek on his while running her fingers through his hair. His hands rounded her shoulders, explored her smooth chest, and then reached beneath the T-shirt to caress her breasts, small and firm. She twisted her head sideways and kissed him, her tongue darting deep into his mouth. This time, Paul pressed back, hard. He swung around to the front of the chair, lips locked to hers. Picking her up just a little, he gave the chair's legs a shove with his foot. The chair rolled out from under Lin while Paul hugged her tightly, and they settled gently to floor.

Lin wrestled her lips from Paul's. "Wait," she said. Puzzled, Paul stopped and sat up a bit, straddling her. He started to stand up, but she grabbed his arm. "Wait," she repeated. Removing her glasses, her naked eyes shone like bright almonds, striking. Dazzled, Paul didn't see Lin pull the pin from her hair. Straight, and full, it fell across her face and shoulders. "I always wondered how long it was," he said. He reached down and parted the soft tangles, exposing her round face, caressing it like a precious pearl. Lin possessed more intellect and beauty than he'd ever imagined. As she began to undo his blue jeans, he added passion to the list.

The computers, modems, and disc drives sung a chorus of humming, clicking, whirring, and then buzzing. Lin propped herself up on her elbows. The buzzing sound repeated. "Wait! Get up!" She fumbled for her glasses and put them on. Here she goes again, Paul thought. "Someone's inside!" she said. He helped her up.

"Where?" he said.

"Outer office, headed this way."

She ran to a control panel on the wall and flipped a breaker. The lights went out, but the computers and modems continued to flash their LED's in the eerie darkness. Lin pulled Paul down behind one of the workbenches. He could barely see his hand in front of his face.

Paul heard the intruder coming, footfalls growing louder. The room door creaked open. Paul fixed on the LEDs on the wall. As the body of the burglar crossed in front of the LED's, they winked off and on, giving Paul a rough idea of the man's size and position. He was big. Lin and Paul held their breath as the man passed to within a few feet.

Paul tried make out the man's exact position, but could not. In a moment, the intruder might spot them. Paul leaped from beneath the workbench, staying low, aiming to tackle the man by his legs. But Paul hit only one of the intruder's legs, bringing him to his knees for a few seconds. Paul landed on the floor, on his back, helpless, his position revealed. The unsteady silhouette of the intruder hovered overhead.

Paul tried to get to his feet. There was a loud bang, a whizzing by his ear, a pinging on the floor. He gave up trying to stand. He'd only make a better target. Before the gunman could regain his footing and fire a second round, Paul somersaulted across the room and dove behind the end of the workbench. The second shot rang out and thudded into the wooden bench above his head.

A siren outside grew louder. The invader ran from the room, his heavy footfalls echoing down the hallway. Paul got up and groped along the wall for the breaker box. He found it. One long lever angled opposite the rest, and he flipped it toward the others. The lights came on.

Lin sat in the far corner of the room, under a table beneath banks of CPUs and monitors. Cross-legged on the floor, she clutched a wireless keyboard in her red-knuckled hands. Shaking, her disheveled hair shimmered over her face.

"Are you OK?" said Paul, running to her.

She didn't answer. He took the keyboard from her, and helped her to a chair. With a pocket comb, he gently combed and parted her hair. Two policemen entered the room, guns drawn. "What happened here? Everyone all right?"

Paul and Lin gave the initial report of what everyone presumed was an attempted burglary, and the policemen ran a quick computer check. Once they discovered Paul was out on bail, they contacted the arresting officer, Jackey McCann. So it wasn't long before Jackey showed up at the door with several detectives and a forensic team.

The detectives began to hunt for bullets, shells, and fingerprints. They dug one slug out of the wall, one out of the workbench, and retrieved several shell casings. Try as they might, there were no prints to be found. The intruder had gained entry to the office through the front door, somehow defeating the digital combination lock. There was no sign of forced entry.

Jackey was dressed in civilian clothes, and looked like she'd been off duty when the call came. "Powers, I'm not even sure that it's legal for you to be here, but I'm damn sure it's not a good idea."

"I'm here to examine the video that led to my arrest. I see no reason why I can't question its validity."

"And?"

Paul shook his head. "Nothing to report."

"I have to assume this is a random burglary, or perhaps related to some other Sentry business. But I can't rule out the unlikely possibility that it has something to do with your arrest. We will investigate fully. In the meantime, would you like police protection?"

The last thing Paul wanted was a nosy police tail. "No thank you. For the time being, I'll watch my own back."

During the intrusion, Lin had overcome her fear long enough to trigger Sentry Security's standard client alarm software, using a keyboard. The alarm program sends out a burglary in progress message to the 911 operator. Paul had Lin to thank for his life.

In the time it took for the detectives to process the scene, Lin managed to calm down. After Jackey and the rest of the police left, Lin sat back down at the graphics workstation and checked the output to her query. Paul examined the hole in the workbench where the bullet had been that barely missed his head. He stared at the hole, transfixed, until his eyes lost focus. But the image lingered, burning into the deepest recesses of his mind. His thoughts raced.

"It's me they're after," said Paul.

Lin swiveled her chair around. "It was probably just a burglary. He must have thought the office was closed. He didn't expect anyone to be here. We surprised him."

Paul shook his head, turning toward Lin, forcing his eyes back in focus. "No. He was a pro. He knew how to bypass a digital door lock. I'm on to something bigger than a simple product tampering."

"What are you on to?"

He shrugged. "I wish I knew. And another thing, assuming he was after me, how did he know I was here?"

"Did someone follow you from the hospital?"

"No, I'm sure I wasn't followed. Somehow, he knew my plans. It's like he read my mind."

Lin pointed a finger at him. "You, Dr. Powers, are paranoid. Someone could have overheard us at the party."

"I don't think so," said Paul. "Who knew I'd be at the party?"

She threw up her hands. "Ah, what's the use?" She returned to the graphics terminal. "You know, it's lucky we've got an entry buzzer to let us know when customers come in. But it's not enough. I never thought about it before, but Sentry Security has a security problem."

"Will you call your father?"

"Not yet. I'll replace the front door lock first with something more secure."

Paul decided to call Natasha, thinking that she should be up by now. He rang her phone six times before she picked up.

"Hello?" said a sleepy voice.

"Natasha, it's Paul. How are you feeling?"

"Quite a headache, dear, but otherwise all right. Made quite a fool of myself, didn't I? Thank you for taking such good care of me."

"Yeah, you're welcome. Did you find out anything useful?"

"No, Paul. But I put out a lot of feelers. Someone will help us."

"Yeah, sure," he said, unconvinced. "Any calls for me?"

"Oh, yes, I almost forgot. Unger left a message while I was sleeping."

"Donald Unger, the birthday boy?"

"Uh-huh. Call him."

Natasha gave Paul the phone number. Before Paul hung up, he told Natasha briefly about Lin's efforts to examine the video, but not about the gunman. Paul didn't want Natasha to worry about him. He called Unger's office and waited for his secretary to put Unger through from a cellular phone.

"Powers?" Paul thought Unger sounded agitated. He spoke fast, his voice raspy.

"Yeah, I'm here."

"Something you said to me, about the killer. How he always stays one step ahead of you, like he's reading your mind."

"What's happened?"

"Well, I lost an important negotiation recently."

"Yeah," said Paul. "I heard you talking about it last night."

"Like they knew my thoughts. Just like you said. And now Wallick's in deep."

"Anthony Wallick?"

"We're close friends. Someone bought out Bay Area Credit right under his nose. But Wallick's California scouts were the only ones who knew Bay Area was ripe for purchase."

"Who bought it?"

"World Development Industries, the same ones who outbid me."

"Who are they?"

"A wealthy South American investment and development company. Based out of Colombia. Nobody knows much about them."

"Obviously, they have good intelligence. So?"

"More like espionage. That's why I called you. Wallick said the same thing you did. He felt like World Development Industries had read his mind and gotten to the prize before him.

"How did Wallick take it?"

"Badly," said Unger. "He's a mess. Stress caused his Meniere's to act up. He's so dizzy today he can hardly stand."

"Meniere's Disease?"

"Yes, that's what they call it."

Paul thought it strange. Wallick has chronic vertigo. This is usually accompanied by impaired hearing. But Wallick hadn't missed a word of conversation at the party, in spite of the music and high background noise. This made no sense, unless he is an expert lip reader.

"Have they ruled out an acoustic neuroma?"

"You mean a brain tumor? Yes, he had an MRI scan recently. It was clean."

"That's good," said Paul, "Glad you called me, but I'm not sure what to make of all this. Call me if you learn anything else."

"I will," said Unger. "And mark my words, some very weird things are going on in this town. Watch your ass. Don't trust anyone."

The line went dead. Paul stared at the receiver, trying to make sense of Unger's call.

"Paul!" Lin called. "Look at this."

He hung up the phone and rushed to the graphics workstation, standing behind Lin as she played for him a segment of Thrifty Mart video from several years ago. A man in a dark coat walked down the painkiller isle, put some medication in his coat pocket, and then turned back, leaving the aisle the way he came. As he turned, his face became visible briefly. He had the same body as in the original, incriminating video, but a different face.

Paul couldn't believe it. "How's this possible?"

Lin froze the man's face on the screen. "Your face must have been digitally substituted for the original."

"Any clue where they got my face?"

"No. Could have taken a video of you anywhere. But there's more. Watch." She started the video clip again from the beginning. The man walked down the isle, pulled medication off the shelf, and then put the medication into his coat pocket. Then he took medication from his pocket and put it on the shelf.

"What just happened?" Paul asked, dumfounded.

"Video voodoo," Lin said. "I just reversed a small part of the action and seamlessly spliced it in digitally, so that the subject appears to be putting drugs back onto the shelf."

"So, he was actually a shoplifter," said Paul. "Ironic, he gets away with stealing, and I get charged with murder. No justice. Who has the skills to do this?"

Lin swiveled around. "Only a computer expert." She grabbed Paul's arm. "But they'd have to do it here. Steal the DVDs from the vault, break the security passwords, and come and go without anyone knowing."

"It has to be an inside job," said Paul.

She released his arm. "Only Father and I can open the vault and input passwords." She shook her head and frowned. "It can't happen."

"But it has."

"How could anyone else get this information?" Lin asked.

"I don't know," said Paul. "That's what both of us need to find out." He knew his freedom and the future of Sentry Security depended on the answer.

A sudden incredible thought crossed his mind. It had been coalescing since the phone call from Unger, but Paul had tried to deny it. Wallick, Unger, and he had something in common besides the fact that someone had discovered their innermost thoughts. All had undergone one or more MRI brain scans.

Paul felt ridiculous. How could MRI scans have anything to do with subsequent events? There was no way an MRI scan could read someone's thoughts. All three men had different neurological problems from different causes. Wallick had Meniere's Disease. Unger had spongiform encephalopathy. And Paul had a brain tumor. The diverse illnesses argued against any coincidence.

But now someone had used information that could only have come from Lin or Twi Chang. Lin's father had hydrocephalus, water on the brain, and also got an MRI scan. Paul found it difficult to dismiss this as coincidence.

Muhammadan, the chief medical examiner, had a sudden neurological problem, a cerebral bleed, and he received an MRI brain scan, too. Muhammadan thought he found an irregularity in the cyanide levels in Z's blood, but the repeat analysis had been normal. According to Poulos, the assistant, Muhammadan used incorrect data. But what if the doubly encrypted data banks at the medical examiner's office had been tampered with? Poulos said tampering with the database was impossible. Just as impossible, no doubt, as creating a video of Paul in the Thrifty Mart.

And what of Michael Buchanan's multiple sclerosis? He'd misplaced fifty million dollars, transferred into untraceable offshore accounts from right under his nose. Someone must have stolen Buchanan's passwords and account numbers to pull the caper off. And Buchanan had gone through the MRI scanner several times.

"Paul," said Lin. "Are you all right?"

He snapped to attention, realizing he'd been staring blankly into space. "It's the MRI."

"What?" Lin cocked her head sideways, as if at the new angle Paul might make more sense.

"Trust me, all this revolves around that machine, somehow."

"How?"

"I don't know." He shook his head. "But digital graphics is your specialty. We need to take a closer look at the Lakeside MRI scanner. It's kept in a separate building because of the intense magnetic field. How can we get inside?"

Lin stood, took him in her arms, and kissed him. "Relax," she said. "I have the key. Lakeside Radiology is a client."

She began unbuttoning his shirt. "Now, where were we?" she said, planting wet kisses on his abdomen.

"I was admiring your gorgeous eyes for the first time," he said, removing her glasses.

"Careful with those," she said, "I'm blind without them."

"Don't worry," said Paul, setting the glasses down gently on the workbench, "it's all done by feel from now on."

She pulled him to the floor, onto his back, caressing his exposed chest. They quickly undressed each other, intensely, without pause, as if everything since the interruption had been foreplay. The clicking and whirring of electronics, playing like frantic techno music, accompanied their breathless sighs.

CHAPTER 14

The Lakeside Radiology MRI building looked different in the overcast, starless night. At this hour, 2 a.m., Lin and Paul felt they'd be less likely to bump into hospital staff. Paul parked his truck on the street a few blocks from the hospital. Many staff members knew his truck, and he didn't want anyone to know he was there. Before they'd left Sentry Security, Lin had scanned the truck for hidden GPS transmitters. There were none. She also insisted they turned off their cell phones, just in case. Paul now realized his paranoia was contagious.

They slowly approached on the deserted walkways around the hospital, walking in the shadows cast by sparingly placed sodium vapor lights. The hospital provided enough light to find the way, but not a penny more. Lakeside had a busy emergency room. Fortunately, the ER entrance was on the side of the hospital opposite the MRI pavilion. The overflow parking lots surrounding the MRI structure stayed mostly empty at night. Fine drizzle coated Lin and Paul with a wet film as they reached the front entrance.

During the daytime, an underground tunnel connected the MRI building with Lakeside to keep patients and staff safe from the elements. A theoretical danger of cancerous mutations from intense electromagnetic fields necessitated locating the MRI building away from the main hospital. Another danger, more real, but seldom acknowledged, that of an explosion or fire from a meltdown of the supercooled magnet, made a separate building an even better idea.

The MRI magnet also interfered with nearby electronics and patient monitors, making it essential to keep all but specially shielded devices at a safe distance. Also, metallic objects placed too near to the magnet became deadly projectiles if caught by the magnetic field and drawn to its center.

Lin let them in and inactivated the alarm. Except for the front office, the place had no windows. A dim light had been left on in the main office, but they didn't dare to turn on additional lights. Once inside the inner control chamber, they lit the lights.

The control room had two cubicles with view screens on the wall and dictation machines for the reading of MRIs. Against the wall, shielded stacks of hard drives held prior MRI scans. Beyond the hard drive data management area and behind a partition, a control desk overlooked the scanner through a thick glass window.

Paul peered through the window. The darkened scanner looked like an Egyptian sarcophagus ready for the Pharaoh's corpse. The huge magnet and its electronics made up most of the square bulk of the scanner. A movable patient platform protruded a few feet from a narrow tunnel in the center of the machine.

Lin noticed the active status of the scanner. "It's on," she said.

"They have to keep the magnet on at all times, cooled down to minus three-hundred and eighty-five degrees by liquid nitrogen," Paul said. "If the coolant fails, there's a backup system. If the backup system fails, they lose a multi-million-dollar magnet, and perhaps this whole building along with it."

"What if they want to shut the thing down?" Lin asked.

"A safe shutdown takes a long time. They can do a fast, emergency shutdown, but the magnet might get fried."

"Why does it need to be supercooled?"

"Supercooling produces a superconducting environment of very low resistance in which electrons can travel unimpeded. This is essential for the magnetic sensors to function."

She sat down and booted up the control station computer. It took her only seconds to defeat the crude password protection and start examining the database. "It might help if you tell me what I'm looking for."

"I'm not sure," said Paul. "Anything out of the ordinary."

"I don't know what's ordinary for an MRI scanner," said Lin. "I don't even know how it works."

Paul forgot Lin was a brilliant computer scientist, but not a doctor. She didn't have a clue as to what MRIs were. "Basically, the magnet aligns all the body's magnetic poles for an instant. A small amount of energy is given off as electrons when the molecules realign. This energy varies for each tissue type. The computer subtracts the magnet's interference and the electronic background noise, and uses the remaining data to construct a three-dimensional, black and white representation of the body's magnetic signature."

"A digital image?" said Lin.

"Yeah. Ultimately, they're no different from the digital images you work with. The trick is using digital subtraction mathematics to remove noisy background interference that would otherwise drown out the body's tiny, electromagnetic signals."

Lin gasped. "The mathematical algorithms must be intense. Who ever figured them out?"

Paul smiled. "Dr. Z created the digital subtraction formulas used today. He was brilliant in applied mathematics and physics."

"You've given me an idea," she said. Her fingers danced on the computer terminal. First, MRI views of a knee came up. Then the images disappeared, replaced by a stream of alphanumeric data.

"Can you actually read that garbage?" said Paul, pointing to the screen.

"Yes, kinda. This system has a very large hard drive. Apparently, it's used as a buffer to hold the MRI data until it's transferred to storage. I'm sorting through leftover files to get a feel for the system. I haven't found any brain scans, yet. All knees and abdomens."

"Come on," said Paul. "I want to look at the front office computer." They left the control room and huddled around the desktop PC in the office.

"Can you look up patient names?"

"I think so."

Compared to the advanced mathematical algorithms Lin had been manipulating on the MRI computer, Paul knew the desktop PC would be child's play. She worked her magic, and after a few moments, a list of names started appearing on the screen.

"So, all these people had MRIs?"

"Yes"

Paul saw Wallick, Chang, Buchanan, Unger, and Muhammadan. "Can you go further back? Just list the brain scans."

"OK."

He watched the computer screen list patients who'd undergone MRI brain scans at the Lakeside facility. Some of the most influential players in Bellevue showed up on the list, including the mayor and the chief of police.

Lin whistled softly. "Wow, it reads like a list of who's who in the Northwest. How could the whole town be sick in the head?"

"Yuppie medicine," said Paul, "A side effect of good insurance, perhaps. An MRI brain scan for every headache." Even as the words left his lips, part of him thought Lin was on to something. It seemed like too many brain scans had been done in the last twelve months. But Paul had no idea what an acceptable number of brain scans might be for the population of Bellevue. Then a familiar name flashed onto the screen. "Stop it, there."

Paul pointed to the screen. "I can't believe it. Benjamin Hinkley had an MRI brain scan, too, almost a year ago. He also took care of Dr. Z. There are too many coincidences surrounding this MRI scanner."

"Oh, oh," said Lin. "I'm beginning to believe you. Hinkley took care of my father, too."

"That's the final blow." He pounded his fist on the desk.

"What do you suggest?" She leaned back in the chair, tilting her head, looking up at him.

"I think I need another MRI brain scan, right now."

Her brown eyes filled the thick glasses. "What?" She arose from the chair and faced him squarely. "Now you're going too far. Tell me, who's supposed to operate the MRI for you?"

Paul smiled.

"No way," she said, shaking her head. "I mean, I'm not qualified."

"RTFM," said Paul, computer-speak for Read The F***ing Manual. "It's just a big computer. You're a computer scientist."

She threw her hands up. "I don't believe this."

"Besides," said Paul, "You two seemed to be getting along fine a few minutes ago." She sat back down, elbows on the desk, covering her face with her hands.

Paul walked up behind her until he felt her warmth. He leaned over and spoke softly. "Look, we've got to see if anything out of the ordinary happens during brain scans with this machine. You can stop the scan at any time if you like, and we'll both leave. What could go wrong?"

Lin didn't budge.

"OK, don't help me. Just call your father and tell him someone altered the DVD, but you don't know who or how."

She stood up slowly. "You're crazy," she said, "Do you know that?"

Paul shrugged. "So, you admit I need a brain scan."

Lin laughed nervously. "Let's find that manual," she said.

They found the MRI manual below the control room desk. A thick layer of dust proved conclusively that manuals were not made for people who really knew what they were doing. The manual consisted of three sections the size of telephone books with explanations and warnings that varied from simplistic to intricate. The books included advanced circuit diagrams of the magnet, superconductor sensors, motorized platform, and cooling systems. Paul knew Lin hadn't made it through the MIT Computer Science Department without the ability to assimilate huge amounts of knowledge in minimal time.

Paul tried to read some of the manual, but it might as well have been in Greek. Instead, he decided to inspect the MRI unit. He removed his mini pocket tool and placed it on the control desk along with his belt, truck keys, watch, cell phone, and loose change. All metal objects had to stay away from the MRI magnet. He also removed his wallet, because the MRI would wipe clean the magnetic strip of any credit cards brought into the scanner room.

"All in," Lin said. Following Paul's lead, she piled her metal possessions on the control desk. This included a silver necklace on which hung a Yin-Yang circle, the curved teardrop Yin interlocked with the identically shaped Yang. In the center of the bulbous portion of each teardrop was a single diamond. The diamonds sparkled like two tiny eyes.

"That's beautiful," said Paul.

"Thank you. Father gave it to me on my sixteenth birthday. I love it."

Once Paul entered the main chamber of the MRI unit, the air seemed charged and thick. On the room-sized square box that comprised the MRI, he noted side panels attached with plastic thumbscrews for easy access. He removed one of the side panels, not knowing what he expected to find.

The inner compartment was an enigma of bundled wires and coolant tubes. Even if something abnormal had been thrown in, Paul realized he'd never find it. He avoided touching the coolant tubes, as they were so cold they'd burn off his skin on contact. He replaced the first panel and opened another.

The second opening gave him a good look at the sensor array. The electronics sat in the midst of the coolant system and looked like something right out of a sci-fi novel. Paul knew the sensors contained sophisticated computer chips that formed the heart of the MRI.

Again, the inspection was unrevealing, and he felt he'd seen enough. He prepared to put the panel back on. Before he set the cover in place, he noticed a small, engraved marker bolted next to the sensor array. Pushing his face almost into the machine, he read: *Replace only with parts from World Development Industries 1-800-555-9000.* This didn't surprise him, as multinational companies often had a hand in everything from high finance to high technology.

He left the MRI room and waited for Lin to finish familiarizing herself with the technical specifications of the MRI scanner. After about an hour of study, Lin closed the last volume.

"Well?"

"Piece of cake," she said.

Paul pushed a button on the MRI table and it slid out of the machine. He positioned himself on the table, with his head in a foam headrest. Absolute immobility was essential for a successful scan. Lin secured a Velcro strap around Paul's forehead and another strap around his chin. Then she gave him a generous kiss. "Tying you up holds a certain fascination for me," she said, her crescent-shaped eyes smiling.

"Careful, I'm still dangerous."

"Uh-huh. Now hold still."

Lin pushed another button on the table, sending Paul headfirst into the hollow central core of the scanner, her beautiful face drifting out of view. He heard her footfalls, and then the closing of the exit door. Paul couldn't turn his head to see her through the window to the control room.

After what seemed like forever, a voice boomed, "Are you ready?" Lin had addressed him through the loudspeaker system from the control room.

"Let 'er rip," Paul gave her a thumbs-up.

The scanner came to life, like a mighty leviathan awakened from a deep sleep. Banging and clunking, the sensor array did a noisy dance around his head. The tunnel seemed to be constricting around him, but he realized this was an optical illusion. A fine tingling began in his skin, a subtle vibration. The air carried a faint smell of ozone and petroleum lubricants. He thanked God he wasn't claustrophobic. In about fifteen minutes, it was over.

As soon as the monster quieted, he could wait no longer. With the sound of tearing cloth, he released the Velcro bonds and ran into the control room. Lin worked the keyboard with breakneck speed. The digital sections of Paul's brain displayed on one screen, flipping every five seconds to the next deepest view. The images sliced through his brain like a razor sharp knife through a tomato. On one section, he recognized the pea-sized tumor that threatened his life. Thankfully, it looked quiescent.

Lin seemed captivated not by the digital images, but by another screen on which alphanumerics scrolled by rapidly.

"Incredible." She poured over the screen. "There are volumes of data here. But..."

"Paul grabbed a second chair and sat next to her. "But what?"

"Too much data," she said.

"What?"

"I've isolated two components of the data stream." She pointed at the screen. "Only about half the data is being used by the computer to construct the digital images, the rest is extraneous. It makes no sense."

"Can you separate out the extraneous data?"

"I'm trying," she said. Paul noted sweat on her upper lip. "It may be possible ... yes, there." She sat back, staring at the screen, face flushed.

Paul scratched his head. "It looks exactly the same to me. Could it be some kind of echo, or backup redundancy?"

"Possibly," she said, "But it reminds me of something. Can't place it, but it's on the tip of my tongue." She removed her heavy glasses and closed her eyes. Paul stared at the gobbledygook on the screen. If Lin couldn't decipher it, he never would. Her high cheeks flattened, relaxed. She looked like she was meditating.

"ADSL!" she shouted, springing suddenly to life. She nearly slid off the chair. "That's it!"

"Excuse me?"

"That's where I've seen it before." She put her glasses back on and attacked the keyboard with vengeance.

"You want to explain?" said Paul, running his hand through his hair.

"ADSL, Asymmetric Digital Subscriber Line. ADSL technology is used to send large amounts of data over standard phone lines at high speed, especially useful for digital images. It's the same system we use for some of our security accounts."

Paul stared at the screen. He realized Lin might be one of few people who could have recognized the extra data, and discovered its significance.

"It makes sense," said Paul, "Radiologists sometime send the digital images over phone lines to a neurosurgeon, or a neuroradiologist in another location, for a second opinion. Can you read the data?"

"No, it's encrypted," she said.

Paul thought for a moment. "The second stream of data might be identical to the first, converted to ADSL format for phone transmission and encrypted for patient confidentiality."

Lin nodded and sighed. "OK, so, nothing out of line about it. But what's this?" She pointed at the screen. Paul saw the same incomprehensible gibberish.

"Another irregularity?" he asked.

"There's another stream of ADSL data here. Paul, this is weird."

"What?"

"This data appears to be incoming."

Paul felt a sudden chill. "Why would data be flowing into the MRI? Where is the incoming data coming from?"

"That's even weirder. It's not coming from the local Lakeside Hospital network." She kept hurriedly imputing commands.

"Can you isolate the source?"

She stopped, holding her hands open over the keyboard. Biting her lower lip, she one-fingered the keyboard a few times. "There is a remote phone link," she said, "and encrypted data is flowing both ways, right now."

"Can you tell where the data's going?"

"If I use the internet here to gain remote access to my computer at Sentry, I can access our tracer utilities."

Paul gave her shoulder a gentle squeeze. "You're a wonder."

"Oh, so you only like me for my brain?" An eyebrow went up.

"And the container it comes in," Paul said softly, planting a wet kiss on her ear.

She giggled. "That's better. I'm in. Running the trace now. Wow, bounced me out of the country."

"Where are you?" He held his breath.

"Telephonos de Mex, the Mexican phone system."

"Mexico?"

"No. It's just a node. I'm trying to pass the Mexican system. Fortunately, it's not very sophisticated. Give me a few minutes."

Paul took another breath. He tried to put the pieces together. Lakeside had an MRI machine that secretly communicated with a distant source, uploading and downloading data. Half of the important people in Bellevue had undergone brain scans in this machine. Many of these people ran large corporations that had been hit with espionage, theft, or scandal. And Dr. Z, a pioneer of MRI technology, had been murdered. There had to be some connection, an answer to the puzzle. If he only knew where to look.

"I'm out of Mexico," said Lin, "Routing through the Western Hemisphere. The end."

"Where are you?" Paul crowded in front of the screen. She glanced sideways at him and tapped the glass surface of the screen with her finger. Tap, tap, tap. Above her sculptured black fingernail he read the name.

"Colombia. Can you be more precise? Can you get the city?"

"Not possible. Colombia has great electronic security. You can thank the high standards of the drug cartels for that." She looked at him, tilting her head sideways, and ran her fingers gently over his cheek. "So, what now, crazy man?"

Paul recalled Z's Colombian hunting trips, and the two buyouts by World Development Industries, a Colombia based corporation. And now he'd discovered World Development Industries made the MRI, or at least the sensors.

"How's your Spanish?" he said.

Lin shook her head. "I don't speak Spanish, why?"

"Do you have a passport?"

"Yes, I..." She pushed away from him. "Oh, my God!"

"I speak it fluently," said Paul, "Había estudiado en la esquela."

"Paul, you're out of your mind."

"We already know that."

"What are we going to do in Colombia?" she asked.

"Hunt doves," he said. "And whatever else we can find."

CHAPTER 15

As soon as Paul stepped on the Atlanta-bound Delta jet, he realized he'd violated the conditions of his bail. It was a miracle, or more likely bureaucratic incompetence, that he hadn't made the no-fly list. He half-expected a warrant for his arrest to be waiting in Atlanta, or at the next stop, Miami. He knew he'd probably be arrested on the spot when he returned to the United States.

In exchange for purchasing plane tickets for Paul and Lin, Natasha had insisted on calling attorney Milton Freeman. Milton had drafted a letter of intent, which he planned to reveal if the authorities discovered Paul missing. The letter emphasized Paul's intention to return to the country to stand trial. Milton hoped the court would accept the letter instead of issuing a federal arrest warrant.

Milton's letter stated that Paul had material reason to believe that evidence needed to prove his innocence existed outside of the country, and that Paul had a right to all such information. Milton took the tack that Dr. Z may have been deliberately targeted for execution, and Paul wished to retrace Z's steps in the final months of his life. Paul hoped Milton's efforts paid off, because arrest warrants for bail jumping didn't look good at trial.

So far, Paul hadn't been charged with domestic terrorism. Since he was not considered a flight risk, his passport had not been revoked. Most likely the judge never expected Paul to make bail.

The five-hour layover in Miami seemed unbearable. But they left Miami without incident, flying four hours on Avianca, and landed in Cali, Colombia in the late afternoon. After clearing customs, they stood outside the baggage claim area, waiting for Augustus Francobar, the lodge guide at Hacienda de las Palmas. Lin's white T-shirt was stained with sweat, and her beige jeans were dirty. She sat on her one bag and waited. Paul paced, gagging on the car exhaust. The taxi drivers tried to solicit them for a ride, but Paul begged them off with a polite, "Gracias, no, por favor." He'd heard that tourists, who got into the wrong taxi in Colombia, could end up penniless in a back alley. Or worse.

After an hour and a half, Paul almost gave up hope before a battered, vintage Land Rover pulled up to the curb, and a man emerged who Paul instantly realized must be Francobar. Tanned as dark as dirt, his skinny, muscular legs bounded to the pavement. They were covered with scars. He wore khaki shorts, heavy boots, and a desert camouflage shirt. The bright sun beat upon his wide-brimmed gaucho hat, the dark shadow concealing his face, turning it into an eerie silhouette. When he reached out his sinewy hand to shake, he tipped his head upward enough to let the sun light his face. It was dark and taut, like sun-dried leather. Little lines covered his cheeks and forehead, like cracks in desert sand.

Paul took the man's hand and shook it. His grip caused bone-crushing pain, and he stared at Paul with dark brown eyes.

"Mr. Francobar, I assume," said Paul. "I'm Dr. Paul Powers, and this is my traveling partner, Lin Chang." Francobar didn't shake Lin's hand, but it was just as well. He probably would have broken it.

"G'day mate, ma'am," he said, touching the edge of his hat.

"You're Australian?" Lin asked.

"Everyone's from somewhere, love," he said, a wide smile with blinding white teeth shining from the darkness under his hat. "You're not originally from the colonies, I'd venture."

Lin laughed. "Oh, but I am. My father's from Hong Kong."

"Ah, you got me there, sweet. That all you hauling?" He gestured toward the two bags.

"Z said you provide everything," said Paul.

"'Deed I do. Bad thing that. Nice guy he was." He grabbed a bag in each hand and shook his head. "Were you mates?"

"He was like a father to me," said Paul.

"I never knew him," said Lin.

"Hop in, make yourself at home." They took the rear bench seat as Francobar stowed the bags in the back, and then got behind the wheel. Paul noticed a shotgun propped up on the passenger seat. Francobar looked briefly in the rearview mirror, catching Paul's gaze for an instant.

"You get used to it around here," he said, starting up the Rover and pulling into the airport traffic.

"Excuse me?" said Paul.

"The killing."

"Oh."

"Every morning, there's a bunch of bodies in the street. That's Cali."

Lin sat up straight. "Who's killing them?"

"Banditos," said Francobar, jerking the jeep through traffic. "Move yer ass, mule!" he yelled out the window while honking the horn. Then he looked at Lin through the rearview mirror. "Oh, sorry, lady. It's therapy, you know."

"Can't the police catch the bandits?" Lin asked.

Francobar burst into laughter. "They are the bandits, love."

Lin's forehead wrinkled. "How long is the ride?"

"About an hour and a half from here, ma'am. No worries."

Paul and Lin tried to relax and take in the view. Paul noted they'd left the Cali inner city, and the surroundings changed rapidly to suburban, with large patches of countryside. Modern utilitarian buildings gave way to dirty white stucco. Francobar turned off the main road, leaving the blacktop behind in favor of hard-packed dirt.

"I thought the lodge was in the town of Buga." said Paul.

"Outside of Buga, in the wetlands," said Francobar. "Buga's the oficina de correos."

"What?" said Lin.

"The postal stop, love. Drink in the country," he said, gesturing out the window. They'd certainly entered the country now. The city smog yielded to fresh air that seemed much too sweet. Huge, thick, green grasses filled the fields on either side. A billowing smokestack stood out on the horizon a few miles away. A few sweaty workers toiled nearby.

"What's the smokestack?" Lin asked.

"Trapiche."

"Translation?"

"Dead doves," said Francobar.

Lin looked at Paul with confusion. "A sugar refinery," said Paul. "They're growing more sugar cane. It's bad for dove hunters. The doves like corn, the old staple. No corn, no doves, no hunters."

"Yup, that's the way of it," said Francobar. The sugar cane fields ended and cornfields began. Thousands of white and gray doves flew overhead. "Ah, that's better. Bad enough they plant cotton, tobacco, and coffee. But now there's sugar, weed, and coke. Birds gonna starve."

"What will you do?" asked Lin.

"Move to Bolivia, maybe. Hate to leave the hacienda. We're almost there."

The land turned to wetlands, and the birds seemed to be everywhere.

"So many beautiful birds," said Lin. "The flocks are spectacular. I hate to kill them."

"It's win-win," said Francobar. "Farmers need shooters to thin the flocks and save the crops. It's a service, love."

The road grew muddy. In the distance, a structure popped up from the middle of the marsh. The road continued toward the building, with no turnoff. The road had apparently been constructed for the sole purpose of reaching Hacienda de las Palmas. Francobar had probably cut the road himself.

Hacienda de las Palmas was a rectangular, two-story affair of white stucco, with wooden decks wrapped around both floors. About an acre of golf-course-quality grass surrounded the building. A split rail fence surrounded the entire compound, beyond which scrubby brush and marsh grass spread out for as far as the eye could see. A few old maple trees shaded the house on three sides. The trees looked foreign to the environment, but seemed healthy and well-tended. Tall, earthen pots with cactus and desert flowers lined the tiled walkways and the decks.

Inside, the ground floor of the lodge contained one great room full of furnishings that had been rough-hewn from old-growth hardwoods.

"Enjoy it," said Francobar, setting down the bags. "Last bit of the rain forest, I'm afraid. Next hacienda may be plastic." His white smile flashed.

Paul respected Francobar. He'd carved an existence out of land in the middle of a wilderness, and he kept his sense of humor in the face of destructive forces of an indulgent civilization that favored sweets and drugs over all else. Francobar lived the life he cherished, and would find another place to start anew rather than be destroyed by common vices. He'd celebrate the joys of nature until the forests and the fields themselves were ripped from his beneath his feet.

The large wooden dining table could easily accommodate twenty people, and the tall, chairs, stuffed with padding, were built for comfort. A long couch, musty with the wild scent of many hunts, faced a ceiling-to-floor fireplace made of massive rocks. Overhead, mounted and stuffed birds demonstrated the biggest and the best that Buga had to offer. Old rifles and shotguns, and even a bow and arrow, hung on the walls.

The kitchen occupied the entire area opposite the fireplace. Tough, well used pots and pans hung from wrought iron hooks on an oval shaped frame, suspended from the ceiling by chains, like a chandelier. Shiny rows of long knives also hung from the iron fixture. They were arraigned in size order and sharpened to perfect edges.

A woman entered behind them. Dark, wavy hair hung to the middle of her back, her long dress, a print of yellow desert flowers, covered all but her feet. Her face, dark and soft, beamed with the freshness of youth. Her lips were thick and moist, like succulent slices of fruit. The round brown eyes projected self-confidence, toughness, and limitless energy.

"Ariel, these are our new guests, Dr. Paul Powers and Lin Chang. Please show them to their rooms."

She smiled, a tiny, friendly smile, without showing teeth. "Welcome to the hacienda," she said softly, "You were friends of Z?"

"Close friends," said Paul.

"I am sad he is gone, we had much fun here."

"I too, am sad," said Paul. "He was a wonderful man."

She nodded, and then gestured out the door. "Let me show you where you will stay." They followed her outside. A staircase to their left followed the wall of the house to the second level. It led to a verandah that circled the entire second floor. They turned the corner and she opened a door. There was no lock or key.

Paul thought this lack of security curious in the land of banditos. But he supposed a lock wouldn't stop bandits nearly as well as a shotgun. Isolation gave the hacienda all the security it needed. Thieves wouldn't be stupid enough to rob a hunting lodge.

Inside, a king-size bed with canopy filled the middle of a large room. The rest of the room contained comfortable looking stuffed chairs and a desk. It had the same rustic look of the great room below. French windows opened to a lovely view of the grounds.

"August will bring your bags. Dinner is in one hour." She bowed slightly and departed, closing the door.

"It's very nice," said Lin, putting her arms around him. "But where's your room?" She smirked.

Paul drew her close and gave her a soft kiss. "I thought you'd feel safer sleeping with me, so I only asked for one room."

She ran her hands underneath his shirt. "Don't you think a lady should have some say in the matter? I kinda like Francobar, very buff, don't you think?"

"Not my type, besides, I think he's taken. But Ariel is quite beautiful." He kissed her deeply. "You are stuck with me, and we have an hour before dinner."

She pushed him away. "Oh, no. I need a shower. You dragged me on this wild goose chase, and I'm not sure why. So, I go first."

Paul backed away, letting Lin get cleaned up for dinner. She had a point. He wasn't sure what they'd come for, or what to look for. All he could do was retrace Z's steps and hope for a clue as to how he'd spent his final days. Something connected this place to the Lakeside MRI, the cold pill murders, and to Z's untimely death. The answer had to be here; he just didn't know the question. Pumping Francobar for information seemed like a logical place to start.

Lin cleaned up well. Her soiled travel clothes yielded to a fresh white blouse and crisp, black slacks. The outfit showcased her slender torso and gave her a look of childlike innocence. Her dark hair accented the black and white motif. It was a clever look, at once modern and old-fashioned.

Paul gave Lin a hug. She smelled fresh. He cleaned up and put on a simple checkered work shirt, red and black, and a pair of light brown pants. Together they headed downstairs to the lodge's great room for dinner.

Ariel served dinner family style to the four of them. There were no other guests. She filled the table with baskets of home-baked breads and fresh fruit. The fruits looked tropical, but unfamiliar, with several obviously belonging to the banana family. The first course consisted of viudo de pescado, fish soup, made with a variety of local fish, green bananas, and manioc, a type of local cassava. This was served with a home made hot sauce that brought tears to Lin's eyes and left Paul's tongue on fire.

Light dinner conversation centered on the preparation of the meal and prospects for a good hunt in the morning. Francobar briefly described the area they'd be going to and the weapons he would provide. Lin conceded that she had never hunted before, and Francobar promised to give her expert instruction.

Ariel pointed out that the main course of barbequed lamb, cooked to perfection, had been prepared from fresh local lamb. The lamb was served over rice with chorizo sausages, beans, and avocado slices. Bottomless pitchers of aguapanela, a home made super sweet lime drink, and cheap red wine conspired to give Paul's head a buzz. Ariel's arroz con coco, coconut rice pudding, spiced with lemon and cinnamon, made the perfect dessert and ending for the meal. The soft, creamy texture was comfort food for Lin and Paul, cleansing their pallets and leaving them satisfied and sleepy.

Paul and Lin complemented Ariel on the exceptional meal, and they retired to the giant couch by the fireplace in the great room. Ariel tidied up after the meal and excused herself for the night. Colorful stuffed pheasants and snowy white doves hung on the rustic wooden walls, wings spread, frozen forever in various stages of flight. A bright fire sparked and crackled, the sweet earthy scent of burning wood filled the room. The couple sank into the comfortable couch, bellies bulging and heavy. Francobar joined them by the fire, settling into one of the overstuffed chairs.

"Can you tell me about the hunts you had with Z?" Paul asked.

Francobar stood up. "I can do better than that. I'll show you some pictures."

He retrieved an album, sat down next to the couple on the couch, set the book down on the coffee table, and began to flip though it. In one picture, Z held a stringer with perhaps fifty doves. In another, he crouched behind the blind, waiting for the birds to show. One action shot caught the flash from the barrel of the shotgun, a Remington. Paul examined the photo closely.

"That was Z's gun, wasn't it?"

Francobar looked at the picture. He hesitated. "Well, yes, yes, I believe so. He loved that gun, never shot without it."

"Did you ever provide him with a gun?"

Francobar shook his head. "Never, Z wouldn't hear of it. Took a lot of paperwork and a couple of bribes to get the gun into the country, but Z insisted." Francobar smiled.

Paul took the album and examined it closely. Then he handed it back to Francobar. "Do you have any other pictures of Z?"

Francobar glanced at Paul for an instant. His smile faded, lips a thin line. He shook his head. These are the last of them, forever, I'm afraid."

Paul remembered Natasha said Z went on several hunting trips to Colombia without his gun in the last few months before he died. Either Natasha had been mistaken, or Francobar had lied. Paul wondered if Francobar had played host to Z and a woman. Maybe Francobar had hidden these incriminating pictures elsewhere. After all, his business was to sell hunts, and he'd asked no questions when Paul requested a single room with Lin. Undoubtedly, Francobar would look the other way if Z brought a mistress to Colombia. Perhaps Natasha's suspicions were correct.

"We'd better turn in, now," said Francobar, "I'll be getting you up before the sun tomorrow."

And with that, Paul and Lin said good night and returned to their room. They changed for bed, sunk onto the plush bed, and fell asleep in each other's arms.

CHAPTER 16

In the morning, Ariel knocked gently on the door to rouse them. A cool breeze filtered though an open window from the dark fields beyond. The first dim twilight made silhouettes of the maple trees, terra cotta pots, and cacti outside their window.

"I hate hunting," said Lin, "if I have to get up this early."

"That's when the birds get up," said Paul. "Get up. I'm sure Ariel's made us a marvelous breakfast."

And she had, although it was simple and basic. Everything seemed as fresh as possible. The air smelled of home-baked bread. No doubt Ariel had risen early to start cooking. Various biscuits and muffins were offered, complemented by home-canned jams, hot, hardboiled eggs, and bananas.

Ariel had set down pitchers of orange juice and dark local coffee.

"Incredible," said Lin. "You're an amazing hostess."

"Gracias," said Ariel, pouring Lin some coffee.

Francobar had also risen early, and busied himself packing the Land Rover. He stopped briefly, shotgun in hand, and grabbed a hard boiled egg, skillfully holding and peeling it with one hand. He bit into it like an apple and finished it in a few bites. From his closed fist, the crumpled shell poured onto a saucer like grains of sand. "Almost ready, mates. Early hunt's the best, you know."

Paul wondered if it had rained, because the road seemed muddier than yesterday, a stark contrast to the desert-like surroundings. Flying insects swarmed around small puddles of wet earth.

Francobar hurriedly finished packing up the truck and the hunters piled into the Rover. Paul sat in front and Lin took the back seat. The cargo area behind the back seat of the truck held ammo, a cooler with lunch packed by Ariel, a thermos with several gallons of cold water, and four shotguns attached to a rack on the ceiling. Two matching steel gas cans in padlocked metal cages hung outside on the back of the truck. A spare tire sat in the luggage rack on top of the Rover, chained and locked.

Lin had dressed smart, in blue jeans, hiking boots, and a mid weight jacket to fend off the cool morning air. Paul wore his shooting jacket, made of soft leather and covered with ample pockets for shells and other supplies, including his passport, wallet, and cell phone. His heavy brown khaki hunting pants had reinforced padding in the seat and knees, and many zippered pockets. They both brought hats to keep off the searing afternoon sun.

Fifteen minutes into the drive, on a curvy, hilly section of road, Francobar slowed. He rolled his window all the way down and stopped the truck.

"Why are we stopping?" Paul asked.

Francobar opened his door partway and leaned over to examine the dirt road. "Heavy trucks, probably military, very recent."

Lin leaned forward in between the front seats. "A problem?" she said, eyes wide.

Francobar shut the door and started up the Rover slowly. "No worries, love. Settle back, I'll handle it." As they rounded the next curve a large green military truck came into view. It blocked the narrow dirt road. The back of the truck, a canvas-covered cargo hold, faced the Rover. Two soldiers in green and brown camouflage uniforms stood on either side of the vehicle with automatic weapons hanging from shoulder straps. They held up their hands.

"Pare! Pare!" shouted one of the solders. Francobar stopped the truck about ten feet from the roadblock. He got out and walked toward the soldiers.

"Paul, I don't like the look of this!" said Lin, biting her bottom lip.

"Keep cool. Francobar probably gets this all the time. He's a survivor. We'll be OK," said Paul, trying to sound confident while his mind played out worst-case scenarios. Suddenly, he felt sorry for dragging Lin on this dangerous adventure. He was a fugitive with a serious cancer and had little to lose. Lin had a whole life ahead of her and it was unfair to put her in danger. Worse, he was falling in love with her. If she was harmed in any way, he would be damaged, too. It was selfish of him to bring her along.

Francobar stood by the soldiers, talking for about ten minutes. Paul wished he could hear the conversation. The more animated solder seemed agitated. Below his black mustache sunlight sparkled off a metal tooth as he shouted at Francobar and gestured, pointing alternately at the Rover and the green truck. The other soldier shifted his hands restlessly on his machine gun.

Finally, Francobar turned and headed back to the Rover. He passed the driver's window. "No worries. Just stay put," he said from the side of his mouth as he passed without making eye contact. Pulling a key ring from his coat pocket, he unlocked one of the gas cans and pulled it from its cage. Walking over to the side of the soldier's truck, he emptied the gas into their tank. Then he walked back to the Rover and stowed the gas can in its cage. The two soldiers climbed into the military vehicle and drove off, leaving the hunting party alone on road.

"Never send 'em off empty-handed," said Francobar, climbing back into the driver's seat. "That's why I carry extra petrol." He smiled and started up the Rover as Paul and Lin took one collective sigh.

After a half hour drive on muddy roads, they arrived at a clearing in front of a cornfield. Great flocks of doves arose like locusts and swarmed in the distance. Near them stood a battered pickup truck, filled with decoys, nets, two by fours, and tools. About a dozen young, dark boys in tattered shorts stood in various places around the clearing. A blind had been constructed from wood and camouflage netting. The blind had a configuration like a three-sided lean-to. Several men could easily sit or crouch behind it. One of the boys ran over to Francobar. He smelled of hot sweat and was so dirty as to be almost indistinguishable from the muddy field. It was the perfect natural camouflage.

"Solamente los dos hoy, Miguel," Francobar said.

"Sí jefe," Miguel replied. He ran off, returned with two old folding chairs, and set them up behind the blind. Francobar handed Paul a Remington twelve-gauge and started to hand Lin a Mossberg. She held up her hand.

"Not this morning, please," she said, "I'm not quite ready. I'll watch Paul shoot for a awhile."

Francobar nodded and withdrew the shotgun. "You're gonna fall for it, love. Nothing quite like connecting with the prey." He returned to the jeep to fetch ammunition, piling up several boxes of it behind the blind. "That'll fix you for a few hours. See that ridge?" He pointed across the marshy field to a gentle hill that arose like the bank of a river, about a hundred yards away. "I'm gonna help the boys set up a blind behind the hill. I'll do some shooting from there, drive the birds your way."

Paul nodded. "Yeah, all right. I'll start from here." Paul knew it made sense to flush out the birds. But he thought it odd for Francobar to leave his guests so early in a hunt. Francobar and several boys hopped into the Rover. It climbed the hill and sunk out of sight on the other side. The rest of the boys piled into the old pickup, packed tightly, sitting in the open cargo bed. Paul watched as the pickup took off up the hill, brown boys bouncing on the flatbed until the brush swallowed them up. Lin and Paul stood alone behind the blind.

"Paul, shouldn't he be assisting us or something?"

The slight morning breeze had stopped. Now the hot air stagnated, and the equatorial sun drew sweat from their pores. Lin angled her wide straw hat to block the rays from her pale face.

Paul adjusted the brim of his baseball cap and gazed at the ridge behind which the Rover disappeared. "He'll be back," said Paul, trying to sound reassuring, but he wasn't sure.

"Paul, I heard you have a knack for getting into trouble, but I didn't believe it, until now. I have a bad feeling about this."

"Don't worry. Francobar's a professional. We came here to retrace Z's steps. He hunted with Francobar, so let's hunt."

With that, Paul loaded five rounds into the twelve-gauge, and pocketed about a dozen more in his hunting jacket. He sat on the chair behind the blind, and motioned to Lin to do the same. To any dove approaching over the wetlands, they'd be invisible. But there were no birds in flight.

After a few minutes, a distant shotgun blast rang out. "This is it," said Paul. "He's flushing them toward us."

Sure enough, a few moments later a cloud-like flock of doves soared skyward from behind the ridge, headed higher at three o'clock. The gray and white birds flew madly, noisy wings slapping like waves on a rocky shore.

Paul stood bolt upright, raising the shotgun to shoulder level, picking a bird, tracking it. Fire and smoke blasted from the shotgun barrel as the gun kicked Paul's shoulder. And then a bird tumbled in a ball of gray, pellets and feathers, spiraling, falling downward, out of sight in the brush. The rest of the doves changed directions, zig-zaging frantically. No longer did the flock glide in formation. The birds traveled randomly, while Paul continued to track them, knocking down several more from the sky. They fell like shells in a fireworks finale, complete with the heavy acrid smell of gunpowder.

"Don't we need a dog to retrieve the birds?" Lin asked.

Paul lowered his shotgun. "No, the boys will do it." He scanned the area, but there was no sign of Francobar or the boys. The doves were gone, and in the sudden, eerie silence, he heard his breathing. His pulse quickened.

"Then where are they?" said Lin.

Before he could answer, Paul saw a flash on the ridge and pushed Lin to the ground, falling on top of her. A loud blast followed, and debris fell from the camouflage net. "Oh, my God! They're shooting at us!" Lin shouted.

"Stay down," said Paul, reloading the shotgun. He wondered if banditos had overtaken Francobar and were now after Lin and him. Or maybe Francobar had set them up. But why? There was no time to figure it out. They needed to survive first or nothing would matter. Another shot rang out over their heads. They felt the breeze from the buckshot.

Lin lay on the ground, face down in the mud, trembling.

Paul spread out on his belly, propping himself up on his elbows, straining to see where the shots came from. He leaned over and spoke into Lin's ear. "OK. They're using shotguns, not very powerful or accurate at this distance. They're not trying to kill us, yet, so they must be trying to pin us down."

He filled the stock with five rounds, and shoveled as many shells from the ammo boxes as he could, stuffing them into his pockets. Then he gave a handful to Lin. "Take as many as you can." She filled her pant pockets with shells. "I'm going to provide you with some cover fire. You've got to get into the brush on the other side of this field. Beyond the brush, a few miles back, there's a sugar plantation. You can get there, hide in the cane fields, and get help from someone at the mill."

She grabbed him around the waist. "No, I'm not leaving without you! Who's going to cover for you? You'll be trapped."

More buckshot passed overhead. Paul pushed Lin away. "I don't have time to argue. Go. I'll find another way out, trust me."

"Not this time. We go together, or not at all."

Paul rolled onto his back next to Lin, clutching the shotgun to his chest. "Next hunt take a shotgun when it's offered." He smirked.

"There will never be a next time."

"OK. We go together. You hang on and be my eyes, I'll run backward and put down some cover." She nodded.

"Ready?"

"Yes."

Paul stood up, and started firing toward the ridge. The opposing fire ceased. Lin grabbed him by his belt at the back of his pants and pulled him toward the brush. Paul's fifth shot rang out twenty feet from the brush. He turned forward.

"Run! Stay low. Dive. Hurry!"

They crouched and ran, buckshot whizzing all around them. A few feet from the brush, Lin dove in, followed by Paul. Thistles on the desert-like scrub tore their skin and clothing. Woody stems penetrated their hands.

Paul lifted Lin from the ground. "Get up. We can't stop now. If we stay still, they'll find us. It's at least a few miles to the sugar plantation."

They walked as fast as they could through the thick brush, hunched over. They dared not stand upright. Dehydrated from the exercise and the hot sun, they grew so thirsty that their tongues felt like lumps of dirt. A few times in the distance, they heard a car and voices shouting. Always, they headed away from the noise. Paul took his bearing from the sun, and they continued in what he thought was the direction of the cane fields. Thorny brush cut through their clothing, bloodying their arms and legs. Pain coursed through them from the cuts, like a thousand little knives slicing their skin. Insects attracted to the bloody stains engulfed them in buzzing clouds of ever increasing haze. The voices in the distance still pursued.

Paul reloaded the shotgun, but there was nothing to shoot at. Firing the gun now would only serve to give away their location.

Lin staggered and fell to her knees, gasping. "I, I can't walk anymore. It must be a hundred degrees. You go. Send someone back for me."

Paul knelt down. "Oh, so now you want me to go alone? Make up your mind. I'm not leaving you here." He dropped the shotgun and put her right arm over his shoulder and continued walking, assisting Lin forward. Paul lost all track of time. His vision wavered, and he stumbled, taking Lin down with him again and again. Panting, his tongue hung limp and dry. A waterfall of sweat poured from every pore, soaking his clothes. Insects, no longer content just to swarm, began to feed on him without mercy. He had no energy to fend off the biting bugs, and the constant pain helped to drive him onward.

No longer able to walk continuously, he stopped when needed, partially set Lin down, then picked her up and walked some more. But the intervals of walking grew shorter, and his rest periods longer. Lin went limp, dead weight, but he continued to carry her forward, rest, and carry her again. Until he found he could not lift her any more.

Down on his knees, he tried to coax Lin to her feet. "Lin, get up, we've got to go. Lin, please." But she didn't respond. She lay still in his arms, unconscious. He couldn't leave her, but he no longer had the strength to carry her. Grabbing her by the ankles, he dragged her a few feet, rested, and dragged her again. The prickly underbrush ripped at her flesh and her clothes. Paul couldn't catch his breath, the air passed hot and dry through his mouth, burning his lungs. He pitched face down in the sticker bushes, and struggled to raise himself, but he could not.

Gasping, face impaled on the thorny undergrowth, he thought if he just rested for a moment, then he'd continue. They would both continue. Continue together. Yes. He closed his eyes. The heat broke suddenly and a chill passed through him like a wave, along with a loud roar, a deafening ocean. For an instant, he felt good, even the cuts no longer hurt. He felt entirely at peace. Somehow he belonged here, with Lin, in this spot, and he knew they'd be here, forever.

CHAPTER 17

Jasmine and musk drifted through a deep recess in Paul's head, like a sultry breeze, flavorful, exotic. He smiled and pain pulled at his cheeks, bringing him to consciousness. It took a few minutes for his eyes to focus in the dim light, and longer for him to realize he was on his back, on a cold, hard floor. Above hung a billowing tapestry inlaid with gold, a picture of hunters with bows, arrows, and rocks closing in on some large, strange beast.

Feeling beside him, he noted a cloth covering the hard surface on which he lay. The material, thick and woven, felt like hemp, or some similar natural fiber. He could perceive the room now, a small chamber, perhaps ten feet on a side, decorated with hanging tapestries. If there was a door, he could not detect it. But he suspected it existed behind one of the hanging curtains.

With great difficulty he forced himself into a sitting position. Every fiber of his body responded with stiffness and pain. In the distance, he heard a faint murmur, like water falling, or many people talking at once. The sound created a steady tone in his ears, like static on a phone line. Beside him he found an earthen pot with a bluish liquid, and a wet sponge made of tightly bound scraps of cloth. Looking down at his legs, he was shocked to find his clothes gone, replaced by a one-piece, dark brown robe that seemed to be made from fine, tightly woven wool.

He remembered the dove hunt, and running into the brush, trying to reach the sugar plantation. They hadn't made it. So where was he, and what had happened to Lin? Slowly, he rose to his feet. Dizzy, he staggered to the wall, grabbing it for support. Pulling aside the wall hanging, he found the wall had been constructed from stone. Dim flames from an oil lamp provided the only light. It felt like he'd awoken in the bowels of the earth, or perhaps he'd been magically transported back in time to a medieval castle.

He needed to find a way out of the room. Groping as he crept along the wall, his hand at last pushed past the barrier. As he'd suspected, one of the tapestries covered a doorway. But to where? He stepped out into a dark, narrow hallway. Like the room he'd left, the hallway had been constructed from stone, and decorated with hanging curtains, but sparsely. The low ceiling curved, and he realized the passageway was a tunnel.

He felt like a spelunker, winding through solid rock, a rare oil lamp providing barely enough illumination to see the way. The stone floor sent a chill up his legs through his naked feet. He wondered if he was miles underground, although he might just as well be on the upper floor of some kind of windowless structure. But where was this place, how did he get here, and how long had he been unconscious?

The answers, he knew, might be waiting at the end of the tunnel. After thirty feet it branched and he stopped at the junction, wondering. Left or right? He walked a few feet down each branch and listened. The noise seemed louder on the right, and definitely came from human voices. But there was something odd about the tone and cadence of the voices that he couldn't fathom. Still, he needed to find out where he was, and if there were people here, they would be likely to know.

Then it occurred to him that someone had just tried to kill him, and nearly succeeded. What if the people he was headed toward were the very same ones he'd almost died trying to avoid? Maybe banditos had kidnapped him, hoping to extort ransom from his family. In Colombia, Paul knew, this was a popular crime. Perhaps, he thought, he might be better off taking the branch that led away from people.

He stood still for a minute, fixated on the trail junction, wondering which path to take. After a deep breath, he entered the right branch and headed toward whatever civilization inhabited this strange environment. And there were other branches, too. Each time he paused, listened, and chose the route that brought the voices closer. The eerie intonations grew louder and more melodic, a song, low-pitched, vibrating the tunnels like a wind instrument.

Finally, the tunnel opened onto a circular, stone balcony, and the voices boomed from below. He looked down upon forty or so hooded figures, in a triangular formation, dressed in the same robes as the type he now wore. They were surrounded by dozens of stone monoliths, each with a smoldering flame on the top. The monoliths contained elaborate gold inlay, and must have been worth a fortune. Paul realized the hooded figures were some kind of monks, chanting in religious supplication.

Their voices arose in unison, rolling through the open chamber, combining with an explosive, but gentle force. Each note boomed and lingered, joining in brotherhood with the notes before and after, the room pulsating joyously, alive, like an animal beseeching the heavens. No one led the group, yet they produced a harmony so complete it seemed of one emotion, one voice.

Paul looked for a way down from the balcony to the floor below. He found it, a magnificent staircase of polished stone, so slick he had to hold on to the railing to keep his footing. Quietly, he descended the stairs, winding down to the chanting monks.

After reaching the main level, he took his place behind and to the left of the group. From this position, he could see in front of the crowd. The chanting continued unabated as he joined the ranks, the faceless, hooded monks paid him no mind. Clearly, the mediation would not be interrupted on his account.

Although no one led the group, Paul could now see that one monk sat in front on a waist-high pedestal, facing the group. His hands folded serenely on his lap, and his head remained bowed and motionless. The group seemed to be drawing strength and guidance from this one individual. It was like a psychic connection.

Paul had read about strange religious cults that possessed extrasensory skills, but he didn't believe in such things. None of these cults had ever demonstrated their so-called extrasensory skills scientifically. Until Paul saw the proof, he'd remain a skeptic. But what was a religious cult like this doing in the middle of Colombia? Of course, Paul didn't even know if he was still in Colombia.

All good things must pass, and Paul suspected that even devout worshipers needed to eventually stop worshipping long enough to eat and sleep. So he waited. Listening to the monks chant, he became immersed. For an instant, he traveled outside of himself, and looked back at a being filled with confusion and fear. His emotions, pure and unfiltered, crystallized before his eyes for a split-second.

Eerie self-realization scared him. It was more than he could take right now. He pulled himself back to what he perceived as the real world, and filled his mind with thoughts of finding Lin and the truth behind Z's murder. But he now understood these monks lived in a different reality, a strange one. The chant intoxicated, tempted, and transported the listener to the precipice of an alternate reality.

When the chanting finally ended, the monks stood motionless for a long time, in silence. Paul dared not speak, partly out of respect, but also out of fear. As strange as the monks seemed, he was the real stranger here.

The group began to disperse, paying no attention to Paul, even though he stood, hoodless, scratching his head in bewilderment. When the group had left, only Paul and the hooded figure on the pedestal remained. Paul walked slowly toward the monk, inhaling deeply, the air smoky from the pillared torches above. Musky incense drifted in.

"Approach," said the monk, lifting his head to reveal an old face, bald head, and scraggly white beard.

Paul walked to within a few feet of the man. "Sir, may I..."

"Silence!" He held up his hand.

"You're American, a hunter. But now you are hunted. Moritz found you on a prayer walk, exposed, left for dead. Although we forbid it, he brought you here. He is young and less inclined to follow the old ways." The wrinkled face smiled a bit, his teeth glistened, long and white. "We could not take you to the police. They are not to be trusted. What is your name?"

Paul started to answer, but became dizzy and staggered.

"Sit down, take care, you are returned from the dead."

Paul sat on the edge of the stage-like platform, looking up for a moment at the splendor of the chamber as seen from the leader's position. "Paul Powers, an American doctor. And I had a traveling companion, Lin Chang, a small, Asian woman."

"I know nothing of your companion."

"She couldn't have walked away, I'd been carrying her for miles."

"Banditos take Americans for ransom," said the old man.

"Thank you for rescuing me," said Paul. "Is there somewhere I can make a phone call? I seem to have lost my cell phone."

"You had no possessions when Moritz found you. You can get a phone in the village. It is a short walk better made in the cool morning air. We have no phones here. Brother Moritz will take you there in the morning. You can do no more now. Rest here tonight. Please take almuarzo with us. That is where our tongues loosen up. We have many tales to share, and few who'll listen."

The old man was correct, Paul realized. He'd have to gather his strength and regroup in the morning. If Lin had been kidnapped, the banditos would treat her well and keep her alive until her father paid the ransom. He'd heard that kidnappers in Colombia were gentlemanly and businesslike. On the other hand, if Lin had escaped, he'd have to find her, somehow.

Dumb luck and the morning constitutional of a young monk had saved him. Francobar may not have been as lucky. Paul wondered if bandits had ambushed Francobar and then come after his rich American clients. Paul might as well show respect to the monks and avail himself of the cult's hospitality. Maybe they'd know something about Dr. Z and his last few hunts in Colombia.

CHAPTER 18

The monks did not deprive themselves when it came to eating. A long slab of rock, raised about a foot off the floor, served as a dining table. Seating accommodations included the same type of woven mat Paul had woken up on not long ago. But there were plenty of soft pillows, and the monks sat in a variety of relaxed postures around the table, kneeling, cross-legged, and sitting on the pillows.

Unlike the orderly community of the religious ceremony, the monks chattered continuously, laughing, drinking, and shouting at one another across the table. It was more like a medieval feast than a devout ceremony.

Platters were heaped high with grilled steak, chorizo sausages, and fried pork rinds. Small bowls of hogao, a spicy homemade sauce, were placed strategically so that no one would have to reach very far to grab a spoonful of the condiment. Paul found the hogao excellent for bringing out the flavor of the meats. The sauce was loaded with partially fried tomatoes and onions. Several large bowls of red beans and brown rice passed hand to hand. Sliced avocado and rows of fresh tropical fruits filled rectangular metal trays that ran lengthwise down the center of the table.

On Paul's right sat Brother Moritz, a fresh-faced man of about twenty. Dark-skinned and jovial, the others treated him like the most irreverent one in the group, and he seemed to enjoy the distinction. Paul remembered the leader saying that Moritz had violated the rules against taking in outsiders in order to save Paul.

"I want to thank you for taking me in," Paul said to Moritz. "I know you broke the rules."

Moritz shrugged. "They all consider me a rebel. I have to live up to my reputation. Besides, you were in desperate need at the time."

"How did you find me?"

"I walk many miles every day in the cool morning air, until the heat of the day. Exercise is part of my personal meditation. I found you quite by accident."

"Please tell me about it."

"You were face down in the dirt a few miles from here. At first I took you for dead. I checked for identification, but you had none. No possessions at all. I thought you'd been robbed and your body dumped by banditos. This is a frequent event around here. But then you stirred a bit and it startled me. I carried you back."

"Did you see any sign of Lin, my traveling companion?"

"I'm sorry, I did not. There were some old tire tracks in the dirt, that's all."

"How long was I unconscious?"

"Many hours. You were overheated and dried out from the sun. I wet you down and fed you juice until you revived."

"I owe you my life," said Paul.

"You owe me nothing," said Moritz.

Baskets of warm pandebono, a corn bread rich in cheese and eggs, came right out of the oven. Paul tasted the pandebono, and found it to have the perfect texture, at once both creamy and course. Other baskets were heaping with fried banana chips, apparently the local equivalent of American potato chips.

The monks ladled out ajiaco, the local version of chicken soup, from a steaming iron kettle. Moritz put a bowl of the hot, yellow soup in front of Paul.

"As part of your treatment, you must have ajiaco," said Moritz.

Paul sniffed the bowl. The bittersweet aromatic tang of Guasca, an indigenous herb, arose from the vapors. The hearty chicken, corn, and potato medley was thick and meaty. Paul followed the monks' lead, adding avocados, and stirring in generous helpings of cream. This was the monks' version of mother's cure-all chicken soup. Paul felt his strength returning.

The monks had their own microbrew ale, and aguardiente, a fiery, anise flavored drink, made mostly from sugar cane. Paul sampled the aguardiente. It exploded in his mouth, sweet and hot, taking his breath away for an instant. He came up for air, realizing the potent drink must be half alcohol. Fortunately, a pitcher of cool water was nearby. He quickly doused the flames.

"Brother Moritz," said the monk to Paul's left, reaching out a hairy arm holding a mug laden with drink. "You brought this outsider for almuerzo, perhaps you should entertain him, too? You want to be entertained, yes, yes?" said the hairy monk, nodding at Paul and prodding his shoulder with an overflowing mug. Moritz shook his head, indicating Paul should not answer. But before Paul could think of a response, a wave of pounding on the table began. "Brother Moritz, tell this American tourist who we are," shouted a voice from the unruly crowd.

The ruckus grew louder and louder, with catcalls of "Tell him, Moritz" mixed with laughter, until Moritz took the pandebono from his mouth, stood up, and held up his hands, palms out. The room grew silent, a few muffled laughs died out. All but Moritz resumed eating.

"Let me remind you of traditions older than any of us. Three thousand years before the birth of Christ, we, the Muisca, flourished in this rich valley. Chibchachum, the creator of the universe, watched over us for centuries. Bachué, Cuza, Bochica, Nemcatacoa, and Chiminigagua protected us. Heaped in gold in ancient times, our culture passed beyond material needs of the flesh and developed advanced discipline of the mind.

We are the descendants, the last of the Muisca, proud keepers of this discipline. But you eat like a bunch of pigs."

Deafening laughter arose in the room, and degenerated into many different conversations. Moritz sat back down.

Paul couldn't believe what he'd just heard. "Muisca? As in El Dorado, the lost city of gold? Please don't take offense, but I thought the Muisca culture had died out, and the gold was a myth."

Moritz smiled. "Myth is what you believe. The Muisca culture lives in us. Of that I am certain. As for the city of gold, I can't say."

Paul drowned his pork rind in hogao sauce and bit off a piece. It was delightfully crisp and tangy. "Who built this place? How did you come to be here?"

"These are ancient Muisca burial chambers, tunneled deep into the mountain. The method of construction is still a mystery. Try the ale, our special blend."

Paul complied, filling his earthen mug with frothy brew from the pitcher before him. "I thought the Muisca buried their dead with riches? Gold, jewels, enormous wealth, what happened to it?"

"Guagueros! Grave robbers. But at least they left us these empty chambers, well hidden, with little wealth left to tempt the banditos."

The ale was dark and hardy, pleasantly burning his throat on the way down. He licked the froth off his moustache. "What did you mean by 'advanced discipline of the mind'?"

Moritz swallowed a piece of chorizo sausage and washed it down with ale. "The Muisca culture had the leisure to spend improving the human mind. Many of our accomplishments have not been duplicated by others, even in these modern times."

"Please explain this to me," said Paul.

"You wish to learn all about Muisca mental power before the meal has finished?" Moritz laughed.

"No, just give me a sample, an idea of what's involved."

"Ah, a taste. Yes, well, give me a moment." Moritz finished sucking the succulent pulp from a couple of bright orange uchuvas, a grape-sized tropical fruit. He spit the empty skins from his mouth, discarding the husks and their parchment-like leaves in a pile on his plate. Juice ran down his chin and hands. Moritz wiped his fingers on his robe.

"Since you are a doctor, let's try something you will appreciate. Take my pulse." He offered his wrist.

Paul felt the young man's wrist. His pulse bounded at about seventy-five beats per minute. Paul had to count seconds silently because he'd lost his watch along with everything else.

"What speed would you like it?" said Moritz.

"I don't understand."

The young monk smiled. "Pick a number, for my pulse."

Paul knew setting the heart rate was under subconscious control, the conscious mind had no say in the matter. But he decided to play along. "Sixty per minute."

"Count it again."

Paul counted the man's pulse again, sure it would be the same, but it was not. Moritz's heart now beat sixty times per minute. Paul thought it must be some kind of magic trick. He looked the monk in the eyes. "Fifty per minute," said Paul, and he counted again.

The beat slowed immediately to fifty per minute. "One hundred and ten." The pulse sped up to one hundred and ten. Moritz pulled his hand away.

"There is your taste," he said. "Did you enjoy it?"

"I'm amazed. And you do this by controlling your thoughts?"

"The Muisca mental discipline is much more than just controlling one's thoughts. It is our religion, our commitment, our life. We spend much of our time in contemplation of a single word, concept, or feeling. It is our path to enlightenment. Western science calls it mind control, a narrow view."

"I apologize," said Paul.

Moritz smiled and held up his hand. "No need."

"You have an amazing culture," said Paul. "These mental powers should be studied using western scientific method."

The monks at the table laughed at Paul's last remark. Dumbfounded, Paul asked, "What is so funny?"

Moritz poked at Paul's shoulder. "Pay no attention to them, they are stupid monks. They laugh because our mental powers are already being studied, and they pay us well."

"Who is studying you?"

"American scientists, at WDI."

"World Development Industries?"

"So, you've heard of them."

"Yeah, I have. What do you do for them?"

"We think."

"Explain."

"I can not. They do not tell us everything. We think of whatever they ask us to while they study us."

"How do they study you?"

"With a monitor, a large machine."

"Do you lay on a table with your head in a tunnel?"

"Yes, in a sealed room."

"Do they let you take metal objects into the room?"

"No."

"I understand," said Paul. Obviously, Moritz had described an MRI machine, but didn't know the name for it.

"Can you give me an example of something they ask you to think about?"

"Anything."

"Like?"

"A word, a number, a color, a feeling. They say think of four and we think four. They say think of red and we think red."

"For how long do they ask you to think of each thing?"

"For minutes, or for hours, or for days."

"After my phone call tomorrow, I'd like to go to World Development Industries. I want to see this machine. Can you arrange that?"

Moritz shook his head and the room quieted down. "Do not ask me this. It is forbidden. We go only when we are summoned."

Paul dropped the topic. Moritz seemed frightened at the mention of an unofficial visit to World Development Industries. Paul decided to concentrate on recovering Lin first, then he'd find a way to get inside World Development Industries. Maybe later, away from the rest of the group, Moritz would at least tell Paul the location of the World Development Industries facility. Bringing outsiders into the enclave had also been forbidden, but Moritz had broken the rule and brought Paul inside.

World Development Industries had to be nearby, since the monks worked there on a regular basis. The other monks accepted Moritz's radical nature, and even relished in it. No doubt Moritz added some excitement to the day to day routine of monastic life.

Paul drank ale and listened as the monks told stories of their boyhood and villages they grew up in, and they laughed at the slightest provocation. These men truly enjoyed life, study, and camaraderie. Later, Moritz guided Paul back to the chamber in which he'd awoken. He sunk onto the cloth floor mat and fell soundly asleep.

CHAPTER 19

Paul awoke to the low rumblings of the morning chants. He was surprised to find his freshly washed clothing, or the tattered remains of it, in a neatly folded pile by his head. Someone had left it there during the night while Paul slept. After dressing, he put the robe back on over his clothes. This time he waited politely in his room until the murmurs stopped and he supposed the meditation session had ended. Then he wandered the labyrinth looking for Moritz.

Paul needed to get out of the monastery, to a telephone, and perhaps to the police. The words of Francobar and the old monk kept ringing in Paul's head. The men had warned Paul not to trust the police. How would he proceed without cooperation from the authorities? For all he knew, corrupt authorities might be the ones who'd shot at him and Lin.

Paul decided he'd best avoid the police, and get in touch with Twi Chang and Natasha for advice. He would have to call Natasha for help, anyway, since he no longer had any money or a passport. Finding Lin was a priority. Then he needed to get into World Development Industries. Location and surveillance of the secretive World Development Industries complex was essential.

Yesterday Paul wondered if Francobar had been attacked by bandits. But today, after sleeping on it, Paul suspected he'd been set up for an ambush by Francobar. The man knew every inch of the terrain, making it unlikely an enemy could sneak up on the hunting party without Francobar's help. The guide had survived for years in the land of banditos and corruption. He knew the system. Either he'd been paid off or threatened.

Who would have the power and motive to coerce a strong, well-armed, savvy man like Francobar? Why did Paul's presence in Colombia pose a threat to anyone? Paul felt the attack must be related to his murder investigation. Something was rotten at Lakeside Hospital. It involved MRI scanners, Z's death, and the mysterious rogue company World Development Industries in Colombia. Maybe the Northwest cold pill tampering was part of some elaborate cover-up. Paul struggled to make sense of it all.

"You slept well, Dr. Paul?" Moritz smiled roundly in the corridor.

"Yeah, yeah, I did, but I have to leave now, I have to look for my companion and..."

"And you intend to visit WDI?" said Moritz. The smile faded from his face, his eyes darkened, and his cheeks stretched tight. For the first time, the jolly man looked scared.

"What? What is it?" Paul asked.

Moritz put his right arm around Paul, and held him close, speaking softly into his ear, "Be careful of that place, it is not what it seems. I do not understand what use they put our powers to, and it frightens me."

"You believe the company is evil?"

Sweat beaded up on the monk's forehead. "The enlightened one believes these westerners have been sent by ancestral spirits to help us survive these materialistic times, but..."

"I understand," Paul interrupted. "Say no more."

Moritz heaved a sigh of relief and released his hold on Paul. "I will take you to Pueblo Viejo, the old village, a few miles from here. You can find lodging there, and telephones for sale in the tienda. You can wire money to the cambio. And you will find no shortage of fresh food from the street vendors. There are few policia in Pueblo Viejo. This is good. Do not ask policia for help. If a ransom is asked for your friend, her family will know. Pay it right away. The secuestradors are honorable. Trust them to return your friend unharmed, or kill her if you don't pay."

Moritz handed Paul a stiff folded piece of paper. "Here is the map you asked for." Paul quickly took the paper. Then Moritz handed Paul a small stack of cash. American bills. "Here, you will need this."

"I can't accept that."

"Please, take it. I have little need for it here. Your quest is true, your companion in trouble. Such an adventure requires money. My journey is a spiritual one."

"Thanks. I'm so very grateful for your kindness."

"Besides, you could use some new clothes." Moritz grinned.

The young monk packed a large cloth sack with fresh bread and fruit. The red cloth edges of the sack formed a shoulder strap for easy carrying. Paul slipped the map into the bag. Around Paul's neck, Moritz slung the strap of a teardrop-shaped leather boda bag filled with water and tied with a leather lace at one end. Then he led Paul out of the monastery.

Paul's eyes squinted painfully at the bright sunlight, and he began to sweat immediately. Without the protection of the caves, the temperature soared. The caves were partially concealed behind a series of rolling hills, so they had to scramble between the folding walls of the hills to reach the nearest road. Along the way, prickly cactus-like plants bit at Paul's ankles, while Moritz seemed easily able to avoid the annoying barbs.

At the edge of a dirt road, Moritz bid Paul adieu, pointing him in the direction of Pueblo Viejo. The young monk turned away, pulling his brown hood over his head and slinking away like a phantom, disappearing into the folds of the rolling hills.

Paul knew he would never be able to find his way back to the monk's enclave. The obscure approach and entrance to the underground monastery helped to keep it secure from tourists and bandits. The monks, it seemed, did not go out much, except for their excursions for the World Development Industries research project. It was a miracle that Moritz had found Paul in the first place.

After hours on the road with only insects, crows, and an occasional passing flock of doves for company, Paul reached a dirty row of stucco buildings that could only be Pueblo Viejo. What a strange sight he must look in his monk's outfit as he entered the village. He would be mistaken for one of the monks from the enclave, assuming the local people knew about the monastery. With so little entertainment in the remote hamlet, Paul felt sure the locals must know about the religious group. He hoped the locals did not fear or dislike the monks. And how would they react when they discovered an American in monk's clothing?

People on the street seemed to pay him little mind as he made his way past dirty children throwing stones into a bucket, and street vendors sleeping in folding chairs next to small carts full of vegetables. Old, wrinkled women dressed in faded, mismatched clothing, shuffled through the street, stopping when needed to squeeze and examine the produce. Straggly dogs wandered lazily, panting, their tongues hanging. Other dogs slept in doorways or chased chickens down alleyways.

A dilapidated sign above a two-story building read: *La Casa Invitada*, which Paul translated to: *The Guest House*. He entered the front room, a hallway with a counter built into the wall. The proprietor entered the hallway from a door on the left, a dark, emaciated-looking bald man. Food clung to his face, and he held a cloth handkerchief. Wiping his face clean, eyes wide, he looked Paul over. Likely he'd never seen an American monk before, and certainly not one looking for a hotel room.

"¿Qué? You are Chibchas? ¿Chibchas Americano? ¡Ay, Dios mío!" He threw up his hands, turned and began to walk away

Paul realized Chibchas must be the local name for the Muisca, and the innkeeper was obviously not comfortable with monks. "No, I am not Chibchas." The man turned around. Paul grabbed the left sleeve of his monk robe with his right hand

and shook it. "Solamente la ropa. I got this robe from them," he said.

"What do you want?" said the man, eyes squinting.

Paul asked for a room. "Necesita un cuarto, por favor."

"Ay. ¿Por cuántos días?"

The man wanted to know how many days Paul intended to stay. Paul hadn't thought about it before. He thought it better to play it safe. Ten days ought to do it. "Diez."

"¿Verdad, diez días?" The innkeeper leapt to attention and waved a set of keys in the air. "Bueno, ándele," he said, jerking his head in the direction he wanted Paul to go.

It seemed Paul had made himself into an instant preferred customer by choosing to stay so long in Pueblo Viejo. The old man led Paul to a Spartan room, a single bed, lumpy mattress, a sink with trickling cold water, and down the hall, a toilet and shower. The shower was no more than a hose with a handheld sprayer attached, and a moldy plastic curtain. A couple passed by in the hallway, a short, pot-bellied man with a tall, buxom woman in a skin-tight dress.

In the room, Paul opened the drawer of a small night table by the bed. Inside the drawer, he saw a Bible in Spanish, used syringes, and a long piece of rubber tubing. The room's rickety cafe table had a hot plate with a metal pot on top. A cockroach in the sink drank lazily from the dripping faucet. The open rusted window overlooked the dusty street below.

The old man smiled broadly, his mouth full of gaps and gold, admiring the room as if it were the finest guest quarters in the house. Which in all likelihood, it was.

"Perfecto," said Paul. "Gracias."

The proprietor turned stiffly, his ancient bones incapable of speed, and he disappeared down the hall. There was no signing a ledger, no ID, no deposit, and no questions. For the time being, Paul appreciated being anonymous. He was reasonably certain that the price would be right.

He needed to keep a low profile in this small town. As such, his first task was to rid himself of the monk's outfit. He figured much of the damage was already done. News of the presence of an American monk would spread like wildfire across Pueblo Viejo.

He left the robe in the room and set out in his old, tattered clothes for a visit to the tienda, the general store. It was a short walk through the dusty streets. There were no sidewalks and he had to dodge a steady stream of motorcycles and light trucks that sped by and didn't seem to care about pedestrians.

Two laughing boys with handfuls of candy ran out of the tienda as Paul entered. Despite the dilapidated condition of the squat, stucco structure, Paul found the store to be deceptively large and well stocked. This made sense, since the tienda was a monopoly in Pueblo Viejo. Shoppers crowded the aisles looking for bargains, and mostly ignored Paul. Already he was attracting less attention in his tattered hunting outfit then when he wore the odd monk's robe.

He purchased a fresh pair of blue jeans, a work shirt, a sturdy pair of hiking boots, new belt, the usual underclothing, and a wool jacket. He also picked up a cell phone, preloaded with an hour of talk time. After buying necessary toiletries, a few bottles of water and some sport drinks, he headed back to the hotel. On the way back he bought fresh fruit, bread, and cheese from the street vendors.

In his hotel room, he activated the cell phone and had the operator reverse the charges for a call to Natasha.

"Paul, where are you?" Natasha asked. "Are you all right?"

"I had an interesting few days," said Paul. "But I'm ok. I've lost track of Lin. I'm afraid she may have been kidnapped."

"Yes, Paul. She has."

A chill ran up his back. "What can you tell me?"

"A ransom of one hundred thousand dollars has been demanded for Lin's release."

"My god!"

"Twi Chang is getting the cash together and waiting for further instructions. Of course, he's beside himself."

"Is Lin OK?"

"She spoke to her father briefly. She's being treated well."

"I'm in Pueblo Viejo, near Buga, at La Casa Invitada. Contact Twi Chang and ask to have Lin brought here after the ransom is paid. Find out if there is anything I can do from this end to help."

There was a long pause on the line. "That will be a hard sell, Paul. Her father wants her on the next plane out of Colombia. And he's already rather tired of your help."

"I understand," said Paul. "But tell Twi Chang that the future of Sentry Security depends on what we find in Colombia. I believe the company has been breached somehow by World Development Industries, a multinational corporation based near here. All I don't know is how and why. I need Lin to help me uncover the truth."

"Twi Chang will never go for it," said Natasha. "I believe you're on your own."

Paul stared at the peeling paint on the walls. He wasn't sure if he could go on by himself.

"There is a federal arrest warrant out for you," said Natasha. "You'll be thrown in jail the moment you return."

"So Milton's letter was worthless?"

"No, the judge delayed the warrant at first when you were discovered missing. Until…"

"Until what?" Paul asked, bracing himself.

"The cyanide was traced back to a batch that disappeared from a University of Washington research laboratory, about three years ago."

Paul took a deep breath and then sighed. "While I was in residency there, and doing research. Perfect! The smoking gun every prosecutor dreams about." His legs went wobbly, and he collapsed on the sagging bed. The bed springs moaned. "If I had the cyanide now, I'd wolf it down and be done with it, save the government the trouble."

"Don't lose hope, Paul. The cyanide trail links you to the murders, but still doesn't prove anything. Did you find out what Val was really doing in Colombia?"

Paul thought about the mysterious appearance of Val's special Remington in the hunting photos. "So far as I can tell, Natasha, Val was hunting doves."

There was a pause on the line. "Is there anything I can do for you Paul?"

"Yes, talk to Twi Chang. Convince him to send Lin to me. And wire me some funds to the local cambio, the currency exchange in Pueblo Viejo. I've lost my passport, so tell the cambio to use my social security number for verification. I'll text it to you later."

"Of course. Anything else?"

Paul thought for a moment. How was he going to get in to World Development Industries?

If Moritz was correct, the place didn't allow any visitors. "Natasha, I need a courier to bring me a package, a special package. It might take a few bribes or some cunning to get it into Colombia."

"I know someone who can help with that," said Natasha. "He's almost family, and he's well connected. Demitri Yurchenko."

Paul swallowed. Years ago Dr. Z had introduced Paul to Demitri Yurchenko, a tough Russian mobster that went by the nickname Mr. Clean because he'd never been arrested. He was rumored to be a jack-of-all-trades, from hit man to smuggling. Paul would never want to be on the wrong side of Demitri Yurchenko. Natasha was correct. Demitri was the right man for the job.

"Yes," said Paul. "Demitri is perfect."

"So what's the package?" asked Natasha.

"Contact Horace Yardley at Edward Rose Pharmaceuticals. Tell him I'm calling in a favor. Tell him I need product, lots of product, ready to use, and user friendly."

"Paul. I don't understand. You're not making any sense."

"Horace will know what I mean. Demitri can pick up the package from Horace and bring it here.

And call Twi Chang and offer to have Demitri carry the ransom money, too."

"Good idea, Paul."

"But tell Demitri to bring Lin to me after she's set free."

"I'll do my best. Be careful."

"I will. Goodbye."

He ended the phone call. There wasn't much more to do now except wait and see if Lin was returned to him, or put on the first plane home. It seemed likely that Twi Chang would do his best to get Lin out of Colombia in a hurry.

Paul didn't blame Twi Chang a bit. Colombia was a lawless and dangerous land. But if World Development Industries had somehow compromised the security of numerous corporations, it would take a computer security expert like Lin to follow the trail.

Paul realized all his problems revolved around computers or digital media, or both. The tampered Thrifty Mart video, an obvious security breach, had turned Paul into an international fugitive. Cyanide levels in the chief medical examiner's computerized database may have been altered, which muddied Paul's investigation into Dr. Z's death. The Lakeside MRI, infallible and accurate, communicated digitally in a most peculiar way with a remote source in Colombia. And Paul's MRI scan results might condemn him to an early death. The cyber world had somehow turned against Paul. Deadly digital data had crossed over from cyberspace and pursued him in the real world.

All these digital computer events seemed connected somehow to activities at World Development Industries, which had an uncanny interest in the ancient mental disciplines of Muisca monks. Besides studying monks, World Development Industries had made a killing in venture capital markets by gathering spectacular intelligence on its competitors.

Paul needed Lin's help to continue the investigation, because they were looking for someone with equal or greater combined computer and medical expertise. Only a computer expert in digital media, graphics, and medicine could be behind all these strange events. There had to be a short list of qualified suspects. If Paul combined his medical knowledge with Lin's computer savvy, they had a fighting chance to get to the truth. He didn't have a prayer without Lin's help.

Paul knew firsthand of Natasha's awesome power of persuasion, and he hoped she'd be able to convince Twi Chang to buy his only daughter's freedom and then send her right back into the lion's den.

If Twi Chang agreed to use Demitri as intermediary in the kidnapping, Paul would stand a better chance of keeping Lin from leaving Colombia. Demitri had a special talent for forceful persuasion. He would cross any line to get the job done.

CHAPTER 20

Paul awoke to a sharp rapping on the door. Dim early daylight filled the room. He rolled off the uneven mattress, already conscious of many aches that would follow him through the day. The door was deadbolted from the inside, although a good swift kick could most likely breach the flimsy old frame. Paul hesitated, and the pounding resumed.

"Who is it? Who's there?"

"Información para Doctor Powers."

Paul hurriedly unbolted the door and turned the knob. But before he could open the door, it flew into him and knocked him down. He looked up into the twin barrels of a sawed-off shotgun held by a small, dark man in a black overcoat.

"¡Cuidado! Careful Doctor! Be very quiet!" He entered the room and kicked the door shut behind him. "Do not move!" He walked quickly around the room, and then peeked out the window. Slowly, he lowered the gun.

"Relax," he said. "I'm a friend." He extended a hand and helped Paul to his feet.

Paul brushed the dust off his pants with his hands. "Strange way for a friend to start a visit."

"It was necessary," said the intruder while pacing around the room. He bolted the door shut, returned to the window and looked out. His greasy, shoulder-length hair hid his face from Paul's view. The invader's black silhouette stood motionless, shotgun dangling at his side.

"Who are you?" Paul asked, backing away.

"I'm a lawyer," said the stranger, leaning on the window, still looking outside. "In your country, I might more properly be called a bounty hunter. But that is not the right word for what I do."

Paul sat on the bed. He assumed the bounty hunter had come to take him back to the U.S. on the federal warrant. Maybe Paul's quest was over, and he would never finish his investigation or get to the truth.

The lawyer reached into the pocket of his overcoat, pulled something out and tossed it to Paul. He caught it, a fine silver chain with a teardrop shaped yin-yang charm and two small diamonds, one in the center of each teardrop.

Paul jumped to attention. "This is Lin's!" said Paul. "Where is she? Is she all right? How did you get this?"

"Stay calm, doc," said the lawyer. "I represent a reputable local businessman. I'm here to negotiate your friend's release. She is perfectly comfortable, and will be returned unharmed when the ransom is paid. I'm here to give you instructions."

Paul sat on the room's one wobbly wooden chair. He clutched the necklace tightly in his hand. "So what are your instructions?"

The dark figure moved closer, his brown pockmarked face came into view.

"A courier is coming later today with your money. After he arrives, I'll call you to tell you where the exchange will take place. You'll make the exchange alone, no courier, no police. If these instructions are not followed exactly, your friend will be killed. Any questions?"

"Just one. You'll need my cell phone number."

The lawyer smiled. "I already have it."

"No questions then."

The lawyer backed up toward the door, unbolted it, and left. Paul figured Natasha must have given his new cell phone number to Twi Chang, who in turn gave it to the kidnappers. Hopefully, it was Demitri bringing the cash, because the tough Russian had surely been through this kind of shady transaction before. Paul was nervous about making the exchange himself. Too much could go wrong and he was poorly prepared to deal with surprises. Lin's life was at stake and he had to succeed.

Paul ate breakfast off the street vendors as he made his way to the nearest currency exchange. Natasha had come through, wiring him enough cash for another trip to the tienda. This time he bought several backpacks, rain gear, a disposable camera, and a cheap pair of binoculars. He also picked up some additional clothing. Lastly, he grabbed a bottle of aguardiente, the local hard liquor, thinking he might need a drink to calm his nerves before the day was over. Then he returned to his hotel room and waited for the courier.

The wait gave Paul time to run through events again in his mind. He lay back on the sagging bed and tried to reason. He decided for the moment to stop focusing on links in the cold-medicine deaths, the corporate espionage, the odd MRI data, the monks, and the activities of World Development Industries. Instead, he asked himself, what kind of person could be involved in all these strange events? What would be their profile?

First, the suspect would have to be a computer expert in digital graphics and applied mathematics. Second, they'd have to be a medical expert in diagnostic radiology and MRI scanning. Third, they'd have to have access at the university level to cyanide. Fourth, they'd have to be associated with both Seattle and Colombia. Paul realized he was looking for someone just like Dr. Z, maybe a colleague, or a rival who might have wanted Z dead.

Paul wondered if there had been any postmortem evidence to support the theory that Dr. Z had been singled out for murder. Paul sat up on the bed and called the King County Medical Examiner's office. He wasn't sure if Joff was back on the job, so he asked for Poulos and reversed the charges. After half a dozen hang ups and some stonewalling by the executive secretary, Poulos finally got on the phone.

"Powers? Where the hell are you? I heard you're on the FBI's Most Wanted list. For the record, I don't believe you killed anyone. But I could get in trouble just for speaking to you."

"Don't worry. I'm far, far away. How is Joff?"

"Much better. He's working part-time now, recovering."

"Good. I want to ask you some questions about Z's autopsy."

"Sorry, I can't help you because there was no autopsy."

"What?"

"It was an unusual case. We had days to study his impending death. Detailed physical exams, X-rays, CT scans, ultrasound, MRI scans, EEG, hundreds of serial blood tests, and more."

Paul couldn't believe it. "So you signed off on it?"

"Yes, there were no doubts about the cause of death. And Valdimire's living will stated a personal objection to autopsy or cremation. He thought of them both as desecration."

"So you signed his death certificate? Death by cyanide poisoning?"

"No, I used my prerogative to waive the autopsy. Hinkley signed the death certificate and supported my decision to pass on Z's autopsy. I needed a break anyway, Joff was down, and I had my hands full with all the other victims. Not enough staff. Damn budget cutbacks. Why do you ask?"

Paul sighed. "I was hoping to get some insight into whether Z might have been targeted for murder. But I guess that won't be possible now."

"I'm sorry, Paul. But if it helps, I never found anything to suggest that Z was a target. And that's all I know."

"Yeah."

"Anything else?"

Paul almost said goodbye, then it struck him. "Do you still have Z's blood samples?"

"Of course. We save some for legal evidence on all unsolved murder cases."

"I want you to run a test for me."

"For what? We ran everything."

"No, you didn't. You didn't run everything."

"Paul, you don't understand. I can't run tests for you. You're a fugitive. You have nothing to lose. It's not legal. I'll lose my license."

Paul was determined to not go away empty-handed, even if he had to bluff. He could use the young medical examiner's paranoia as a weapon.

"I have evidence of mistakes made in your office," said Paul. "If you don't run the test for me, I'll email the details of those mistakes to your superiors."

"You wouldn't!"

"I'm a fugitive. I have nothing to lose. You said so yourself."

There was a moment of silence. "What test do you want?"

"Check the samples for vitamin B12."

"What?"

"You heard me. I want a vitamin B12 level. Can you do it?"

"A simple test, yes, but it will take some time to get the samples out of evidence and run them discreetly. And then what?"

"Text the results immediately to me at this number. And if anyone asks, I just called to check on Joff."

"I don't know what you think you're doing, Powers. I'll do it under one condition."

"What's that?"

"Don't call me again!"

"Agreed."

"Good luck." Poulos ended the call.

The rusty bedsprings moaned as Paul lay back down and stared at the cratered ceiling. A lost cockroach wandered above, upside down on the uneven sheetrock, continually changing directions, going in circles. Paul closed his eyes and tried to clear his mind. Every new answer raised another question, and he found it hard to turn off the flow of ideas. Fatigue finally overtook him and he fell soundly asleep.

CHAPTER 21

In the afternoon, Paul awoke. The short nap had recharged him. He paced around the room and looked out of the window every few minutes. A steady stream of pedestrians dodged noisy street traffic and diesel fumes arose from below. From directly overhead, the sun burned through haze and stifling humidity. He began to wonder if anyone was going to show.

The hours passed painfully and slowly. He eventually stopped pacing and pulled the room's one chair up to the window and positioned himself to have a wide view of the street. Then he spotted a broad-shouldered man. A clear path formed in front of the man as people stepped back into doorways or crossed the street to avoid him. In spite of the heat, the imposing figure wore a black suit and carried a backpack. Paul realized, as the man came closer, that he was Demitri Yurchenko.

Paul watched Demitri disappear from the street into La Casa Invitada. The expected knock on the door came a minute later. Demitri entered without even a hello and bolted the door. Moving quickly around the room, he pulled closed the dingy window curtains. A handgun bulged beneath his dark coat, and his backpack had a red tag that read: *Diplomat*.

"Dr. Powers, we meet again." Demitri scanned the room, his scarred face frowning. "Russian gulag is better than this."

"I know," said Paul. "But it makes a good safe house, if you don't mind whores and heroin addicts."

"Good people."

"I'm glad they sent you, Demitri."

"You know I do anything for Val and Tasha."

"You brought the package and the money?"

"Both."

"Any trouble getting them in?"

"Nyet."

"How?"

Demitri took off his backpack and twirled the red tag. "Diplomatic pouch, no customs inspection. I have friends in Russian embassy."

"And the money?"

Demitri held up the backpack. "Cash. All here. Mr. Chang wants his daughter back."

"I need Lin here," said Paul. "I'm hoping you'll make that happen."

"Sorry, doctor." Demitri set the backpack and himself on the bed. He patted the bag. "Trade cash, take girl home. Simple."

Paul pulled the chair up to the bed and sat facing Demitri. "No, not so simple," said Paul. They want me to make the exchange. The kidnapper's lawyer paid me a visit." Paul shook his head. "I don't think I can do it."

Demitri's open palm struck Paul's face like a baseball bat and nearly knocked him off the chair. Paul's ears were ringing as he clumsily struggled to keep his seat. Demitri could move surprisingly fast for a man of his bulk.

"You will do it," said Demitri. The scar across his forehead pulsed. "Do not cross these men, or your comrade is dead. These kind of people I know. Cowards. More scared than you."

Paul's cell phone rang. Demitri snatched it from Paul's hands and put it on speaker.

"Hello, doctor," said the familiar voice of the sleazy lawyer. Listen carefully and everything will go fine. Take the money and go out the back door of La Casa Invitada and follow the path. It's an old road that will take you to an abandoned well about a mile away. It's El Centro, the old village center. No one goes there anymore. Sit on the rock wall by the well and wait for me. We'll make the exchange there. And come alone. Do you understand?"

Demitri looked at Paul and nodded. "Yeah," said Paul. "I'll do as you say." The lawyer ended the call.

Demitri pulled a smaller backpack out of his large one. He handed it to Paul. "One hundred grand, be careful."

Paul slung the innocent-looking nylon pack over his shoulder, shaking a bit.

Demitri grabbed Paul by both arms. "Steady. You have one shot. Keep to plan and your comrade comes back alive. Stay cool. They are watching me. But I will help if I can."

Paul didn't think Demitri could help, because he couldn't afford to be seen leaving the hotel room and risk ruining the exchange. Paul couldn't believe it had come down to this. He was on his own, about to walk into the woods in the middle of Colombia with one hundred thousand dollars on his back, hoping to save the life of a remarkable woman with whom he'd just begun to fall in love. And saving her life might be his only chance to save himself.

He made his way out the back entrance of La Casa Invitada, and easily found the overgrown path that started behind the building. It was an old dirt road, long unattended, and choked with weeds. The lightly trafficked footpath ran in the old right-sided tire groove, but the left-sided groove was mostly obscured. Brush and trees lined the old road, along with discarded tires, oil drums, bags of garbage, and a rusty set of bedsprings.

Paul walked for what seemed like a mile before he saw what had to be the well, and the old city center. A big bore rusted pipe stuck out about four feet above the ground, with an outlet and a huge valve. The control wheel for the valve had long since been removed. On the ground, a round wooden cover about four feet across surrounded the pipe, capping the old well hole. Half of the wooden boards were missing or rotten. Around the wooden well cap was a stone wall, partially collapsed. The stones had been placed one at a time by hand, without mortar.

Paul could imagine a simpler time long ago, before the internet and modern plumbing, when the villagers had gathered around the well to draw water and share news. He sat on the stone wall and waited, hoping that the reputation of Colombian kidnappers for good conduct was well deserved. He prayed that no one robbed him before he had a chance to make the exchange. Without the money, he'd never see Lin alive again.

The trees behind Paul rustled and he jumped up. A pair of colorful birds flew from the branches, chirping excitedly. An insect buzzed by his ear and startled Paul again. He scanned the area but didn't see anyone. Then he sat back down, trying to slow his rapid breathing. He couldn't afford to lose his nerve now.

Paul noticed that the abandoned road he'd taken to El Centro continued on past the well in the other direction. From that direction, a dark sedan approached. The car stopped about fifty yards from the well, but close enough that Paul could make out at least three people inside. There were two in the front seat, and one in the back. The front passenger door opened, and the unmistakable dark, greasy visage of the lawyer emerged. He walked slowly toward the well carrying a gray metal suitcase, nervously eyeing both sides of the road.

Paul stood up and stood his ground, waiting for the lawyer to approach. Sunlight pierced the approaching man's long hair, lighting up his face. His pockmarks stood out like moon craters. A few feet from Paul the lawyer stopped.

"Muy bien, doctor. You follow directions well. Now show me the money."

"No," said Paul. "First, you show me Lin."

The lawyer squinted in the sunlight and put his suitcase down on the rock wall. Without taking his eyes off Paul, the dark man raised his right hand in the air and waved. The driver's door of the car opened. A tall man with a baseball cap and dark glasses came out and opened the back door. He reached inside and pulled out Lin, gagged, her hands bound behind her back. Paul met her gaze. Even at this distance seeing her made his spirits soar and gave him the confidence to go on.

The driver pushed Lin back into the car, slammed the rear door, and then returned to the driver's seat. Paul took off the backpack and handed it to the lawyer.

"It's all here," said Paul.

The lawyer handed the backpack back.

"No. You count it. Here," he said, and opened his empty suitcase on the rock wall.

Paul opened the backpack. There were twenty bundles of hundred-dollar bills, with fifty bills in a bundle. Paul counted each individual bill in one of the bundles without breaking the band, and put the first bundle in the case. Then starting at two, he counted just the aggregate bundles, until all twenty filled the suitcase. The lawyer pulled out several of the bundles at random and flipped the edges of the bills with his thumb like they were decks of playing cards. He seemed satisfied. After putting all the cash back in the suitcase, he closed it, picked it up, and turned toward the car.

Again the driver came out of the vehicle and retrieved Lin from the back seat. This time he started walking toward the well. Paul and the lawyer walked down the road to meet Lin and the driver halfway. When the four were face to face, the lawyer paused for a moment and then stepped past Lin. Paul held his breath and took Lin by the arm. Sweat dripped down the sides of his face. The air was still. No birds. No bugs. No wind.

A loud reverberating boom cracked the silence, and repeated. Paul was drenched in blood and pain stabbed his right arm. The lawyer dropped the briefcase and pitched over backward, falling on Paul and knocking him off his feet. Paul lost his grip on Lin. The driver grabbed Lin and the briefcase and ran for the car. Paul tried to get up, but he was pinned by the dead weight of the lawyer's body. It took a few moments for Paul to roll the body off.

Paul got back on his feet just in time to see the car take off with Lin and the money. Then he noticed a high-powered rifle pointed at his chest from a few feet away. The rifle was in the sinewy hands of Augustus Francobar.

"You're nothing but trouble, mate," said Francobar.

"So my suspicions were correct," said Paul. "You did set me up." Paul grabbed his painful right shoulder and discovered a hole in his clothing. It seemed the bullet had just nicked him. He was covered with blood, but too much blood to be from such a minimal wound. The lawyer on the ground moaned, face down in an expanding red puddle. Paul realized that he was soaked in the lawyer's blood.

"I planned to get rid of you on the hunt," said Francobar. "And feed the sheila to the kidnappers. But then that damn aborigine came along."

"And you couldn't kill him," said Paul. "Because you're working for World Development Industries and they would frown on you killing one of their prized monks."

Francobar lowered the rifle. "You're a smart one. Fellow's got to make a living, you know. Doves are drying up. I like the hacienda and I'm too old to start over. WDI pays me to handle the locals and keep out people who ask too many questions, like you."

"Maybe Z got curious, too," said Paul. "And World Development Industries poisoned him? Maybe you helped to set him up?" Paul figured he might as well ask questions now, since he was about to be shot. This was his last chance to find the truth.

Francobar laughed and raised the riffle. Sunlight glistened on the barrel of the riffle and on his toothy grin. "Smart you are, but not that smart. I had nothing to do with Z's death."

"So what do they do at World Development Industries?"

"I haven't a clue, doc. And unlike you, I'm smart enough not to ask."

Paul held up his hand. "Wait! Maybe World Development Industries could use a doctor with research experience, especially one that's a fugitive and needs to disappear for a while. They might even pay you to recruit me."

"Nice try, doc. But it's less complicated to just shoot you."

Francobar raised the rifle up, looked down the barrel, and aimed for Paul's head. Paul closed his eyes and thought that at least his death would be painless. Maybe that was better than dying of cancer, or rotting on death row.

Paul heard the shot and then a thud that shook the earth. He opened his eyes. Francobar was on his back, on the ground, rifle in his hands, motionless. There was a gaping hole in his left chest. The bushes behind Paul rustled, and out stepped Demitri, with a .45 caliber Glock pistol.

"You are injured, bleeding?"

Paul shook his head. "No, just a scratch. The blood's mostly his." Paul pointed to the lawyer, who was writhing on the ground. He was clutching his neck, trying to scream, but it came out as a whisper, too soft to hear. Paul knelt down and put his ear close to lawyer's lips.

"Ayúdame," said the lawyer. "¡Por favor, no quiero morir!"

Paul quickly examined the wounded man. He had a hole in his right upper chest. Bubbling bloody froth percolated out of the chest wound with each gasping breath. There was no exit wound on his back. He was bleeding steadily from the right side of his neck where another bullet had gone completely through, leaving two holes.

Paul realized that the bullet that had nicked his shoulder must be the same one that had passed through lawyer's neck. The wounded man was trying to hold his hand over the bleeding holes in his neck. From the persistence of the bleeding, Paul guessed the bullet must have torn a major artery in the neck, probably the right carotid. The man's neck was swelling.

"He's dying," said Paul. "Bleeding out. Worse, he's also bleeding into the soft tissues of his neck, and the swelling is pressing on his windpipe. He's choking to death."

Demitri knelt down beside Paul. "You must not let him die. If he dies, your comrade dies."

"I don't understand," said Paul.

"I know these kind of people. All family. This one may be a brother or cousin. They will want him back. Trade him for the woman. They have the money now. If he dies, they will kill her for revenge."

"He needs to go to a hospital," said Paul, shaking his head. "What can I do?"

"You are a doctor. Do what you do. At a hospital he will die or go to jail. Return him alive and they will take him to a special hospital where police ask no questions."

The lawyer's lips turned blue, and he made a screeching sound as he struggled to suck in each breath. He flailed his arms wildly.

"Do you have a knife?" Paul asked.

Demitri reached down, under his right pant leg, and pulled out a short dagger.

"Hold him," said Paul

Demitri wrestled both of the agitated man's arms to the ground, and pinned him at the waist. The lawyer's neck was so wide now that his head seemed to rest directly on his shoulders. Paul used his left hand to hold down the wounded man's head. Then Paul put the tip of the dagger in the lawyer's neck, in the front entry wound, and sliced the skin all the way around to the exit wound.

A jelly-like blood clot the size of an apple squirted from the incision and the swelling of the lawyer's neck instantly decreased. He took a deep gasp of air, coughing and sputtering.

"Gracias, Dios," he said in a hoarse, squeaky voice.

Paul cut off a strip of the man's shirt, balled it up, and shoved it into the wound. "Let go of his left hand," said Paul to Demitri. The Russian released his iron grip. Paul put the lawyer's hand on the improvised packing. "Hold this," said Paul.

Demitri got up, walked over to Francobar, and grabbed the body by one arm and one leg. Then Demitri bent over, lifted the body, and flipped it over his shoulders, right on top of his backpack. He walked to the well, kicked out a few of the rotten planks in the wooden cover, and dropped the body into the hole. A minute later, he did the same with the rifle.

Paul helped to hoist the wounded lawyer onto Demitri's shoulders. They hurried back toward La Casa Invitada. While they walked, Paul held the dressing on the lawyer's neck wound. It was full of dirt, saturated with blood and still oozing.

Francobar might have ruined any chance Paul had to get Lin back. Paul's only hope now was to keep a criminal with two critical gunshot wounds alive long enough to make an exchange. Lin's life depended on it.

CHAPTER 22

The injured lawyer left a trail of blood all the way back to La Casa Invitada. The trio entered the back door of the hotel, and started up the stairs with the gasping man on Demitri's back. The dark head of the proprietor peeked out of his office door. His eyes opened wide and he shook his head. "No me diga nada. Nada, nada," he said. Then he retreated into his office and slammed the door.

In the room, Demitri bent over and rolled the wounded man onto the bed. Blood instantly appeared on the white sheets. Paul's hands were blood soaked as he tried to compress lawyer's neck wound and slow the bleeding.

"Hold this for me," said Paul to Demitri. The Russian sat on the side of the bed and held pressure on the bloody dressing. Paul reached for the lawyer's wrist and took his pulse. The man's skin looked ashen gray.

"It's no use," said Paul. "He's lost too much blood. His pulse is weak and rapid. If he doesn't get at least some IV fluid, he's going to go into shock."

"Keep him alive, doctor," said Demitri.

"I can't. He needs electrolyte replacement."

Demitri's bushy eyebrows went up. "Electric lights?"

"No," said Paul. "I'm talking about electrolyte solution, salt and fluid replacement. If we had a few bags of replacement fluids, we could keep him going for a while."

Paul took his cell phone from his pocket and put it on the nightstand next to two large bottles of sports drinks. He looked at the dying man's bleeding neck and Demitri's big, hairy hands.

"They will call," said Demitri.

Paul stared at the two bottles on the nightstand next to the cell phone.

"What is it?" said the Russian.

"An idea," said Paul. He opened the drawer and pulled out the long piece of rubber tubing, undoubtedly left by some lonely heroin addict who needed an arm tourniquet that he could tie off with his teeth. That must be as bad as life gets, Paul thought, when you don't even have a friend to help you shoot up.

Paul moved to the side of the bed opposite Demitri, up by the lawyer's head. Then Paul passed one end of the rubber tubing through the left side of injured man's nose and continued to feed it in.

"Swallow this, swallow, swallow," said Paul. But the lawyer coughed and gagged on the rubber tube and spit the advancing end out of his mouth."

"No," said Paul, as he pulled the rubber tube back a bit. The forward end of the tubing disappeared back into the dying man's mouth. Paul shoved the tubing forward again "Swallow this if you want to live."

This time the lawyer began to swallow as Paul pushed the tube inch by inch into the man's nose. Several feet of the rubber tube disappeared into the wounded man's nose until only about half a foot of tubing remained.

"If I only had some tape," said Paul.

Demitri took Paul's hand and pressed it against the bleeding neck wound. "Hold this," said the

Russian. He took off his backpack and rummaged around inside. Out came his bloody hand with a roll of gray duct tape. Demitri resumed holding the neck compress and handed the duct tape to Paul.

Paul took the duct tape, looked back at Demitri, and squinted.

"Is for my business," said Demitri, shrugging his shoulders.

The sports drinks had funnel-like spouts on top for sipping while exercising. Paul unscrewed one of the spouts, broke the paper seal, and reattached the spout. Then he crammed the end of the spout into the open end of the rubber tubing. It was a tight fit. He wrapped a few turns of duct tape around the bottle, but left the tape on the roll. Above the head of the bed, he saw a picture hook from a picture that had probably been stolen long ago.

Paul unrolled and tore off a few feet of the tape, enough to hang the bottle upside down from the picture hook above the lawyer's head.

Paul held out his hand. "Your knife."

Demitri retrieved the sharp dagger from his ankle sheath. Paul grabbed the plastic bottle securely and punched a small hole in what was now the top of the inverted bottle. Air bubbles arose in the clear fluid as the water level started to decrease.

"The electrolyte fluids will be absorbed rapidly by his stomach and intestines," said Paul. "It will keep him from going into shock and buy us some time."

The neck wound bleeding had slowed a bit, and the lawyer's skin color changed rapidly from ashen gray to brown.

"He's looking better already," said Paul. "But I'm going to have to do something to stop the bleeding. He needs a clean dressing." Paul opened a bottle of plain water, emptied it into the pot on the hotplate, and turned the burner on. With the dagger, he cut strips out of the bed sheet and stuffed them into the pot.

Paul observed the lawyer's progress. He continued to improve. His breathing slowed, rich brown color returned to his face, and his pulse felt strong. Paul prepared, attached, and hung a second bottle of the sports drink. He went back to check on the new dressing. The water was boiling.

"Doc, something happening," said Demitri.

The lawyer was gasping for breath, but couldn't seem to get enough air. His lips turned dark blue and he clutched his chest. The man's pulse felt rapid and weak. Paul opened what was left of the lawyer's shirt. Then Paul put his ear on the right side of the struggling man's chest, next to the frothy, bubbling chest wound. Bloody mist sprayed onto Paul's face from the open wound, and he could smell the lawyer's breath.

"No sound on the right. His right lung is collapsed. Probably full of blood and air. And now it's putting pressure on his left lung, collapsing it." Paul shook his head. "I'm afraid there's nothing more I can do for him here."

Demitri grabbed Paul's arm with a vise-like grip. "Do not give up. He must not die. Do what you need to do."

"He needs a chest tube," said Paul. Then it struck him. "Give me the knife."

Demitri let go of Paul's arm and handed him the dagger. Paul left the room and ran down the hall to the bathroom. Cockroaches scattered for cover as he flipped on the bare bulb hanging above. He grabbed the shower hose and cut it off at the control valve, leaving the showerhead still attached.

He ran back to the room with the showerhead swinging on the end of the hose.

Paul stuck the cut end of the hose in the boiling pot of water. Then he cut off the showerhead on the other end. The remaining piece was about three feet long. From his bag of groceries he retrieved the aguardiente, opened the bottle, and poured some on the wounded man's lower, right chest, and on the dagger.

"Nostrovia," said Demitri.

Paul looked at the bottle. Demitri nodded and Paul took a big gulp. The fiery liquor burned his throat with a bitter taste. He handed the bottle to Demitri. The Russian took a drink and then put the bottle on the nightstand.

Paul removed the end of the hose that was in the pot of boiling water and stuck it in one of his plastic bottles of plain water to cool it. "You better hold him," said Paul.

Demitri sat on the lawyer and pinned him to the bed.

Paul inserted the blade of the dagger into the lawyer's lower, right chest, above a rib. The man thrashed but couldn't move under Demitri's weight. A muffled scream was all that the air-starved lawyer could manage. Paul twisted the dagger's blade to open the stab wound. Without removing the knife, he shoved the clean end of the shower hose about a foot into the man's chest cavity.

Blood exploded from the far end of the hose and sprayed the opposite wall of the room. After the initial purge, bubbly bloody froth continued to ooze from the hose onto the floor. Paul secured the hose to the lawyer's chest with duct tape, and then stuck the other end in the plastic water bottle, and put the bottle on the floor. With each breath the lawyer took, air bubbled out the end of the hose into the water bottle.

The improvement was miraculous. The lawyer's breathing slowed down and he lay quiet on the bed. The blue left his lips. His pulse slowed and grew stronger.

"Gracias, doctor," said the man.

A new blood stain expanded on the bed like a halo around the lawyer's head. A few minutes without pressure on his neck wound had caused the bleeding to accelerate.

"We've got to stop the bleeding," said Paul. He'd come too far to lose the man now.

"I am not doctor," said Demitri.

"Duct tape him to the bed. Arms, legs, and head."

"OK. This I know," said Demitri, and he proceeded to expertly secure the lawyer to the bed.

After another trip to the grocery bag, Paul added a toothbrush and dental floss to the boiling pot. Then he washed his hands in the sink with soap and cold water.

Paul used the dagger to pull out one of the strips of cloth from the boiling water. After it cooled a bit, he soaked it in aguardiente and began cleaning the neck wound. The screams of the lawyer were no longer muffled, but Paul found them reassuring.

Demitri assisted, holding supplies and handing Paul whatever he needed. Paul's cell phone beeped. Demitri grabbed the phone and flipped it open. "Text message from U.S.," he said.

"I'll deal with it later," said Paul.

Paul explored the neck wound with his fingers, wiping the fresh blood out of his way with a strip of the clean cloth. He used the pulse of the bleeding carotid artery as a guide. He figured that the artery would be intact, that the bullet had only nicked it, leaving a small hole. Since the carotid artery was a large vessel, he reasoned that if it had been totally severed, the lawyer would have bled out and died a long time ago.

Finally, Paul had the carotid artery at his fingertips. He slipped a finger under the artery, lifted it up, and slid the handle of the toothbrush underneath. With the artery suspended, he ran two strings of dental floss underneath. Then he pulled one string up toward the man's head as far as it would go, and one string down in the other direction. Paul tied knots in each piece of dental floss and the bleeding stopped. He knew the neck and the brain had enough redundant blood supply that this one artery would not be missed.

He removed the toothbrush, dressed the wound with the clean cloth, and secured the bandage with duct tape. A little blood still trickled from the lawyer's neck, but the life-threatening bleeding had stopped.

Paul checked his cell phone. The text message was from the assistant King County medical examiner, Poulos. It read: *Vitamin B12 levels are way up, off the scale. I have no explanation. Good luck. Poulos.*

Paul handed the phone back to Demitri, who then read the message before closing the phone.

"What does this mean?" asked Demitri.

Paul stared blankly, his eyes lost focus. "That when nothing else makes sense, look for the impossible."

Demitri shrugged his shoulders and shook his head. The cell phone rang, and Paul's eyes snapped back into focus. Demitri flipped the phone open and put it on the speaker.

"I'm here," said Paul.

"Is my brother alive?" said a voice.

"He's OK for now, but he needs to get to a hospital as soon as possible."

"Let me speak to him."

Demitri held the phone by the wounded man's head.

"Carlos," said the voice. "¿Está bien?"

"Vive. El doctor hace lo que puede. Quiero va al hospital."

Demitri pulled the phone away.

"OK, he's alive," said Paul.

"Return Carlos to us, or we kill the woman."

"Of course. But I want you to know that we didn't shoot him, the shooter was aiming for me."

"I know," said the voice. "We all have enemies."

"Let's keep this simple," said Paul. "Bring Lin here and you can pick up your brother. Send two men. You'll need them to carry Carlos out. Agreed?"

"Agreed," said the voice.

"And as you already know, my courier is armed and dangerous. No guns, except ours, or the deal is off. I don't want any more bloodshed."

"Understood."

Demitri closed the phone. He ripped the tape off the lawyer's head, arms, legs, and waist. Then the dark suited, broad shouldered Russian leaned over the lawyer and grabbed his chin. The man's eyes opened wide.

"Your blood is already on my suit," said Demitri. "Do not run." As he removed his hand, he gave the lawyer's chin a painful pinch.

"No, señor," said the lawyer, shivering.

Both bottles of sports drink had finished going into the wounded man. Paul disconnected the last hanging bottle from the nose tube. He propped the man's head up with pillows and held a bottle of water to his lips. The lawyer drank the water like a man in the desert.

On the floor, the hose from the lawyer's chest bubbled in the water bottle. The water turned the color of a blush wine from slow, continuous bleeding. Red staining also appeared along the edges of the neck dressing. Paul hoped the lawyer's family would arrive soon to claim him, before he bled to death.

There was a knock on the door. Paul hesitated. Demitri pulled out his Glock and aimed it at the door.

"Open it," said the Russian, waving his handgun at the door.

Paul walked over to the door, unbolted it, and jumped out of the way. The doorknob turned and the door began to open. Demitri held the gun ready. A teenage boy stood in the doorway, with shorts, T-shirt, and sandals. Demitri lowered his gun. The boy walked in and over to the lawyer. Paul closed and bolted shut the door.

"¿Está bien?" said the boy.

"Bien, mas o menos," said the lawyer.

The boy stuck his hand out the window and waved. Paul ran to the window, but aside from the usual assortment of locals on the street, he saw no one. Then there was a knock on the door.

Demitri raised the gun again and walked over to the door. He unbolted the door and then held the gun with both hands. The door opened and Lin walked into the room with a young boy behind her.

Dirty, with disheveled hair, wearing the same clothes as the day of the dove hunt, she nonetheless looked rested and fit. She ran into Paul's arms, clinging to him tightly, burying her head in his arms.

"Lin, thank God you're OK," said Paul. "I thought your father wouldn't want the kidnappers to deal with me at all. I thought he'd insist that Demetri pay the ransom and take you out of Colombia."

"He did insist," she said, raising her head to meet his gaze, her eyes bright.

"I don't understand," said Paul.

"When I found out you were still alive, I knew you wouldn't quit looking for the truth. I couldn't leave you here to face this alone. You need my help to clear your name. I'm the one who insisted that you pay the ransom yourself. I didn't want Demitri to take me home."

"You're disobeying your father."

"Yes, I am." She grabbed his face in her hands and kissed him hard and long. Paul pulled the necklace from his pocket and gazed into Lin's almond eyes as he put the silver chain around her neck and fastened the clasp. Lin twirled the charm and smiled.

"Mr. Chang pays me when I bring you home," said Demitri. "It is my job."

"OK," said Lin. "You can take me home after Paul is done in Colombia. And then you will get paid."

"I had enough of this gulag," said the Russian. "Why should I wait?"

"I'm out on two million dollars bail," said Paul. "You can return me too, after I'm done here. If I get my bail back, I'll give you half. If not, I'll match whatever Mr. Chang pays you."

Demitri smiled. "OK, good business. Short time delay. One week, no more. And I stay with you. Then you both go home with me."

Paul nodded. Demitri helped the two boys hoist the lawyer off the bed while Paul held on to the chest hose and drainage bottle. The two teenagers stood on either side of the lawyer. Then they draped one arm each of the wounded man over their shoulders and held him upright between them. With a free hand, one of the boys took the drainage bottle from Paul. Demitri helped the trio out of room and locked the door behind.

"I heard you were with monks," said Lin.

"Later, it's a long story. Were you treated well?"

"Yes, the bandits in Colombia are gentlemen, although I must have been in bad condition when they found me, because I don't remember much."

"You passed out," said Paul, "I carried you for as long as I could until I collapsed."

"So what now?" she asked.

"Do you feel up to a little investigative field work tomorrow?"

"Sure, after I shower and get some clean clothes. Where are we going?"

"World Development Industries, corporate raiders, maker of fine hardware for MRI scanners, and employer of Colombian monks." Paul picked up the severed showerhead from the floor. "But first, about that shower."

CHAPTER 23

In the morning, Paul leaned out the window of the hotel room. A cluster of vendors hung out near the front of the hotel, waiting for the Americans to come out. The presence of the foreigners in Pueblo Viejo was no secret, and they'd become instant and involuntary celebrities. The street vendors knew they'd get business from the travelers, because there were few other places to eat in Pueblo Viejo.

The prior evening, a cash payment from Paul had smoothed everything over with the hotel proprietor. The owner proved to be very resourceful. He'd no doubt had violent incidents to clean up before. Cleaning up messy crime scenes was a competitive growth industry in Colombia.

An hour after Paul settled with the owner, a man who called himself the Cleaner arrived to service the room. The Cleaner had a crew of a dozen or so young boys and girls skilled in the removal of blood and other bodily fluids. In about an hour they had restored the room to its original awful condition. They even repaired the shower. When they left, it looked like the bloody encounter had never happened.

Lin looked radiant in the morning after her shower, her baby face freshly scrubbed. Paul supplied her with a light brown man's shirt that hung like a skirt from her tiny waist. She tucked in the shirt, and rolled up the long sleeves to make them fit. Lin's hunting pants and hiking boots were still in good shape. Paul outfitted Lin and himself with the backpacks he'd purchased earlier, the binoculars and disposable camera, and a few other items from the room.

The proprietor had given Demitri a mattress so he could sleep on the floor. He'd been offered his own room, but didn't want to lose sight of Paul or Lin. Paul felt much safer with Demitri sleeping in the same room.

The Russian had gotten up early and was standing over the sink, scrubbing the bloodstains out of his suit. The suit looked much better. Demitri obviously had experience removing blood from clothing.

They left the hotel and dined on fruit and freshly baked breads, a hodge-podge of flavors more interesting and probably healthier than the usual morning Bellevue fare. Paul and Lin bought wide-brimmed straw hats made locally to help with the blinding sun. Demitri chose a black fedora, Panama style. After eating, they stopped at the tienda for more supplies. They bought a compass, water bottles, and a coat for Lin.

Back on the street, they bought bread and hard cheese from the vendors, made crude sandwiches, and stashed them away in their backpacks for lunch.

Paul pulled out and opened the map given to him by the young monk Moritz. It was on a single page of while paper, handwritten in ink, barely legible in the bright sunlight. Lin and Demitri held edges of the paper and they all stood around and studied the map.

Paul took off his hat and scratched his head. "If this is to scale, then World Development Industries is over ten miles from our present position."

"That's too far to walk in this heat," said Lin. "It'll be ninety degrees by mid-afternoon. And I haven't seen a taxi in this town."

"Have to hire driver," said Demitri.

Paul traced the line out of town on the map. "According to this, the main road west out of Pueblo Viejo goes a few miles to Buga, then about six miles to the Rio Cauca. The company headquarters are on our side of the river, the eastern bank, about three or four miles north of where the main road crosses the waterway."

"I don't see any other roads running north along the river from there," said Lin.

"Roads always follow river," said Demitri.

"Probably there are roads," said Paul. "They're just too small to be on this map. The Rio Cauca is one of the biggest rivers in Colombia. There must be secondary roads."

Lin let go of the map. "If we get a ride west to the river, we can walk a few miles north from there. I'm up for that."

Paul nodded. "Makes sense. And there's enough traffic on the main road for us to catch a ride back when we're done at World Development Industries in case our driver doesn't wait for us."

"What is plan?" Demitri asked, letting go of the map.

"Reconnaissance. We get in. Look around. Take pictures. And get out."

"Good plan," said Demitri.

"What are we looking for?" said Lin.

"I want to know what goes on at World Development Industries."

"How are we going to find a driver?" Lin asked.

"This I can do," said Demitri. "Come with me."

Paul and Lin followed the Russian closely as he walked down the dusty streets of Pueblo Viejo. After a few blocks, they stood outside of a windowless stucco building that was pockmarked with bullet holes. Painted on the side was the faded name Cantina de Oro. The two O's in Oro looked like gold coins.

Lin stopped. "I'm not going in there," she said, pointing to the battered metal door.

Demitri turned around. "You go with me. Stay close."

Lin folded her arms and stood her ground.

"It's all right," said Paul. "Demitri is a professional. You know computers, he knows this."

Demitri opened the door and entered the bar. Paul held the door for Lin. She threw her hands up in the air, shook her head, and followed Demitri inside.

The first thing that hit Paul when he entered Cantina de Oro was the smell. If desperation mixed with desolation had an odor, the fragrance would be called Cantina de Oro. Paul thought it must be a combination of dirt, urine, beer, and vomit. He doubted that even the Cleaner could remove the stench.

Thankfully, light was dim inside the windowless bar, because the more Paul saw, the more revulsion set in. Tinny Latin music played from an old jukebox in the corner. Even though it was early in the day, the Cantina was filled with twenty or so customers. No doubt they were locals, regulars meeting in the Cantina like kids at a clubhouse. Minus the innocence.

At the long wooden bar, several dark tattooed men in white shirts with rolled-up sleeves hunched over beers in the shadows, their overgrown moustaches drowning in the froth. They had the look of young men grown old before their time, with muscled arms and graying hair. The bartender was short and round, with a loose black cowboy shirt and matching studded hat.

Others sat at one of several flimsy round metal cafe tables, on matching chairs. A few were slumped over, unconscious. Two young women circulated around the room chatting up the men. Both women had skintight dresses and too much makeup.

In a sudden eerie silence, everyone turned to check out the strange trio as they entered the room. After a few moments, one by one the bar patrons lost interest and returned to whatever they'd been doing.

All except one. At the far end of the room, a man put a small shot glass to his lips, threw his head back, and finished the drink in one gulp. As he arose, he stumbled a bit and then kicked the chair out of his way. His arms were covered with curling flames in old green ink. The fellow had a thick head of sandy hair, golden tan skin, and a faded dagger tattoo on his neck.

Paul guessed the man must be at least six foot tall, and all muscle. He lumbered over and walked directly up to Lin. "Muy bonita, señorita," he said. "We don't get many like you here. Can I buy you a drink?"

Lin froze.

"She doesn't want a drink," said Paul

"The lady can speak for herself," said the man. "You're bothering me, gringo." He moved to within inches of Paul. Sweat dripped from the man's forehead. He reached his hand out and gave Paul's chest a shove. A sudden silence in the room was immediately broken by a thud as the man hit the floor, on his back, unconscious.

Few in the crowd had seen Demitri's lighting-fast fist. Demitri stepped over the body and waved for Paul and Lin to follow. Activity in the room quickly returned to normal.

"You were right," said Lin, stepping over the body.

"I told you." Paul nodded. "He's a pro."

Demitri led them to three empty wooden stools at the bar. Lin took her place sandwiched in between the two men. Several locals sitting at the counter plied over their beers and eyed the foreigners. Dusty shelves behind the bar were filled with bottles of all shapes and sizes.

"Señor," said the bartender to Demitri. "What can I get you?"

"Three shots vodka," said the Russian.

The bartender reached into a bucket and pulled out three wet shot glasses. He placed them upside down, one in front of each of the foreigners. Then he upended them one at a time and filled them with vodka.

Demitri grabbed his glass and waved it at Lin and Paul. They also raised their glasses.

"Nostrovia," said the Russian, as he sucked down the vodka in one fluid motion. Paul looked Lin in the eyes, touched her glass with his, and rapidly downed his shot. Lin sighed and sipped the harsh liquor slowly, ladylike, until it was gone.

"Anything else?" the bartender asked.

"We're looking for a driver," said Demitri.

"Sorry, I can not help you, señor," said the bartender. He turned away.

Lin looked at Paul. "Now what?" she said.

A scrawny man at the end of the bar fell off his stool. With much difficulty, he picked himself up off the floor. He ran his fingers through his unruly crop of curly brown hair, pulled up his sagging pants, and tugged on his wrinkled white shirt. Then he picked up a bottle of tequila from the counter and staggered over to the foreigners. He tapped Demitri on the shoulder and then weaved his way to one of the empty tables, sat down, and took a swig from his bottle. Demitri didn't respond, as if he hadn't noticed the shoulder tap. He paid the bar tab in American cash and got off the stool.

"Stay close," he said, and headed for the thin man's table. Lin and Paul followed.

The foursome sat at the little cafe table in silence. The man took another drink from the bottle of tequila and wiped his mouth with his hand. He tapped his fingers on the metal table.

"I have a car," he said. "What is it you are looking for?"

"One who asks no questions," said Demitri.

The man sat back in his chair and raised his bottle to his gaunt face for another drink. Demitri snatched it from the man's bony hands.

"And one who can drive," said the Russian.

The man frowned. His finger tapping resumed. "Where do you want to go?"

"Take us west to the river, and then north a few miles if the roads permit."

The man's eyes widened. "¡El Diablo! You are going to the crazy place? I can not take you there."

Paul leaned in. "What do you know about it?"

The man leaned in and lowered his voice almost to a whisper. "Something unholy goes on there, I know. I can't say what. It is a bad place. You shouldn't go there."

"Are there roads heading north along the river?" Paul asked.

"Sí, but roads along the river are bad. You can walk or take a jeep. The Devil doesn't use the roads. Only monks walk on the roads. You cannot get close to the crazy place. They have soldiers."

"What do you mean?" Lin asked. "When you say the Devil doesn't use the roads?"

"The Devil flies," said the man. "I have seen it."

"Drive us to the river then," said Demitri. "And wait for us until we come back."

The man started laughing.

"What's so funny?" Lin asked.

"You will not come back!" said the man.

Lin put her arm on Paul and pulled him backward into his chair. "Paul, maybe we should rethink this," she said.

"No," said Paul. "It's just irrational fear that's keeping the locals from getting close. Don't you see? There's no Devil there, but the story keeps away the fainthearted."

"One hundred dollars American to take us west to the river," said Demitri. "And two hundred more to bring us back."

"We'll walk the rest of the way north and south," said Paul.

"Great," said Lin. "A hundred bucks to hire a drunk driver for a one-way trip to hell."

Demitri looked at the thin man and shrugged his shoulders. "It's the vodka," said the Russian.

The man held his bony hand out to Demitri. The Russian reached to shake the man's hand, but the fellow just snapped his fingers. Demitri put the bottle of tequila in the outstretched hand, and the man drank until he finished off the bottle. He coughed and sputtered, and the clear liquor dribbled down his chin.

"It's a deal, amigo," he said, as he wiped his face with the back of his hand.

"We're gonna need another bottle," said Lin.

"And some glasses," said Paul.

CHAPTER 24

Paul couldn't identify the thin man's car. The body color ran the spectrum from azure blue to rust. It had been reconstructed so many times that most of its original parts were long gone. He surmised it must be some kind of ancient midsized American sedan. The important thing was it still ran. Barely.

The odd foursome piled in. Paul got in the front seat with the driver. The thin man cradled a bottle of tequila in his lap between his legs. Lin and Demitri rode in the back.

Paul turned around and looked at Lin. "Don't worry," said Paul. "He probably drives better drunk."

"Nice assessment, thanks, doctor," said Lin, rolling her eyes.

"In Russia, everybody drives this way," said Demitri.

"It's only eight miles or so," said Paul, "He'll get us there."

As they took off west out of Pueblo Viejo, Paul wondered if the driver would wait for them for the return trip. Paul figured the man would have to weigh the two hundred dollars against his belief that the adventurous trio would be snatched by the Devil.

The road was paved and smooth, but the old car sputtered and backfired, jerking violently from what Paul thought must be a broken ball joint on the front axle. He looked back to see how Lin was holding up. A billowing cloud of black smoke followed the sedan. There were no seatbelts and she was bouncing wildly, clutching the edge of her seat with white knuckles.

"I'm gonna be sick," she said.

He rolled his window down to vent the heat and the fetid smell of alcohol and burning oil. Soon all four windows came down. The ride was painfully slow, as the old engine didn't seem to be firing on all cylinders. An endless stream of cars streaked past them.

"At least he's able to stay on the road," said Paul.

"Good driver," said Demitri.

Their progress slowed briefly as they passed through Buga. The disorderly clash of local traffic, motorcycles, bicycles, and pedestrians lasted for about a mile. Aside from some sidewalks and brightly painted storefronts, Paul didn't think the dusty streets of Buga looked much different than Pueblo Viejo. It only took about ten minutes to leave the town behind. The rest of the road west was mostly open country.

A police car pulled up behind and trailed them.

"Uh, oh. I think we've had it," said Lin

"This could be a short ride," said Paul.

The police car pulled along side on the driver's side. Sunglasses on a dark face in uniform turned toward the lumbering sedan. In a burst of speed, the police car pulled in front of the sedan and vanished in the haze of the road ahead.

"They don't bother with my little burro," said the driver, holding the wheel with one hand and the bottle of tequila with the other. He closed his eyes and took a long drink. Miraculously, they stayed on the road.

"See? Multitasking," Paul said to Lin. "And good with authority."

"Good driver," said Demitri, nodding.

"Oh, God, please!" said Lin, her face ashen.

They reached the bridge at the Rio Cauca and the driver pulled onto the gravel shoulder.

"This is as far as I go, amigos," he said.

They all exited the car and the trio checked and secured their backpacks. The driver leaned against a signpost and drank his tequila. Demitri handed him the hundred.

"You wait here," he said. "Two hundred more to take us back. And all you can drink all night long."

The driver folded the money and stuffed it in his saggy pants. "Gracias, señor," he said. "Vaya con Dios." He made the sign of the cross on his chest. Paul felt reasonably certain they'd never see the thin man again.

The trio started their walk just north of the highway bridge. The first hundred yards were steep walls of concrete, ending on top in bridge supports or thorny overgrowth. There was no road in sight. The Rio Cauca raged below, thirty feet down and a few hundred yards across.

Concrete walls gave way to steep, green, shrub-covered embankments that were impossible to walk on for any length. The river twisted like a snake, so they couldn't see much of the terrain ahead. Every few feet brought new surprises.

"Let's go down to the riverbed," said Paul. "There may be a trail we can follow along the bank."

They carefully picked their way down the steep bank to the rocky riverbed, hanging on to shrubs, sliding on the loose rocks. The sharp shale on the river's edge made for uncomfortable walking.

"Stop," said Lin, panting. She sat down on a boulder on the river's edge. "I need a break. It must be eighty-five degrees. She took off her backpack and splashed her face with the icy river water. "Where's the road?"

Paul stopped and stared north down the river. Beside him, the Russian came lumbering out of the brush on the steep bank, sliding down the last few feet. He walked to the water's edge and scanned the river.

"No trail on river," said Demitri.

"Let's catch our breath for a few," said Paul. "We can only walk a little ways here on the bank,

then we'll have to climb back up and head east
and hope to cross a road that will take us further
north."

"Great. Now we're backtracking," said Lin,
before drinking from her water bottle. "We have
to stay above the river," she said. "On top of the
bank, if we want to see anything. Or we might go
right past it."

"Or stumble into it, unprepared," said Paul.
"Good point. Settled. We rest. Then we climb
back up to the high ground and look for the road
north."

He took off his backpack and sat next to Lin on
the boulder. A few colorful birds flew by along the
water's edge. The river churned and bubbled. The
sound was soothing, the ripples mesmerizing.

"I would find this a beautiful place," said Paul.
"If I wasn't up to my ears in trouble."

Lin took his hand. "We'll get through this,
together."

"Time to go," said Demitri.

They walked along the narrow riverbank for
about a hundred feet before it became impassible.
Then they started the grueling climb up the steep
bank. Lin scrambled up the hill first, loose rocks

flying from her feet. She had to get on her hands and knees a few times to gain elevation. Sparse shrubs provided some unreliable handholds.

Paul tried to dodge the rocks cascading off of Lin's boots, but got he pelted anyway. He made it to the top soon after Lin, but Demitri lagged behind. The Russian moved slowly, testing every foothold, taking tiny steps. Finally, the trio was reunited on top of the embankment, looking down at the river.

"Let's find that road," said Paul. He pulled out his compass and took his bearings. Then he pointed it east. "This is so we don't walk in circles," he said.

Without a trail, they pushed through thick shrubs, thorny brush, trees, and piles of woody blow down. Arms, legs, and backpacks snagged repeatedly in the dense overgrowth. The trek was slow and painful.

After about a hundred yards of slogging through the woods, they came out into a clearing. There were two rutted tracts running north and south with potholes and scattered rocks.

"Hallelujah," said Lin.

"This has got to be it," said Paul. He pointed the compass north.

They trudged up the dirt road for several miles, with Paul in the lead. Although the hike was exhausting, it was infinitely easier than cutting through the woods.

They walked around a curve in the road and Paul stopped abruptly. The others stopped beside him.

"Look at that," said Paul.

A series of poured concrete buildings had come into view, sprouting up in the distance on the rolling hillside, alongside the Rio Cauca. It looked like a child had dropped a bunch of huge building blocks, about a half-dozen, of different sizes.

"Looks more like a fortress than an office building," said Lin.

Paul took out his binoculars and focused them on the distant structures.

"Yeah, I agree," he said. "I only see a few upper-level windows, and those appear to have metal grates over them. The entire complex looks like it's about a mile away, and right on the river. Square shapes, one that's probably three or four stories, and a weird funnel-shaped cement structure as tall as the big building. I don't have a clue what that could be."

Demitri held out his hand. Paul gave him the binoculars. The Russian studied the distant scene carefully. He lowered the binoculars. "Cooling tower," he said. "Like nuclear plant."

Paul felt a lump in his throat.

"Nuclear?" said Lin. "God, Paul. Are they making bombs or something?"

Paul took the binoculars back from Demitri.

"It makes no sense," said Paul. "What's the nuclear connection? This could get very ugly. We've got to get a closer look and get some pictures."

Someone sneezed, and it wasn't anyone in the trio. Another sneeze.

"Someone coming," said Paul in a hushed tone. "Let's get off the road."

They quickly scrambled into the woods, about ten feet off the road, and knelt in the brush. No one made a sound and the woods were still. They heard footfalls shuffling in the dirt, coming around the bend from the place they'd just come from.

A brown-robed, hooded person came into view, walking up the road. The hooded figure stopped in the exact spot the trio had just been standing in. The person's head turned towards the hidden group, the face an indistinct hooded shadow.

Paul held his breath and waited. The hooded form swayed a bit, as if trying to get a better view. Then the lone traveler faced forward, resumed walking down the road, and disappeared around the next bend.

The trio left the woods and regrouped on the road.

"That was close," said Lin.

"A Muisca monk," said Paul, "headed for work."

"What kind of work?" Demetri asked.

"Thinking," said Paul.

The Russian shrugged.

"You're not making sense, again," said Lin.

"Sorry," said Paul. "But I don't really understand it all myself."

To give the monk a big head start, the trio paused before continuing down the road. They were careful to stay well behind the monk, out of sight. About a hundred yards further on, the group ran into an electronic iron gate, complete with a keypad control. The red and white sign on the gate said *Private Road No Trespassing* in English and Spanish.

Paul grabbed the iron gate. "Very bad. Security already and we're still almost a mile away."

"They will be watching this road," said Demitri.

"We may not even get close to the place," said Lin.

"The hell we won't," Paul replied, walking around the right side of the gate. The gate was apparently made to keep out vehicles, but not people on foot. Lin and Demitri hesitated and then followed.

They stayed out of sight a few yards off the road, walking parallel to it in the woods, fighting their way though the overgrowth like before. It was a difficult way to travel.

"I miss that lousy road already," said Lin.

Single file they advanced a few hundred more yards, in silence except for the cracking of the brush as they plowed through. Paul held up his hand to signal a stop. They were so close now they could hear the hum of heavy machinery and smell diesel fumes.

"I need to climb a tree and get a look," said Paul in a hushed voice. The binoculars hung on his neck.

Demitri removed his backpack and squatted. "Get on," said the Russian.

Paul mounted Demitri's broad shoulders, one leg on each side, piggyback style. The Russian stood up, lifting Paul high above the brush. Paul peered through the binoculars.

"I don't see any high-voltage transmission lines like I'd expect to see at a nuclear plant," said Paul.

"Could be underground," said Demitri.

"In this rugged terrain? In Colombia? I doubt it," said Paul. "And between the diesel fumes, smoke, and the noise coming from the small, outer buildings, I'd say I'm looking at power stations, with conventional generators inside."

"Why do they need so many diesel generators going if they're running a nuclear plant?" said Lin. "It doesn't make sense."

Paul tapped Demitri on the shoulder and the Russian squatted again. Paul dismounted. Then it struck him.

"It makes perfect sense," said Paul. "If it's not a nuclear plant."

"Then what is it?" said Demitri.

"I don't know," said Paul. "But I do know that whatever it is, they need lots of electricity and lots of cooling. And they must be using the river water to cool something."

"What now?" said Lin.

"We get closer," said Paul.

They continued to walk through the woods parallel to the road with Paul leading the group. Lin followed behind Paul, and Demitri was the last in line. The brush and trees doubled in density as they got closer to the complex.

Paul wedged his backpack sideways through some trees and then he saw the security fence. This one was meant to keep everyone out. It was about twelve feet high, built from thick, metal cables that were suspended from steel posts anchored in cement. Paul admired the sturdy construction.

He reached out to touch it, but before his hand made contact something bashed his right arm. The blow knocked him over sideways into the thorny brush. It felt like he'd been whacked in the shoulder with a two-by-four. Demitri had punched him hard.

The Russian threw a stick into the fence. It exploded in a shower of sparks, popping off the fence like popcorn. The charred remains of the stick smoldered in the brush.

"Electric," said Demitri.

Paul untangled himself from the brush and got back on his feet. He rubbed his sore right shoulder. Pain from the old bullet wound stabbed at him again.

"Thanks," said Paul. "You saved my life, again. And I never thanked you properly the first time."

The Russian smiled and tipped the fedora down over one eye.

Lin was looking through the fence. "Paul, take a look," she whispered.

And he did. The thick brush and most of the trees had been cleared beyond the fence, and he could see the buildings of the World Development Industries complex. The nearest buildings, which he'd guessed must be power stations, started about three hundred yards from the deadly fence. Metal pipes on the roofs of these nearby buildings belched smoky fumes. A constant mechanical hum resonated from within the structures.

Behind the power stations, rising up three stories, was what had to be the main building. It was one large cement cube, right on the river. The round top of the cooling tower poked up from behind the main building.

"Get down!" said Paul, in a hushed voice. They all got down on their bellies, side by side in the thorny brush facing the fence. A man in a camouflage uniform with an automatic weapon slung over his shoulder walked the perimeter of the nearest power plant. Propped up on his elbows, Paul looked through his binoculars.

"No rank, no insignias. A generic uniform," said Paul.

"Mercenaries," said Demitri.

Paul took out the camera and snapped a few pictures. The mercenary walked around the corner of the power plant and disappeared from sight. The air began to pulsate.

"Do you feel that?" Lin asked.

"Yeah, I do."

The pulsations increased until they were audible, and turned into chopping sounds. A large red helicopter swooped in from above and landed on the roof of the main building. The rotor noise diminished for about five minutes, and then abruptly increased. The helicopter lifted off straight up. It looked like a red streak as it vanished in the haze. The air was still again except for the hum of the generators.

"There it is," said Lin. "The Devil flies."

They lay on the ground in silence for several minutes.

"We have to get in to the main building," said Paul.

"Automatic weapons," said Demitri, "And patrols. We can not fight them."

"It's impossible," said Lin. "What are you going to do, Paul? Just go up to the gate, say hello, and walk right in?"

Paul reached into his backpack and pulled out his monk robe.

"Yeah," he said. "That's exactly what I'm going to do."

CHAPTER 25

Paul stood up, removed his hat, and put on his monk robe over his clothes. He handed his backpack to Demitri. "Hang on to this," said Paul. "And let me see the package that Horace Yardley gave you."

Demitri reached into the bottom of his backpack and pulled out a package the size of a small cereal box, wrapped in plain brown paper. Paul ripped off the wrapping paper and opened the cardboard box.

Inside, the box was lined with white Styrofoam, with contents held neatly in form fitting indentations. It contained four preloaded syringes labeled PF, four preloaded syringes labeled DN, and two unlabeled aerosol spray cans. Lin's eyes widened.

"Paul," she said, "what is that?"

"Drugs?" Demitri asked.

"Yeah, drugs," said Paul. "The best kind of drugs. No time to explain. Now, everyone roll up your sleeves."

"No way," said Lin.

The Russian shook his head. "Nyet, I hate needles."

"Trust me, I'm a doctor," said Paul.

Lin rolled her eyes. "You first," she said.

"So that's the way you're both gonna be?" said Paul. "OK, here goes." He pulled up the monk robe and his left shirtsleeve. Then he stabbed his upper left arm with one of the preloaded syringes labeled DN. "See, I'm still alive," he said.

Lin frowned. "Great experiment, doctor." She pointed a finger at herself. "But I'm not taking any shot until you explain what all that is." Demitri nodded his agreement.

Paul sat down in the brush and motioned for the others to follow. They sat in a circle and Paul placed the open box in the center.

"The four syringes labeled PF contain picafentanyl, a potent, synthetic narcotic. One shot of that would put you to sleep for hours."

"It's anesthesia?" Lin asked.

"Yeah," said Paul.

Demitri reached into the box and grabbed one of the spray cans. "What is in can?" asked Demitri, while turning the can around near his face. He popped the top off the can and accidently released a tiny puff of mist. The Russian dropped the can and his pupils shrunk to pinpoints. He closed his eyes and fell over sideways with a loud crunch as the brush snapped on impact.

"Oh, my God!" said Lin as she rushed to Demitri's side.

The Russian lay on his left side, body limp and breathing slowly.

"Roll up his right sleeve," said Paul. She did.

Paul grabbed the second of the four preloaded DN syringes and injected it into the Demitri's arm. In about half a minute, the Russian took a few deep breaths and sat bolt upright. He grabbed his head.

"What happened?" said Demitri.

"You got curious about that spray can and took a whiff," said Paul. "You wanted to know what was in it."

"Now I know," said Demitri.

"So the spray can contains an aerosol anesthetic?" said Lin.

"Yeah," said Paul. "The spray cans contain an airborne version of the same potent narcotic that's in the four PF syringes."

"And the injection that you gave Demitri was the antidote?" Lin asked.

"Correct," said Paul. "The shots I gave myself and Demitri, from the DN syringes, were depo-naloxone, a narcotic antidote."

"You gave me a shot?" said Demitri.

"Yeah," said Paul. "While you were out cold." Paul picked up another syringe of the narcotic antidote. "So Demitri and I have had our narcotic antidote shots."

"And I'm guessing," said Lin. "That the antidote shot you're now preparing is for me."

"Good guess," said Paul.

Lin rolled up her right sleeve. "Any side effects?"

Paul readied the shot. "Yeah, it will also reverse your endorphins, your body's own natural narcotic-like painkillers. So everything that hurts you will hurt much more."

"Great!" She shook her head. "Give it to me."

Paul injected Lin with the narcotic antidote. She rubbed the injection site. There was now one remaining syringe of narcotic antidote.

"That really stings," she said. She rolled down her sleeve.

"The next one will hurt even more," said Paul.

"Next one?" said the Russian.

Lin pointed at the four PN syringes. "The pica whacha-mi-call-it?" she said. "The super-strong narcotic? Why would you inject us with that?"

"It's picafentanyl," said Paul. He pulled the first narcotic syringe from the box and injected his left arm. "It's excreted on the breath, like alcohol. In an enclosed space or with close contact, exhaled breath will put anyone to sleep who has not had the antidote shot."

"So you are now an anesthesia delivery device?" said Lin. "Like the aerosol can?"

"Yeah," said Paul. "I'm now the ultimate anesthesiologist. My breath alone can put someone to sleep. I am the anesthetic."

She rolled up her sleeve again. "Sounds like a wise self-defense precaution under the circumstances," she said. "Hit me."

Paul injected her arm with the second narcotic syringe. Then he picked up the third syringe of narcotic.

"Demitri?" said Paul.

The Russian sighed. He rolled up his right sleeve and turned his head way left. Paul gave Demitri the shot. He flinched and the color ran from the Russian's face. He swayed a bit and sweat ran down his ashen cheeks.

"Are you OK?" Lin asked.

"I am good," said Demitri. He took a few deep breaths and the color returned to his face.

"So we've all had our shots," said Paul. "And we have both the narcotic and the antidote in our bodies." He held up the spray cans. "We are now immune to this anesthetic spray, and we have narcotic anesthetic on our breath. In close quarters, our breath alone will put someone to sleep."

"How long do the effects last?" said Lin.

"About five hours," said Paul.

Paul stuffed the two aerosol cans in his pockets, along with the remaining narcotic syringe and the last antidote syringe. He stood up and threw the monk-robe hood over his head. The trio walked silently toward the road, where they all expected to find a well-guarded gate.

They were not disappointed. On the road, the electrified steel and concrete fence was broken by a huge motorized gate. It was twelve feet tall, like the fence, and wider than the road to accommodate large vehicles. In the center of the large gate was a smaller gate made for people.

Behind the gate, on both sides of the road, were concrete bunker-like guard posts. Inside each guard post, behind open windows, sat a mercenary soldier with an AK-47 riffle over his shoulder. The dirt road outside the gate transformed into a concrete road at the gate threshold.

Paul led Lin and Demitri back into the brush and then backtracked, moving away from the compound. After traveling about one hundred yards, Paul turned to the others.

"I'll walk down the road from here," said Paul. "Keep close off to the side, and out of sight."

"And you've got to lose the hat," he said to Lin. "Too visible." She took off her straw hat and stuffed it in her backpack.

"Once I'm though the gate," said Paul. "I'll let you both in. Demitri, if I screw up and things go nuts, grab Lin and take her back down the road."

"I'm not leaving you," said Lin, grabbing his arm.

"I will watch out for her," said the Russian.

Lin let go of Paul's arm and he headed through the brush for the road. Lin and Demitri stayed out of sight and headed back toward the main gate.

Paul walked slowly down the road in his monk robe. He shuffled slowly, imitating the relaxed walk of the Muisca monks. He used his brief walk on the path of the monks to calm himself. He'd have to stay focused and be convincing to get into the World Development Industries compound.

The mercenaries carried automatic weapons, and Paul suspected they wouldn't hesitate to use them. Francobar hadn't worried about killing a few Americans to keep them away from World Development Industries. In this remote area, no one would even hear the gunshots.

Paul wanted to get in, get some intelligence, and get out without anyone being killed. He knew they'd never shoot at a monk. The monk robe was his bulletproof vest, his cloak of invulnerability. Or at least he hoped so.

CHAPTER 26

The two mercenaries in the guard station bunkers at the massive gate didn't seem to notice Paul as he came into their field of view. It was as if the robe made Paul invisible. Undoubtedly, the guards had seen so many monks come and go that it didn't impress them anymore. Paul wondered how long his newfound invisibility would last.

He approached to within a few feet of the gate and then bowed his head and stood still. He could smell the acrid exhaust from the power plants and feel the hum of the generators. The two guards exchanged weary glances through the open windows of the guard posts, got up off their seats, and straightened the AK-47 assault rifles that hung on their shoulders.

The mercenary on Paul's left wiped the sweat from his tan upper lip, ran his fingers through the crewcut stubble on his head, and then walked out of his guardhouse. He pointed a finger at the other mercenary, who reached along the inside wall of his guardhouse and flipped a switch before exiting the structure.

The heavy gate machinery came to life and the people-sized door slid open slowly. Paul noticed the toes of his hiking boots sticking out from under the long robe. They were not the typical monk sandals. He pushed the loose fabric forward with his knee to hide the boots.

The guards stood on either side of the cage-like door as it crept open. Paul kept his hooded head bowed and waited until the sliding gate came to rest. He shuffled slowly through the opening, entering between the two guards. The guard to Paul's right lowered his assault rifle, holding it at waist height across Paul's path, blocking his way.

"Your work orders, please," said the guard on the left.

Paul reached into his pockets slowly, pulled out the two spray cans, and held them up, one in each guard's face. A fine puff of mist hit the mercenaries at point-blank range.

"Count to ten," said Paul.

The guards went limp and dropped gracefully on the cement. Paul rolled them over and checked to make sure that they were breathing freely. Demitri and Lin came running through the open gate.

"Nice trick," said Demitri. He slapped one of the guard's faces, and there was no response. "I could use that for my business." Then he started to pick up one of the AK-47s.

"Leave the guns," said Paul. "If anyone finds these two guards sleeping, they won't know what to make of it. But if we take the rifles, we'll have an army looking for us. I'd like to get in and out before anyone knows we're here." Demitri nodded and put the AK-47 down.

"Let's get out of the open," said Lin.

"Yeah, good idea," said Paul.

Demitri and Paul dragged the guards back into their original bunkers, to hide the sleeping bodies from view. Lin found the gate controls and closed the gate. They moved out of the open gate area and off the cement road, into the sparse brush and trees that lined the road. The vegetation offered little cover, but at least they no longer stood out like a parade.

The trio stopped and crouched behind a bush. Paul could see the main building, about fifty yards away, past the two power plants. Heavy transmission lines came in from the north on towers along the east bank of the Rio Cauca as the river twisted through the valley. That's why he hadn't seen the lines before.

Part of the smooth upstream side of the cooling tower peeked over the top of the main building. The tower was attached to the main building, wedged between the building and the river. If he could see the north side of the tower, Paul would expect to see a manmade waterfall cascading into the river.

The base of the three-story main building and cooling tower was right on the Rio Cauca, near the edge of the riverbank, thirty feet above the water. The other buildings had been set back away from the river.

Paul took a few pictures and then peered through his binoculars.

"Transmission lines," said Paul. "The upper ones are high voltage, the lower ones are for data communication. And there's a lot of each."

"Why do they need power plants if they have electricity coming in?" asked Lin.

"Either they have electrical demands that exceed the ability of the Colombian infrastructure to provide," said Paul, "or they have to have backup power available at all times. Or perhaps both."

"Is not nuclear plant?" said Demitri.

"No," said Paul, "Despite the cooling tower, I don't think this is a nuclear facility."

"What now?" said Lin.

"The main building," said Paul. "We've got to get a look inside."

"Ok," said Lin, "but on one condition."

"What?" asked Paul.

"After we get a look inside, we get the hell out of here."

"I promise," said Paul. "One look and then we go home."

CHAPTER 27

The cement road ended at the main building. The trio stayed off the road and advanced slowly from bush to bush. Evidently, their presence had not yet been detected. They still had the element of surprise on their side.

They lay in the tall grass no more than fifty feet from the entrance to the main building. Mercenary patrols walked by frequently, but didn't enter or exit the building. A metal entry door with an electronic lock was the only visible way in or out of the windowless concrete structure.

"Looks like the guards all stay outside," said Paul.

"A good thing," said Demitri.

"How are we going to get past the patrols?" said Lin.

"Same way I got through the gate," said Paul. "Once I'm in, I'll clear the way and signal for both of you to follow me."

"Good plan," said the Russian.

"Yeah, well, here I go."

Paul assumed his quiet monk pose, with hooded head bowed, and walked over to the cement road. He shuffled slowly toward the entrance of the main building. Two brown-faced mercenaries walked past him quickly, smoking cigarettes, talking in rapid-fire Spanish, and laughing. One had an AK-47 machine gun hanging from his shoulder.

Paul approached the metal door and pulled the handle. It was locked. He stood there, dumfounded. Someone pulled his hood off from behind. He turned to find an AK-47 pointed at his chest, and the two guards he'd passed a moment ago.

"Do not move!" said the one holding the rifle.

"You are no monk," said the one who had pulled off Paul's hood. He walked close to Paul and looked in his face. Paul could smell the guard's stale breath and see the pockmarks on his rutted, brown skin. "So, who are you, gringo?"

"I'm the sandman," said Paul, and he blew on the man's face.

The pockmarked man went limp. Paul caught the limp mercenary and hugged him to his chest, putting the sleeping man in the path of the AK-47.

The mercenary holding the rifle moved back, waving his AK-47, looking for a clear shot. He never found one. He dropped to the ground suddenly, a pool of blood spread out on the cement below his body.

Demitri and Lin came out of the brush. The Russian had his Glock in hand, fitted with a silencer, still smoking. He removed the silencer and blew on the barrel.

"Is good for quiet," he said, and put the silencer and his gun away. Then he took the AK-47 from the dead mercenary and examined it.

"Russian made," said Demitri, as he put the rifle strap over his shoulder. "Very nice."

"My God, you killed him!" said Lin.

"Like doctor," said Demitri, shrugging. "I put them to sleep. But they don't wake up."

"We're sitting ducks if we stay here," said Paul. "We have to get inside, before the guards discover what happened. But it's locked."

The door opened and a monk in a brown robe came out. Paul grabbed the open door with one hand and the monk with the other.

"I'm Dr. Paul Powers, a friend of Moritz. We have to go inside and get all the Muisca out, right now."

The monk entered the building and the trio followed.

The room beyond the entry door had hard benches along the walls, and a thick, woven mat on the floor. On the left side, a half-dozen secretaries in red uniforms sat at computer terminals behind a counter. Faux old-fashioned lights provided dim illumination, and the air smelled of jasmine incense. Tapestries of the same type as in the Muisca monastery covered the walls.

Two monks sat cross-legged on the floor in silent meditation, and three others sat silently on the hard benches.

"What kind of room is this?" said Demitri.

"It's a waiting room," said Paul. "For monks."

"Waiting? Waiting for what?" asked the Russian.

"Mother of God," said Lin. "Our driver was right. This is it. The crazy place."

"Everybody out, now!" said Paul. Nobody moved.

Demitri fired a round from the AK-47 into the ceiling. "Get out," he said.

The secretaries and monks ran from the room. A flurry of brown robes and red uniforms jostled each other through the doorway. But the monk Paul had befriended outside the building remained.

"Brother Paul," said the monk. "There are many others inside. This way."

The monk led the trio through a metal door next to the secretaries' station. Paul followed the monk through the door.

The door opened into an expansive, warehouse like space with thirty-foot open ceilings crisscrossed with pipes and transmission cables. A long row of MRI machines filled much of the first floor of the open warehouse. A dozen or so technicians in white coats circulated around the main floor with clipboards, or sat at desks opposite the MRI machines. Paul quickly counted about twenty machines. Half of the machines had Muisca monks inside. Each MRI machine was enclosed in a clear Plexiglas cubicle, and there was a fine metal mesh embedded in the Plexiglas.

Over the MRI machines hung a second floor that was built like a loft, open in front except for a metal railing. The second level was about half the size of the first. On the second level were massive computer towers, workstations, and LCD monitors, with fifty or so busy programmers. A large glass elevator stood out in the middle of the warehouse, with a metal staircase rising beside it.

The third level was only a platform leading to a door, which Paul assumed must access the roof and the helipad they'd noticed earlier. The entry door and the roof access seemed to be the only ways in or out of the warehouse.

Demitri's eyes widened. "What is this place?"

"Welcome to hell," said Lin.

CHAPTER 28

"Let's get everyone out of here," said Paul.

The monk ran through the warehouse, spreading the word to the monks in the MRI scanners. Demitri fired a round from the machine gun into one of the huge LCD monitors on the second level. It burst in an explosion of glass, sparks, and smoke, and got the computer programmers' attention. They all ran down the staircase.

"Get out, get out!" Paul screamed.

There was a mass exodus through the warehouse door, and in a few minutes the entire building was empty except for the odd trio.

"They will come for us, soon," said Demitri. "Do you have plan?"

"Yeah," said Paul. "I'll be right back."

Paul ran to the warehouse door. He opened it in time to see several mercenaries, rifles ready, storming through the main building entrance into the waiting room. Paul covered his face with his brown hood and walked slowly back into the waiting room. A dozen or so armed mercenaries surrounded him. Machine guns pointed at him from every direction.

Underneath Paul's robe, out of sight, he sprayed the two cans of airborne narcotics. The invisible gas filled the room, and the soldier nearest to Paul hit the floor with a thud. Then the adjacent mercenaries went down, like dominos, until they were all unconscious. Two more soldiers entered through the main door and rapidly fell to the ground.

Paul emptied the two spray cans, and tossed the empty cans into the waiting room.

A missile-like projectile flew into the waiting room through the main door and landed with a metallic clank. Paul sprinted back to the warehouse door, dived through, and slammed the door shut. There was a loud boom and the building shook.

"Are you all right?" said Lin. "What was that?"

"Concussion grenade," said Demitri. "To knock you out."

"I'm OK," said Paul. "And I sprayed enough narcotic anesthetic to hold them off for a while."

Paul approached one of the Plexiglas MRI machine cubicles. He ran his hand along the smooth Plexiglas wall and looked at the metal mesh embedded in the clear Plexiglas. Each MRI machine cubicle had an open door in front.

As Paul walked by the open doorway of a cubicle, the syringes in his pockets came to life, tugging violently in the direction of the MRI machine. The powerful MRI magnet was pulling on the metal parts of the syringes. Once Paul passed the open MRI machine doorway, the MRI magnet abruptly stopped tugging on the syringes. They settled back into his pockets.

Lin examined the Plexiglas and metal mesh wall of the cubicle. "It's a Faraday cage," said Lin. "For electromagnetic isolation. The only place the MRI machine's magnetic field can pass is straight through the open doorway of each MRI machine cubicle. It's a clever design."

"Of course," said Paul. "With so many MRI machines, you need some way to keep the magnetic fields from interfering with each other."

"What's going on, here?" said Lin.

"I'm just beginning to understand," said Paul.

Gunshots rang out in the open warehouse, and the noise was deafening. Someone had fired at Demitri from the second floor level. Demitri countered with a barrage from his machine gun. The twang of ricocheting bullets persisted well past the initial gunfire. Plastic and metal parts fell nearby from above. Lights dimmed and flickered in the warehouse, and steaming liquid poured out of one of the ceiling pipes in the far corner of the room.

Lin and Paul got down on the floor between two of the MRI machines. Demitri's rapid response to the sudden gunfire had pinned the shooter down in the stacks of the computer servers above Paul's head. Paul and Lin were below the overhanging second floor ledge, and out of the shooter's line of fire.

Demitri had partial cover behind a desk, but Paul couldn't tell if the Russian or the shooter had been hit. The shooter had lost the element of surprise, and Demitri appeared to be the only one with a machine gun. If the shooter risked exposure by firing again, Demitri might be able to finish it.

Steaming liquid poured onto the floor at the other end of the warehouse.

"What is that, Paul?" said Lin. "Hot water?"

"No. The opposite. Liquid nitrogen. That's why they need the cooling tower. To keep all the liquid nitrogen, the MRI machine magnets, and the computer servers cool. And the backup electricity is so the cooling never fails."

Demitri slumped over and the rifle fell from his hands. He was motionless. Another shot from above hit near Demitri.

"He's down," said Paul. "Maybe dead. And the shooter knows it."

"We're pinned down here," said Lin. "It's just a matter of time until whoever is up there gets us, too."

"Maybe not," said Paul.

"What are you going to do?"

"Play a hunch."

"Oh, God, no."

"I'm sorry," said Paul. "But a hunch is all I've got. I'm so sorry I got you into all this. I never thought it would end this way. I can't tell if I'm the most selfish man in the world for bringing you here, or the luckiest man alive because I met you."

Lin's eyes filled with tears. "I'm with you. No matter what happens."

He kissed her cheek and smiled. "Stay put."

Paul took off his monk robe. It wouldn't protect him anymore. He yelled to the room, "I'm coming out. I'm not armed. My hands are up."

He stood up and made his way slowly into the center of the room, from where he'd be an easy shot for the shooter hiding in the computer server stacks above. Paul stood there, hands raised, facing the hidden shooter.

"You are brilliant," said Paul. "Too brilliant. That's what tipped me off. The profile. Expert mathematician, doctor, research scientist with access to cyanide in Seattle, radiologist. I couldn't find anyone living who fit the profile. So I had to consider the dead. You can come out, now, Valdimire."

A bulky form emerged from the computer stacks above. Down the stairs, with gun in hand, came Dr. Valdimire Zhazinsky, returned from the dead. He walked off the last step. Even his dark beard could not hide his smile.

"Very good, Paul. I didn't think anyone could track me down. That was the whole idea. How did you know?"

Paul moved slowly toward the staircase and the nearest MRI machine.

"I didn't," said Paul. "Until now."

"Very clever," said Valdimire. "But there must have been some clues I overlooked." Z took another step and turned his broad shoulders toward Paul.

"Oh, there was the ampoule," said Paul. "Just a shard of glass. That really bugged me. It was from the cobalt compound you imported from Europe, no doubt. That compound was the antidote for cyanide poisoning that Hinkley told me about. The one that's not available in the U.S. It turns cyanide into vitamin B12. And your blood tested positive for high levels of vitamin B12. You took that cyanide antidote before you gave yourself a small dose of cyanide. There was no way you could have died."

Dr. Z raised the gun and moved closer to Paul.

"But you saw me die," said Dr. Z. "In ICU. That should have convinced you."

Paul backed up to the closest MRI machine as Dr. Z approached. The gap between the two doctors closed.

"The first day you were in ICU," said Paul. "I thought I smelled anesthetic gas on your breath. Hinkley tried to convince me it was cyanide.

But Hinkley must have attached an anesthetic vaporizer to the ventilator, to give anesthesia gas and put you under deep anesthesia. Under deep anesthesia it's normal to have no brain waves, so you would appear to be legally dead. But in your case, it was simulated death."

Dr. Z walked closer and Paul continued to back off toward one of the MRI machines.

"But you saw them shut off the ventilator," said Dr. Z.

"Yeah," said Paul, "But as long as you leave the oxygen on, you can safely turn off a ventilator for a while. Even if you're not breathing, you'll still get enough oxygen to keep you alive. So Hinkley turned off your ventilator and shut down your monitors long enough to convince everyone that you were dead."

"You know nothing!" said Dr. Z, shaking the gun at Paul.

Dr. Z's bushy, black eyebrows cast dark shadows over his eyes. Paul was so close that he could see the red in Z's eyes piercing through the dark sockets.

"I know you found the Rosetta Stone," said Paul.

"What?" said Dr. Z.

"The Muisca monks," said Paul. "They are the Rosetta Stone, the encryption key, without which your work has no meaning."

Dr. Z stared blankly into space. "Yes, yes, they are the key," he said.

"That was your turning point," said Paul. "When you discovered the monks could produce a sustained electrochemical and magnetic pattern from a single thought. The monk's ability to concentrate on a single thought gave you a way to translate every thought into a known electrochemical and magnetic pattern, and turn that pattern into a series of ones and zeros. You're building a digital database of human thought."

"Yes," said Dr. Z. "But it's much more than that. I modified the sensors to scan for multiple biological factors. Chemical, electrical, mechanical, and magnetic. And I incorporated DPI, Deep Packet Inspection, the best data-mining technology known to man."

Paul backed up a few steps more, and Z moved in to close the gap.

"It's like the human genome project," said Paul. "But instead of collecting and mapping human DNA, you are collecting thoughts. And when you're finally done creating your digital dictionary of human thoughts, you'll be able to turn any brain into a digitized, searchable database."

"How ignorant you are," said Dr. Z. "It's even more than that. My search engine works better than the natural one in the brain. I'll be able to access forgotten and repressed memories. Determine the reality of love or criminal intent. Or find out what the consumer really wants. No more lies. No more deception. The potential benefits to society are enormous."

Paul moved back another step, and Dr. Z crept forward.

"You ruined a lot of lives to get here," said Paul. "Espionage to raise funds, murder to drop out of sight."

"Necessary first steps," said Z. "It takes enormous resources to run a project of this magnitude."

"And all that incoming MRI data," said Paul. "I don't really have a brain tumor, do I? You just overwrote the digital data on the MRI brain scans for me and all those executives."

Z shook his head and waved the gun. "Yes," he said. "You're normal, they're all normal. It's just digital image manipulation. It's as easy as touching up a photograph. I could draw a flock of doves on your brain scan." He laughed. "Falsifying an MRI brain scan works well as long as I stick to a diagnosis that no one will open the brain to verify."

Z moved in closer and Paul backed up some more. They were now within a few feet of the nearest MRI machine.

"Blackmail," said Paul. "Extortion, wire fraud, breaking and entering, tampering with legal evidence, murder. Quite the resume you've accumulated. What did you have on Ben Hinkley?"

Z stepped forward. He stood just a few feet from the doorway to the Plexiglas and metal mesh cage that surrounded the nearby MRI machine.

"Hinkley," said Z, smiling. "We all have secrets that we'd rather not share. Let's just say that old Ben has a few antisocial sexual habits that he'd prefer to keep private."

"I see," said Paul, moving back a step. "How did you make people sick? Maybe Spasmol? I thought it was odd that Ben was using Spasmol in his practice. How does that work?"

"Very good pickup, doctor," said Z. "If you liquefy the Spasmol pills, and give the drug by injection, it only takes a tiny bit to bring on the bad side effects. Just a scratch on the skin will do it. And it's undetectable by common blood tests."

Paul moved back another step. He was now in front of the doorway to the MRI machine. He could feel the syringes in his pockets come to life, struggling to go toward the powerful MRI magnet. Z moved in to close the gap.

"So you prick someone's skin with the liquid Spasmol," said Paul. "And they get dizziness, muscle weakness, and double vision. More than enough to prompt getting an MRI brain scan. Then you scan the patient, download the individual's thought database, and leave a false MRI image of some ailment if you want to scan that person later. Like I said, brilliant."

Paul stepped back just past the MRI machine doorway, beyond the influence of the MRI magnet. The syringes stopped tugging on his pockets.

"Almost a shame to kill you after you figured it all out," said Dr. Z. "For the record, I always liked you, Paul."

Dr. Z stretched out his arm with the gun, just past the edge of the doorway to the MRI machine. He started to squeeze the trigger. The weapon fired as it flew from Z's hand into the MRI machine tunnel, nearly taking his fingers with it. The bullet whizzed by Paul's right ear. The gun ended up inside the MRI machine, stuck to the center of the roof of the tunnel, held in place by the powerful MRI magnet.

Paul jumped on Valdimire, trying to knock him to the ground. But the man had the weight and muscle of a linebacker, and he didn't budge. Instead, Dr. Z put his hands around Paul's neck in a vise-like grip. Paul couldn't breathe, and Z's hands felt like a ring of fire. Paul reached into his right pocket where he'd put the narcotic syringe, pulled it out, and jammed the needle through Z's clothing into his left arm. It had no effect.

Paul stuck the needle of the now-empty syringe into Valdimire's left ear. Z broke off his chokehold, screamed in pain, and batted the syringe out of Paul's hand. The empty syringe went flying into the MRI machine.

Paul tried to catch his breath, as Valdimire ran to the MRI machine to retrieve the gun. Z clawed at the pistol, but couldn't pry it loose from the intense magnet.

Lin ran over to Demitri from her hiding place between the MRI machines, and Paul ran to join her. Demitri's bent body was crammed behind a desk. Carefully, Lin and Paul pulled Demitri from his wedged position, unfolded him, and propped him up against the desk in the sitting position. His AK-47 still hung from his shoulder.

Paul glanced back at Z in the Plexiglas MRI machine cubicle thirty feet away. Z had his hands in the tunnel of the MRI machine, still trying to wrestle the gun free from the MRI magnet. He pulled his empty hands out of the MRI machine tunnel, and looked at Paul through the Plexiglas. Z started to walk away from the MRI machine.

From Demitri's ankle sheath, Paul pulled the dagger. He tossed it thirty feet toward the doorway of Z's MRI machine cubicle. The knife flew on a trajectory that would take it right past the doorway. But when it reached the MRI machine doorway, it seemed to freeze in midair for a split second. Then it made an abrupt turn, and shot toward the MRI machine, impaling Z's right forearm. Valdimire howled, staggered, and stumbled backward, bracing himself on the MRI machine. He pulled out the dagger and it flew into the MRI machine tunnel to join the gun.

A series of explosions rocked the warehouse. Several of the MRI machines burst into flames. The caustic smoke of burning plastic quickly filled the room. Sparks rained down from the computer towers above. Paul realized the errant bullets recently fired had disrupted the cooling and electrical safety systems in the warehouse. The emergency systems had not been designed to withstand gunfire.

Valdimire came out of the cubicle and ran for the stairs. Paul let him go. Lin knelt by Demitri, crying. Demitri had several obvious deep chest wounds. Blood trickled from his nose and mouth. He struggled to open his glassy eyes, and smiled.

"Spasiba," said Demitri.

"Why are you thanking us?" said Paul.

Demitri coughed, and frothy blood spewed from his mouth. "For this chance to do a good thing."

"Paul, can't you do something?" said Lin, holding Demitri's hand. Paul shook his head.

Dark blood bubbled over Demitri's lips. "Sometimes," said Demitri. "You have to fight through hell to get to heaven."

Demitri gurgled and went limp. His head nodded, eyes open. Paul felt Demitri's neck for a pulse. There was none. Gently, Paul shut Demitri's eyes and removed the strap of the AK-47 from his neck.

Paul picked up the machine gun.

"Lin," said Paul. "We have to go."

Lin didn't move. "We can't just leave him here," she said.

"He's gone," said Paul. "We can't help him. There's an army of solders with automatic rifles outside the main door, and this place is going to burn to the ground. The air here is almost toxic already. We have to go, now."

Lin wiped her tears and nodded. Paul slung the strap of the AK-47 over his shoulder and took Demitri's Glock from its holster.

"We have to get to the roof," said Paul, as he shoved the pistol into his pocket. "It's our only chance."

CHAPTER 29

Paul and Lin ran up the stairs. The staircase ended on a platform on the third level that was about ten feet square with a metal railing on the left. The door to the glass elevator shaft faced the staircase. To the right of the staircase, a steel door on the wall, with a left-sided, digital combination lock, stood between them and the roof. The door was locked.

Paul pulled the ammunition clip from the AK-47 and inspected it.

"You know how to use that?" asked Lin.

"There's a range I go to in Bellevue," said Paul as he reassembled the rifle. "They give you AK-47s to shoot. They charge for the ammo. Thirty rounds per clip. I'd estimate we've got about twenty rounds left in here. I'll take you to the range when we get back."

"Never know when some training will come in handy," said Lin. "Do you think it will work?"

"Yeah," said Paul. "But the ricochet will probably kill us. Now stand back."

They squeezed into the far left corner of the platform, against the railing, opposite the exit door. Paul fired about a dozen rounds into the lock. The glass elevator shaft exploded, covering them with a million pieces of safety glass. The stale smell of spent gunpowder merged with the acidic stench from the plastics burning below. The bullets barely made a dent in the lock.

"Damn good lock," said Paul, as he brushed off some of the shattered glass. "I can't shoot it off. Can you pick it? It's a computer, after all."

"No way," said Lin. "Maybe with a couple thousand dollars of equipment and a few hours."

Smoke billowed from below and flames reached up from the second floor. Lin coughed in spasms.

Paul looked around the ceiling over the platform. Then it struck him. There it was, right over the door, plain as day. A large bore pipe ran just above the door. It was labeled: *Liquid Nitrogen*. He stared at it.

"What is it, Paul?" said Lin, looking up and then at his face. "I know that look. Nothing good ever comes of it."

"Get on top of the railing," said Paul.

"Oh, God, here we go," said Lin.

She hoisted herself up and sat on the metal railing facing the door. Paul sat on her right, next to her. He raised the AK-47 and fired two rounds into the pipe along the wall right above the door lock. The pipe burst open, shards of metal and insulation exploded over them. A stream of liquid nitrogen poured right onto the lock and flowed under them and off the platform.

"Don't get any on you. It'll burn your skin off on contact," said Paul. "The intense cold should weaken the metal and make it brittle."

He waited about a minute and then raised the machine gun. He aimed at the lock, right through the stream of liquid nitrogen. About half a dozen rounds hit the lock before the machine gun ran out. The lock bent, chipped, and cracked, but did not break off. Paul let go of the AK-47 and it hung from his shoulder. He pulled out Demitri's Glock, aimed it with both hands, and fired over a dozen rounds. Then he tossed the spent pistol over the railing. The lock was damaged, but still intact.

"That's it," said Paul. "I'm empty."

"What now?" said Lin.

"Brute force. Follow me."

Paul slid along the railing until he was no longer sitting over the stream of liquid nitrogen. Then he jumped onto the platform to the right side of the stream and removed his shirt. He wrapped his shirt around the empty machine gun, leaving only the barrel exposed.

He braced the cloth-covered machine gun against the door with the bare barrel inside the stream of liquid nitrogen near the lock. Lin put her hands around his waist and against the door. They pushed together.

"Push, push, push," said Paul, to coordinate their efforts.

The lock splintered and shattered into many pieces and the door opened. Paul dropped the AK-47 and stepped through the doorway, barely squeezing by the steaming waterfall of liquid nitrogen. A few drops of the cold liquid splashed on his naked back. The drops burned like fire.

"I can't move my left foot!" said Lin.

Lin's left hiking boot had strayed into the liquid nitrogen washing over the platform, and the sole was frozen to the metal surface. Paul got down and untied her left boot, grabbed her around the waist, and helped her hobble through the doorway.

On the roof the air was clear and the sun hot. Valdimire stood by the edge of the roof, scanning the horizon. A red helicopter was approaching fast from the west. The dark barrel of a machine gun pointed at Lin and Paul from twenty feet away. It was in the hands of a mercenary.

"You should have stayed below," said Valdimire. "No shooting just yet," he told the mercenary. "Might scare away the chopper." He pointed to the red shape growing in the sky.

"So we have a standoff," said Paul.

Dr. Z shook his head. "No, I'm leaving. You can take your chances with the hired help. I'm sure they'll have a few words with you. This solves nothing, you know. I'll just start over again."

Lin moved close to Paul and put her arms around his bare chest. She held him tightly.

"You knew I'd be using narcotics," said Paul, "You took the antidote, didn't you? That's why my injection had no effect."

"I know everything you've been thinking, remember?" said Z. "You can't outsmart me. You can't outthink me. You never had a chance."

The air began to vibrate, then chop. With a deafening roar the red helicopter began its final approach. Paul and Lin stood about fifty feet away from the helipad. The mercenary and Dr. Z crouched down about thirty feet from the descending helicopter, getting ready to go aboard. Obviously, Z and his bodyguard intended this pickup to be a scoop and run. They were not planning to hang around.

The big red machine landed and the rotor powered down a bit. The passenger door opened, facing Z and the mercenary. The bright flash and pop of a handgun came from inside the passenger door, and the mercenary dropped before he'd even had a chance to get up from his crouching position.

Dr. Z stood up, wide eyed, his jaw dropped. The unmistakable long slender legs of Natasha Zhazinsky exited the helicopter and alighted on the roof like a spider. She came out low, gun in hand, and stood up tall once she cleared the rotor.

With fire in her eyes, she turned to her husband.

"How dare you do this to me?" she said. "You faked your death because you knew I'd never allow you to do any of this."

Dr. Z looked down at the floor.

"I love you, Natasha," said Z. "But I couldn't take you on this journey. There's so much good I can do the world."

She waved the gun and leaned in toward her husband. "Murder, lies, threats, bribes," she said. "You learned nothing from the old country. You're a bastard just like them. You think you know what's good for everyone. You want to dominate the world."

Z held his right hand outstretched. "Come," he said. "We can do this together. We can do it your way."

She lowered the gun and paused.

"No," said Natasha, shaking her head. "This time, I will do it your way."

She raised the gun and emptied half a dozen or so rounds into Z's chest at close range. He fell on roof deck, immobile, on his back, eyes closed. She hovered over him with the gun, and then spit on his face.

Z's eyes popped open. He grabbed Natasha's right leg, pulled it out from under her and brought her down. Then he snatched the gun from her grasp, and started to get on his feet. His tattered shirt opened, revealing a Kevlar vest underneath.

Paul jumped on Z and wrestled him for the gun, knocking him back onto the roof deck. Z lost his grip on the gun. It skittered across the roof deck and stopped when it hit the little cement curb that bordered the roof edge.

The two men dived for the gun, ending up on their stomachs at the edge of the roof. Valdimire got there first, grabbed the gun, and got to his knees at the roof edge. He turned away from the roof edge and aimed the gun with both hands as Paul struggled to get off his belly.

Paul looked up into the barrel of the gun, inches from his face. He grabbed Z under his knees, lifted, and pushed. The gun fired and the bullet flew over Paul's head. Z and the gun toppled backward off the roof, into the raging waterfall of the cooling tower, and the river sixty feet below. He disappeared from sight.

The momentum of Paul's thrust propelled him halfway over the roof edge. He lay on his belly, bent over the edge of the roof, dangling, stunned, and staring into the falling water. Lin grabbed him around the waist and held him in place.

"One look and we go home," said Lin. "You promised, remember?"

Lin helped Paul to his feet, and then he saw the mercenaries.

The mercenaries had pulled a pickup truck up to the side of the building, with a long black extension ladder in the cargo bay. They intended to climb the building to get on the roof. It would only take them a few minutes.

"We've got to get out of here," said Paul.

The trio piled into the helicopter. First Natasha, then Lin, then Paul. He shut the door. The rotor powered up.

"How?" said Paul, to Natasha.

"GPS tracker on Demitri," said Natasha. "Where is he?"

"I'm sorry," said Paul. "He didn't make it."

"Go," said Paul to the pilot. But he didn't respond. Paul leaned forward to look at the pilot. The young man was nodding, limp, and breathing slowly.

"Paul," said Lin, "Natasha's out cold."

Sure enough, Natasha was slumped in her seat with a smile on her face.

"Damn!" said Paul. "It's the enclosed space. Our breath put them to sleep."

The black tips of a ladder could be seen peeking over the far edge of the roof.

Paul reached in his pocket for the last syringe of narcotic antidote. He leaned forward and stabbed the pilot's right arm through his clothing. The pilot didn't respond.

Outside, the top of a head popped up between the black posts of the ladder, then two hands clawed their way up the posts.

"We're not gonna make it," said Lin.

"The pilot's young," said Paul. "Good circulation. Give it a moment."

In less than a minute, the pilot sat up and shook his head.

"¿Qué pasa?" he said.

"Take off, get us out of here, ándele!" said Paul.

"Sí, señor," said the young man, and the helicopter went airborne. They lifted off just in time to see several mercenaries run across the roof.

"What about Natasha?" said Lin.

"Priorities," said Paul. "That was the last antidote syringe. She'll wake up, eventually."

Paul handed a communication headset to Lin, and then put on his own headset and stared down at the Rio Cauca. It ran for miles, a shimmering blue-green ribbon, vanishing in the haze beyond his view. In the distance, black smoke billowed out of the World Development Industries' building. Next to Lin, Natasha slept peacefully, her head tilted back on the seat and propped up against the helicopter window.

Paul adjusted the microphone on the headset, pulling it towards his lips. "Rasputin," he said.

"What?" said Lin.

"Evil Russian wizard of the medical arts," said Paul. "Used his knowledge of advanced medical technology to heal, to control, to overpower, to command others."

"Paul, what are you talking about?"

"They poisoned him, shot him, then drowned him in a river. His body was never recovered. I'm guessing they'll never find Z's body in the Rio Cauca, either. And they'll blame the missing body on hungry animals."

"You sound crazy," said Lin.

"Don't you see?" said Paul, gently grabbing Lin's hand and looking into her eyes. "Many people thought Rasputin was the Devil's spawn, immortal, indestructible, and rotten to the core. El Diablo."

"That's nuts," said Lin, shaking her hand loose from Paul's grip. "Do you really think Dr. Z is Rasputin, or some kind of ageless demon?"

Paul shook his head. "No, I'm more inclined to believe that there are technologically advanced physicians in every age who misuse their knowledge for personal gain, with no moral boundaries."

Lin leaned in, put her arms around him, and held him tightly. They both looked out Paul's window. The helicopter turned, tilting them toward the ground, and the raging river disappeared from sight. The rolling green and brown hills of Colombia flowed beneath them.

"But I still wonder," said Paul.

EPILOGUE

On returning to Seattle, Paul was immediately arrested and put into the Federal Detention Center in SeaTac. Federal agents debriefed him for several hours every day. Milton instructed Paul to be entirely truthful to the feds, but Paul didn't like talking to the agents. They asked too many questions about how the mind-reading technology worked, and how it was implemented. They didn't seem interested in the people who'd been murdered or ruined in pursuit of the dangerous technology.

Three days later, after one long interrogation session with the feds, the guard took Paul to the visitor's room. Lin sat on one side of the table, waiting, dark hair pinned back, manicured nails polished pink. She smiled.

"You look great, rested, happy," said Paul as he pulled up a chair at the table opposite her. She reached out and put her hands in his.

"I'm happy because I get to see you," she said.

"Thank you for coming," said Paul. "You can't believe how good it is to see you. I'm glad you're OK."

Paul felt bad that he'd dragged Lin along on such a dangerous quest. He'd been selfish, just trying to save himself. He wondered if he was truly in love with her, or had they just been thrown together by fate for this one ordeal?

"How are things at Sentry?" said Paul.

"Getting back to normal. Fixing all the security holes. We lost some accounts over the break-in and the video tampering, but most of our customers stayed with us."

"Have you told anyone?" Paul asked.

"About the mind reading?" She shook her head. "No. Who would believe me? If I start talking about that I'll lose all credibility with my customers."

Paul nodded. "Yeah. I'm sort of in the same boat. While the case is ongoing, Milton won't let me talk about the mind reading, either, except to the feds. But when I'm out, I'm going to tell the whole world."

He gazed into her bright brown eyes. Lin's brilliance had enabled Paul to save himself. He had deep feelings for her, and immense gratitude, but was it love?

"When will they let you go?" she asked.

"I don't know," said Paul. "Soon, I hope. Milton says he's working a brilliant angle. I agreed to go along with whatever gets me out of here and back to work."

"Well, when you get out, you need to ask me out on a proper date. No shooting, no kidnapping, no fires. Agreed?"

"Agreed," said Paul.

A guard approached. "Time's up," he said.

Paul let go of Lin's hands. Her delicate fingers slid slowly across his palms and out of reach.

The next day, Paul found out that Milton had changed the whole case from a murder investigation into a discreet matter of public health, and negotiated an agreement.

Judge Ryan, in his chambers with Paul and the necessary attorneys present, looked over the paperwork. "In light of the circumstances and the risks to public health," said the judge, "I find this agreement to be in order and acceptable to all parties. Dr. Powers, do you understand that this agreement forbids you, by order of the court, to discuss the activities of World Development Industries or the safety of MRI scanners?"

Paul looked at Milton. The lawyer shrugged his shoulders. Paul couldn't believe it. Milton hadn't told Paul that he was to be gagged in exchange for his freedom and the return of two million dollars bail. Unfortunately, Milton had it right. It was a good compromise, and a done deal.

Paul nodded. "Yes, I understand, Your Honor," he said.

"Very well," said the judge. "You are released without further conditions, and all bail is to be refunded."

It would be a big adjustment for Paul to get back into his old routine. He'd been preoccupied and it played tricks with his mind. He wondered if he was suffering from post-traumatic stress disorder.

After his release from jail, Natasha lent him the Mercedes, because he couldn't remember where he'd put his truck keys before leaving for Colombia.

He spent hours searching his small apartment, but just couldn't find his keys. He finally gave up and took the Mercedes out to run his errands. Tomorrow, he'd have to call the Toyota dealer and make new keys for his truck.

The first errand on his list was to pick up a new cell phone. His old phone had been stolen in Colombia, and the Colombian disposable had been left behind. He got a new phone and threw the unopened box on the passenger seat. He figured he'd take it out and program it later when he had the time.

The next stop was Lakeside, to check in with the anesthesia group. Paul hoped to get back to work soon and put the entire adventure behind. He checked in at the anesthesia office. They scheduled him to work the next week.

After going to the anesthesia office, he went to the operating room to check his locker. He'd bought a new padlock the week before the cyanide deaths, but in all the confusion he'd left it locked and forgotten the combination. If he couldn't recall the combination in the next few days, he'd call maintenance to cut off the padlock, and then he'd have to buy a new one.

He wanted to thank Horace Yardley for providing the lifesaving package of narcotic anesthetic, so he called Edward Rose Pharmaceuticals from the hospital.

The receptionist answered, "Edward Rose, can I help you?"

"Yes, I'd like to speak to Horace Yardley, please."

There was a pause. "I'm sorry, Dr. Yardley is no longer with us."

"Do you have a forwarding address, phone number, or email?"

"I'm sorry," said the sweet voice. "I don't have that information."

Paul hung up the phone. He wondered if Yardley's generous help had cost him his job. Paul wasn't surprised that a man involved in top-secret work might disappear without a forwarding address. That came with the territory.

Paul wasn't worried about Yardley. A man with his credentials in computer science, biotechnology, and research would always find work. Yardley would be all right.

Neurosurgeon Christine Mason wanted Paul to get one more MRI brain scan to prove there was no tumor. He'd told her he was tumor-free, but he couldn't tell her how that had happened. The last thing he wanted was another MRI scan, but the staff office demanded medical clearance before Lakeside would allow him to come back to work. Christine wouldn't give her OK without another MRI scan, so Paul had no choice but to agree.

The Lakeside MRI machine had been shut down. The official story was a safety recall of all MRI machines with defective parts from World Development Industries. The recall started a mass scramble nationwide to obtain MRI machines from other manufacturers. Lakeside had been lucky to grab a portable MRI machine not containing parts from World Development Industries.

The portable MRI scanner was located in a trailer in the overflow parking lot at Lakeside. Paul's transit through the portable MRI machine was uneventful. Christine reviewed the brain scan while Paul lay on the MRI table.

"I can't believe it," said Christine. "There is no sign of the tumor." She stared down at Paul. Her auburn bangs fell across her face. "How is this possible? Even with radiotherapy I'd see some residual scarring."

"Trust me," said Paul. He looked up at the confusion in her beautiful eyes. "There's a logical explanation. I'd tell you if I could. Please, just sign my clean bill of health or they won't let me go back to work."

"You are neurologically cleared for duty," said Christine. "I'll send a copy to the staff office for your privileges file."

"Thanks again," said Paul.

He walked back to the hospital parking lot and eased into the Mercedes. He took his new cell phone out of the box. It was already fully charged, ready to go. He removed the plastic screen protector, and turned the phone on.

"You have one text message," said the phone.

Paul was surprised, because no one had his temporary number. It would be several days before his old number was ported to the new phone. He assumed the message must be an automated one, from the cellular company, thanking him for buying the new phone.

The message read: *You can't put the genie back in the bottle. Your truck keys are in the drawer with the remotes, your locker combo is 12-23-34, and you really are in love. Welcome home. Horace Yardley.*

Paul stared at the screen and then hit the reply button. The screen flashed bright white as if hit by lightening, and then went dark. The phone was totally dead and Paul couldn't revive it. The unit felt hot.

There would be no phone calls, and it was just as well. Paul had a quiet evening planned at home. And all he wanted now was a few moments alone with his secret thoughts.

Made in the USA
Charleston, SC
08 March 2013